He'd done his best to protect her from himself

And all right—maybe his best was one hell of a poor effort, but he'd *tried*, dammit. He'd never said he was a saint. That was why he'd stayed away from her since the last time—because he knew his limitations when it came to Bailey Flowers.

But then she'd come back into his life. And now she was asking him to destroy the last scrap of feeling she might have for him.

"You shouldn't have come back, Bailey." He kept his voice even, but he could feel a muscle twitching at the side of his jaw. "I told you how it would turn out."

Her eyes widened. "In bed together, or at each other's throats," she said flatly. "And I told you that the second scenario was the more likely one. It seems I was right."

Dear Harlequin Intrigue Reader,

What's bigger than Texas…? Montana! This month, Harlequin Intrigue takes you deep undercover to the offices of MONTANA CONFIDENTIAL. You loved the series when it first premiered in the Lone Star State, so we've created a brand-new set of sexy cowboy agents for you farther north in Big Sky country. Patricia Rosemoor gets things started in *Someone To Protect Her*. Three more installments follow—and I can assure you, you won't want to miss one!

Amanda Stevens concludes her dramatic EDEN'S CHILDREN miniseries with *The Forgiven*. All comes full circle in this redemptive story that reunites mother and child.

What would you do if your "wife" came back from the dead? Look for *In His Wife's Name* for the answer. In a very compelling scenario, Joyce Sullivan explores the consequences of a hidden identity and a desperate search for the truth.

Rounding out the month is the companion story to Harper Allen's miniseries THE AVENGERS. *Sullivan's Last Stand*, like its counterpart *Guarding Jane Doe*, is a deeply emotional story about a soldier of fortune and his dedication to duty. Be sure to pick up both titles by this exceptional new author.

Cowboys, cops—action, drama…it's just another month of terrific romantic suspense from Harlequin Intrigue.

Happy reading!

Sincerely,

Denise O'Sullivan
Associate Senior Editor
Harlequin Intrigue

P.S. Be sure to watch for the next title in Rebecca York's 43 LIGHT STREET trilogy, MINE TO KEEP, available in October.

SULLIVAN'S LAST STAND

HARPER ALLEN

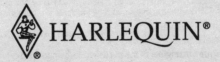

TORONTO • NEW YORK • LONDON
AMSTERDAM • PARIS • SYDNEY • HAMBURG
STOCKHOLM • ATHENS • TOKYO • MILAN • MADRID
PRAGUE • WARSAW • BUDAPEST • AUCKLAND

ISBN 0-373-22632-2

SULLIVAN'S LAST STAND

Copyright © 2001 by Sandra Hill

This edition published by arrangement with Harlequin Books S.A.

® and TM are trademarks of the publisher. Trademarks indicated with ® are registered in the United States Patent and Trademark Office, the Canadian Trade Marks Office and in other countries.

Visit us at www.eHarlequin.com

Printed in U.S.A.

ABOUT THE AUTHOR

Harper Allen lives in the country in the middle of a hundred acres of maple trees with her husband, Wayne, six cats, four dogs—and a very nervous cockatiel at the bottom of the food chain. For excitement she and Wayne drive to the nearest village and buy jumbo bags of pet food. She believes in love at first sight because it happened to her.

Books by Harper Allen

HARLEQUIN INTRIGUE
468—THE MAN THAT GOT AWAY
547—TWICE TEMPTED
599—WOMAN MOST WANTED
628—GUARDING JANE DOE*
632—SULLIVAN'S LAST STAND*

*The Avengers

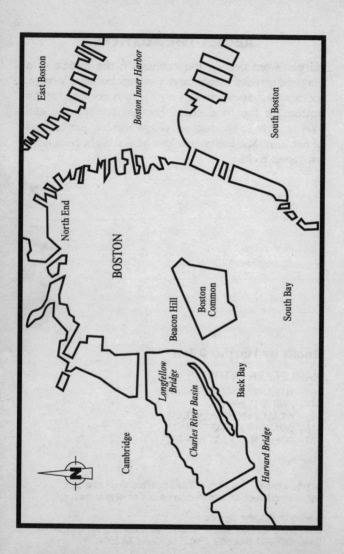

CAST OF CHARACTERS

Bailey Flowers—A year ago Sullivan broke her heart. Now she's back in his life again…with a score to settle and a sister to find.

Terrence Patrick Sullivan—The tough ex-mercenary can't undo the mistakes of his past. But he's determined not to repeat them—and Bailey was his biggest mistake.

Angelica Plowright—Bailey's beautiful blond sister was smart enough to hold out for marriage to a billionaire. She just wasn't smart enough to realize that money isn't everything.

Aaron Plowright—The well-known billionaire is always a popular subject for the photographer's lens—and now his illicit weekend with a mystery woman has been caught on film.

Tracy Weiss—The ambitious attorney has a professional connection to Plowright. It's rumored she has a personal relationship with him, as well.

Ainslie O'Connell—Sullivan's half sister loves him dearly, but she's afraid that history will repeat itself.

For Michael

Chapter One

He hadn't changed at all in one year. He was still the most gorgeous male she'd ever seen.

She might have known, Bailey thought in resignation, crossing her arms and waiting for him to see her standing in the doorway. Telephone receiver cradled on his shoulder, his eyes closed and a wry smile lifting one corner of his mouth, Terrence Patrick Sullivan was in full spate, slouched so far back in his leather chair that by rights he should have tipped the thing over. Long legs were propped up on the paper-strewn surface of his desk.

She gave an audible snort and had the satisfaction of seeing his eyes fly open as his startled gaze met hers.

"Whoever she is, she'll have to call you back," she said dryly. "Hang up the phone, Sully. We've got to talk."

She'd been right. He was even more heart-stoppingly handsome than she remembered, she thought with a spurt of irritation as he gave her a quick glance. Really, that was a big part of his problem. Would women have been throwing themselves at the man the way they had for most of his thirty-odd years if he hadn't been blessed with those dark navy eyes and those thick sooty lashes? Would he have been able to have his pick of female companionship without that glossy black hair brushing the collars of his Armani suits, or the linebacker shoulders that filled out the jackets of those same suits?

Probably, she conceded in annoyance. Because even if he'd had nothing else going for him, Terrence Patrick Sullivan was a charmer. Women adored him. Men liked him. Children trusted him, dogs followed him home, and although he parked his Jaguar near a tree at the back of the building here, she'd seen with her own eyes that the pigeons that roosted in it would spatter everyone else's car except his.

He was pond scum.

"Listen, something's come up, sugar," he was saying into the phone now. "But I'll see you tonight like we planned. Uh-huh, seven o'clock. SWKA, baby-doll."

"I see you still use the old sign-off, as well. But I must have rattled you, Sullivan—it's SWAK, not SWKA." Unfolding her arms and shoving herself from the door frame as he abruptly hung up, Bailey crossed the carpeted floor to his desk. She pulled out a chair and plopped herself negligently down in it. Swinging her own jean-clad legs up, she put her feet on a pile of papers next to his. "Unless you meant Sealed With Kiss A," she added.

"Tara's a great kid, but she's not that big on spelling. I'm doubting she noticed." He met her eyes. "My sister Ainslie's twelve-year-old goddaughter, Bailey. I'm taking her and Lee out for pizza tonight."

"Oh." Now he'd rattled *her,* she thought. She'd known when she'd made up her mind to come here that she would have to hold on to every ounce of self-control she possessed, and already she could feel it slipping away. She took a deep breath. "Why don't we skip the small talk and get right to the—"

"The ever-charming Ms. Flowers." There was an unaccustomed edge to his voice. "It's been—how long—a year?'' He leaned back farther in his chair, and she found herself hoping that this time it would fall. ''So to what do I owe the unexpected pleasure of this visit? Don't tell me— you finally decided to pack in that little fleabag operation of yours and join a real firm of investigators, right?''

''Triple-A Acme's doing just fine, thanks,'' she said evenly. ''In fact, I send *you* business every so often. I figure you need to keep the cash flow steady, what with those expensive tastes of yours. Nice suit, Sully.''

He followed her gaze and flicked a nonexistent speck of lint from the sleeve of his jacket. ''Thanks,'' he said complacently. ''Those Milan tailors know how to do their job.''

''Too bad you don't.'' Bailey took her feet off the desk and planted them back on the floor with a thump. She leaned forward, her gaze hardening. ''Your firm screwed up, Sullivan.''

''My firm screwed—'' Abruptly he swung his own legs off the desk, all traces of good humor gone from his handsome face as his eyes met hers. ''I don't think so, Bailey, honey,'' he said softly. ''You can rag on me about anything else you please—my love life, my clothes, even my character. But Sullivan Investigations and Security is off-limits, unless you can prove what you just said.''

''Angelica was one of the cases I sent your way.'' Her tone was as humorless as his. ''And you're right—whatever else my opinion of you might be, I've always admitted that you run one of the best agencies in Boston.''

''*The* best,'' he interjected. ''Just because you come first in the phone book doesn't mean you beat me out in getting results and clients. Far from it, in fact.''

''I assume that's a dig at the fact that Acme's just a one-woman detective agency.'' She shrugged. ''I'll admit that. The reason I sent Angelica to you was partly because Sullivan's is such a large firm.''

"Multinational, now." He shrugged, too. "I've expanded since you and I last chatted."

On the mahogany desk he had an exquisite Waterford crystal paperweight. For a moment the impulse to grab it and hurl it at him was almost overwhelming. *Chatted?* Bailey thought with dull fury. Was that how he categorized their last encounter?

"I can see you're doing well," she noted tightly. "But that's *your* problem, Sullivan—I think the company's gotten so big you've lost touch with what's going on. You didn't even know Angelica was a client until I just told you, did you?"

"Your sister? Okay, I didn't know, but what's your point, Bailey?" He leveled an unconcerned blue gaze on her. "I can't be expected to be on top of every file we're handling."

"My adopted sister," she said shortly.

"Adopted sister." His usual lazy tone was clipped. "She married Aaron Plowright four or five years ago, going from cocktail waitress to billionaire's wife in one fell swoop, right? So why did you send her to me? Did she mislay some trifling object like a yacht that she wanted us to locate for her without the hubby finding out?"

"No. She thought hubby had a trifling object that he didn't want her to find out about." Impatiently she tucked a stray strand of hair behind one ear. "But Angel never was the smartest girl on the block—just the most beautiful. She came to me first and asked me to tail him."

His grin surprised her. In the tan of his face it was a flash of white, and it was devastating. Even now she could feel her own lips starting to curve in an answering smile. She bit the inside of her cheek sharply enough to keep her expression under control.

"Yeah, he might just have clued in, seeing his sister-in-law popping out from behind bushes everywhere he went,'' he said. ''You're right—not too bright of our little Angelica. Although I don't agree that she was the most beautiful girl on the block, honey. Not when the two of you lived in the same house, anyway.''

It took a moment for her to realize what he was saying. It took a moment only because her brain was starting to turn to mush, she thought in chagrin, the way it had turned to mush a year ago when she'd been around him. It was the grin. She was letting him affect her.

''I never was in Angelica's league in the looks department, Sully, and you and I both know it. I didn't come here for a dose of your patented Irish blarney. I came here on business, so let's keep things on that footing and we'll get along just fine.''

It came out more sharply than she'd intended. He held her gaze for a moment, his own as unreadable as she hoped hers was, and then he let out a long breath.

''So you sent the lovely Angelica to my firm to have her husband followed.'' He pushed aside a stack of papers on his desk and leaned forward, lifting his shoulders a little as if his muscles were tense. ''How do you figure we screwed up? Did Aaron make the tail?''

''Of course not. Your people aren't amateurs.''

Her voice was nearly back to normal again, she noted with surprise. She felt oddly light-headed, as if she'd just picked her way through a minefield and couldn't quite believe she was still in one piece. She'd done it, she thought. She'd finally gotten him out of her system.

''As a matter of fact, Aaron had to go away on an unexpected business trip last weekend, and apparently your—'' She stopped abruptly, her breath suddenly short and her heartbeat speeding up.

''Go on.''

He'd stood up and shucked off the suit jacket he'd been wearing. Now he was unbuttoning the cuffs of his shirt and rolling his sleeves back, his attention focused on the task. His forearms were a dark gold against the white material, and the same tan tone was echoed in the worn leather shoulder holster that slashed across the whiteness of his shirt higher up. He glanced over at her.

"What is it?"

How many times had she seen him shrug off his jacket and unfasten his cuffs in the past? she thought helplessly. The answer came to her immediately—*three*. Three times in the past he'd stood in front of her and lazily started to undress, and those three times he'd kept going. She'd once told him that if the investigation business ever went bust, he could probably make a darn good living as a male stripper. He'd given her a wide-eyed look of protest that had had nothing innocent about it at all, and then he'd taken so excruciatingly long to discard the rest of his clothes that by the end of it she was practically out of her mind with desire for him.

And the next time she'd paid him back in exactly the same way, Bailey remembered.

They'd made love three times together. Well, that wasn't strictly true—they'd spent three nights together and made love all through each of those nights, time and again. They'd made love that last morning, just an hour or so before she'd walked in on the phone call that had negated everything she'd thought they had between them. She swallowed with difficulty.

"Nothing. I just want to make sure I don't leave anything out," she finally said, her tone as professional as she could make it. "Aaron went away on what he said was an emergency business trip, and your operative followed him. Apparently Angelica's suspicions were correct, because when Jackson reported back to her—''

''Jackson?'' He looked up quickly. ''Hank Jackson?''

''Yes, Hank,'' she said impatiently. ''When he reported back to her—''

''You're telling me that Hank Jackson screwed up on a job, honey?'' Despite his casual posture, there was a tenseness about him. ''It didn't happen, sweetheart. Not Hank—he's my best investigator.''

Gone was the man she'd walked in on ten minutes ago, the man whose easy charm had so irritated her. Gone also was the man she remembered from last year. Looking at his hard, set features, Bailey suddenly recalled that Terrence Patrick Sullivan hadn't always worn Armani and driven Jaguars. He hadn't always run a security and investigative firm that was doing so well he had to keep a string of girlfriends just to help him spend his money.

He didn't hide his past, but he didn't talk about it, either. She hadn't known he'd been a mercenary until afterward, when she'd needed to find out everything about the man that she could in order to make some sense of his actions toward her. It had been astonishingly difficult to find anyone who claimed to know the real Sullivan, and even harder to persuade those who did to talk, but digging up information was what she did for a living. Eventually she'd pieced together just enough rumors and half-truths to realize she'd never known the man at all.

He'd been one of the toughest soldiers-for-hire available, she'd been told by a big man in a smoky bar one rainy night. An older man, trim and ramrod straight despite his advancing years, had met her on a park bench in the Common. While throwing bread crusts to the ducks, in a clipped British accent he'd informed her that Sully had been a maniac, always volunteering for the most dangerous missions available and never seeming to take anything seriously. When she'd asked him if he'd ever served with him, the faded gray eyes had met hers as if she was the one who was mad. Every damned chance he could, he'd told her. And if Sully came up to him today and asked him to join him on one last suicide jaunt, he'd sign on with him in a flash, he'd added wistfully.

There had been others she'd talked to—not many, just a handful—but slowly a picture had grown in her mind of a man who was nothing like the Terrence Sullivan he now presented to the world.

She was looking at that man right now, Bailey thought. But that didn't change what she'd come here to tell him. She watched him walk back to the desk and sit down across from her.

"He might be your best investigator," she said flatly, meeting his cool gaze with an even chillier one of her own. "But he made a judgment call that sucked big time, and that's what I've got a problem with."

Even in shirtsleeves and with that glossy black hair in need of a trim, he seemed suddenly remote. She found herself wishing that she'd picked out something more businesslike and intimidating to wear herself. Jeans and a Pearl Jam tee weren't exactly power-dressing, she told herself ruefully. And her own hair kept falling out of the banana clip she'd pinned it up with this morning, in deference to the unseasonable—for Boston, at least—May heat.

Still she had one edge over him. She knew what had happened, and he, by his own admission, didn't. His next action made it obvious he didn't intend to let that state of affairs last much longer.

Leaning forward, he jabbed the intercom button on his phone. "Moira, ask Hank to come in here, will you? If he's not in his office, have him paged." He sat back, his expression grim. "I won't conduct a court-martial of one of my own men without giving him the chance to tell his side of the story, Bailey. But go on. What exactly is it you're accusing him of?"

His attitude was meant to put her on the defensive, but with a tightening of her lips she continued. "Jackson gave Angelica the gist of his findings over the phone on Sunday night. The written report was to follow, along with copies of the photos he'd taken, and apparently they alone were pretty damning. Aaron's 'business meeting' was with a gorgeous brunette young enough to be his daughter. Of course, all of his wives after the first Mrs. Plowright have been young enough to be his daughters, so the age thing isn't surprising," she added. "But they weren't exactly discussing a merger. According to Jackson, they were in the middle of one—a very personal, very *intimate* merger."

"So what's the big problem you keep talking about?" A moment ago, Sullivan's wry smile would have seemed natural. Now she could discern the effort it cost him to hide his anger, and her own temper flared.

"The problem is that Angelica's not the most stable person you could drop a bombshell like this on, even if she did semi-suspect something. Besides which, Jackson apparently gave her the bad news only an hour or so before Aaron himself returned." Bailey's eyes flashed. "A two-bit PI with a mail-order diploma would have known better. He had to have realized what a volatile situation he was creating."

"Then why didn't you try to soften the blow, since you were so concerned about how she would take it?"

"I wasn't there, dammit!" Her features sharpened with frustration. "I was on a stakeout all Sunday night and right up until noon on Monday. When I got home I took a shower and then crashed for a few hours. After I woke up

I saw the message light blinking on my answering machine, and that's when I heard Angel's message from the night before. She'd wanted to talk to me before Aaron arrived home, but I—'' Bailey hesitated ''—I wasn't there for her,'' she finished, looking swiftly down at her hands.

He'd been watching her intently. Now he shook his head, his gaze still on her. ''You can't be around all the time. Besides, after she gets over the blow to her pride, your little sister'll realize that she's looking at a rock-solid divorce settlement. From what you've told me about her in the past, that's probably more to her liking than a diamond eternity band and a bunch of red roses on their next anniversary, anyway.''

''That's the way I thought she'd take it.'' She looked up at him. ''But the message she left on my machine was so hysterical I could hardly make out what she was saying. She said she was going to confront Aaron with the whole thing as soon as he walked in the door.''

''Not wise,'' he said shortly. ''Plowright's got the kind of money that can erase memories. She should have kept quiet about it and let her lawyer get statements from anyone Jackson mentions in his report.'' He frowned. ''Today's Wednesday. Aaron's had time to do a lot of damage control already. Where's Angelica been staying since she turned on the fan and watched everything hit it?''

''That's just it—she's disappeared, and no one seems to have any idea where she's gone.'' Her eyes met his and her voice hardened. ''Jackson's your man, Sullivan. I'm holding you responsible for anything that's happened to Angelica.''

''*If* anything's happened to her and *if* Hank behaved un-professionally, then I'll accept that responsibility,'' he said curtly. ''But maybe you should keep personal out of this yourself, honey.''

Bailey stiffened. "What possible connection could there be between my problem with one of your investigators and the way I feel about you personally?"

"You know damn well what the connection is. It's not Hank Jackson who blew it as far as you're concerned, is it? It's me. *I'm* the one who screwed up big time."

Raking his hair back with one hand in a suddenly frustrated gesture, he held her gaze intently. "I always wanted to call you up and apologize for the way I behaved, but I figured you'd just slam the phone down as soon as you heard my voice," he said softly. "But you're here now. I'm sorry for what happened last year, Bailey. No excuses. I handled things badly."

She stared at him, taken completely off guard. Once she would have given almost anything to hear him say what he'd just said, she thought. For months after, her heart had skipped a beat every time her phone had rung, thinking it might—just *might*—be him. But as he'd said, he'd never called.

She hadn't been able to forget him completely, but she'd gotten on with her life. His twelve-months-late apology shouldn't have the power to rip away the scar tissue of composure it had taken her so long to build up.

But it did. And all of a sudden she was back there in his house, standing in the doorway of his study and clad only in one of his shirts, listening to him methodically pull her world to bits.

Bailey blinked. Her throat felt as if it had a drawstring around it and someone had just tugged the drawstring shut.

"You're wrong, Sullivan. There's nothing personal left at all between us. I'm over you completely." Her voice was barely audible. "Want proof?"

She got to her feet and leaned over the desk until she was close enough to him to lightly grasp the pearl-gray silk of his tie. Sullivan half rose from his chair, his eyes dark with suspicion.

"What the hell—" he began, but she didn't give him a chance to finish. With a swift movement she brought her lips to his. Her tongue darted out and flicked the corner of his mouth teasingly, and immediately she felt a tremor run through him and heard his sudden indrawn breath. Those eyes, which only a moment ago had been narrowed and wary, closed, the thick lashes fanning against the hard ridge of his cheekbones.

Bailey kept her own open with an effort and fought down the dazed languor that she could feel spreading through her. She couldn't keep this up for more than a second or so, she told herself disjointedly. Already the taste of him was spilling through her like some kind of dangerous intoxicant, addictive and seductive.

It had taken long months to break that addiction the last time. She wasn't going to let herself get hooked on it again.

Her hand tightened on his tie. She ran her tongue lightly across his parted lips, forcing herself to ignore the impulse to explore deeper, and finished up at the opposite corner of his mouth with another little flick of her tongue.

"Completely. Over. You," she whispered against his mouth. Then she drew back from him and let go of his tie.

His eyes opened and he stared at her in disbelief, his gaze still slightly unfocused and his breath audibly shallow. She kept her own expression impassive, willing herself not to betray the shakiness she was feeling. She gave him a brief smile.

"So now that you know it's not personal, what are you planning to do about finding my sister?"

He didn't answer her. Instead, he slowly lowered himself to his chair, his eyes never leaving hers. "That was dirty fighting, honey," he said softly. "You've changed."

She sat down herself, her legs feeling as if they couldn't support her a minute longer. "Maybe I have, Sullivan. Maybe you changed me." She shrugged tightly. "You played me for a fool once. I came so damned close to falling in love with you that one more kiss would have done it. I looked at you and saw the person I'd been waiting for all my life—a sexy, gorgeous man with a wicked sense of humor who, by some miracle, was falling in love with me." She paused. "I thought we were two halves of a whole," she added. "I was wrong."

For a moment she thought he was about to speak, but when he said nothing she continued, her tone brisker.

"Anyway, we both know how that turned out. I was a wreck for about a week after, and then for two weeks more I think I hated you. But after a while I realized that was simply the way you were, and to expect anything more of you had been unreasonable of me. You've got a reputation, Sullivan. I was well aware of it before I went home with you the first time."

"I wouldn't go so far as to say I've got a reputation," he said shortly.

"Please." Her smile was humorless. "Of course you do, and of course you know it. You never stay with the same woman for more than a month or so, but that doesn't matter, because the women you date prefer brief relationships. You don't like intense, you like casual. You say that you intend to settle down one day, but no one's putting their money on the likelihood of that happening."

"I see." He looked away, and then back at her, his expression shuttered. "That's quite a list, honey. Anything on the plus side that you can think of?"

She blinked, wondering if she'd imagined the thread of unsteadiness she thought she'd heard in his voice. Of course she had, she told herself impatiently. She hadn't exactly hit the man with any painful revelations about himself.

"On the plus side, you're a damn good investigator," she said smoothly. "Or at least you used to be. That's why I came—"

"Sully?"

The interruption came from the doorway and, looking over her shoulder, Bailey saw Sullivan's indispensable secretary, Moira, standing there surveying them quizzically. The slim, dark-haired woman sounded hesitant.

"Jackson hasn't been in to work for the past three days, and Shirley in personnel says she hasn't been able to contact him at home. It seems that his line's out of order." Moira's expression clouded. "You'd better send someone over to his house to see what's wrong, Sully. I—I've got a bad feeling about this."

Chapter Two

One way or another, Bailey Flowers had been the biggest mistake of his life, Terrence Sullivan told himself, pressing the button for the elevator and slanting a sideways glance at the straight-backed figure beside him. He just wasn't sure what part had been a mistake—acting so out of character as to let himself get involved with her in the first place, or reverting at the last possible moment back to type and letting her walk away for good.

The former, of course, he thought with a familiar twinge of self-disgust. He'd known from the moment he'd laid eyes on her that she was capable of blowing the precariously fragile existence he'd carved out for himself all the way to hell and gone. He'd known she wasn't the type that he'd been so careful to restrict himself to up until then. A few laughs, a couple of heated encounters between the sheets, and the women he usually dated would be casting their big blue eyes around as restlessly as he was, looking for someone new.

Bailey's eyes were the color of water running over stones in a stream. They hadn't glanced around restlessly; they'd been direct and clear, looking at him and only him. Sometimes he'd even had the unsettling feeling that her hazel eyes could look right through him and see everything he'd always kept so well hidden.

The rest of her was a combination of ordinary attributes that somehow added up to beauty. Her hair was a rich, peaty brown, with glints of honey and amber in it. She'd pinned it up on top of her head once, and the exposed nape of her neck had excited him as no blatant display of any other woman's cleavage ever had. Her mouth was wide, and a dead giveaway to whatever she was feeling. She was slim, her muscles had definition, and all in all she was as unlike the kittenish blondes he was used to as possible.

He'd fallen for her like a ton of bricks.

Things had ended badly between them, and it had been his fault entirely. But as brief as their affair had been, there had been moments about it that he'd clung to since she'd walked out on him. One wet afternoon they'd gone to a horrendously bad kickboxing double feature, and Bailey had laughed so hard she'd spilled a jumbo carton of popcorn all over him. Once they'd gone on a picnic, and she'd fallen asleep in his lap under a big shade tree, with the sunlight dappling her features, the breeze stirring those honey-amber strands of hair, and him just watching her, drinking in all the delicate details of her face and stamping them on his memory. He could remember every single time they'd made love—her hands on him, his on her, the scent of her skin and the taste of her mouth and the small shallow sigh she gave just before the two of them reached the limits of their control and soared over the far edge of desire together.

But from her attitude toward him since she'd walked into his office, it was all too obvious she'd kept none of those memories. And if they didn't exist for her, then maybe one day he would lose them, too. Fear shafted through him, bright and painful.

"My sister and now your best operative. Are you starting to see a pattern here?"

Wrenching his thoughts back to the present, Sullivan frowned as the elevator doors opened and Bailey stepped in. He followed her and the doors slid closed behind him.

"Not yet. But there's something taking shape I don't like." He reached over and grasped her shoulder lightly. Immediately she stiffened.

"Hands off, Sully. Like I told you, this is strictly work."

"I know." He pivoted her around to face him. "And like you also said, my firm screwed up. Why don't you go back to Triple-A and I'll call you after I talk to Hank? There's no need for you to be involved in this."

She gave him a blankly incredulous look. "Come again?"

He sighed. "Let's face it, the past half hour just proved we can't even keep up a civilized facade when we're together." He shoved his hands into the pockets of his suit. "Hell, we've got a history, and my part in it isn't anything I feel too proud about. Let me find Hank, locate Angelica, and send you a report when I'm through."

"You're giving me the brush-off." Her voice was disbelieving. *"Again."*

"For crying out loud, Bailey, it's not like that at—" he began, but she cut him off.

"It's *exactly* like that." Her glance flicked to somewhere a little lower than his midsection, and then back again to his face. "Tell me, Sully, are they made of brass? Is that your secret? Because you've got a nerve like I just don't freakin' *believe!*"

Her eyes glinted ominously. "Your conscience is bugging you. *Tough.* Learn to live with it, because this time I'm not going to quietly disappear just to make things easier on you. I'm coming with you to talk to Jackson. You owe me that much, at least.''

The elevator doors opened to the lobby, and the guard behind the desk looked over at them. He gave the man a brief nod and switched his attention back to Bailey.

''It won't work, you and me together, and you know it, lady.'' He shrugged. ''Within twenty-four hours you'll be at my throat or I'll have you in my bed—and neither of those scenarios can have a happy ending.''

''You never know.'' Her tone was ice. ''Why don't we give that first one a shot and see how it plays out?''

He wasn't going to win this one, Sullivan told himself in defeat. He wasn't even sure he wanted to. He took a deep breath.

''Move that sweet butt and let's get going, honey.''

For a moment—just for a moment—the woman he'd once known looked up at him through those clear, brilliant eyes. Then she was gone again.

''Don't push me, Sullivan.'' Her lips tightened. ''I'm in no mood, believe me.''

No matter what she'd said to him, it looked like Bailey Flowers was back in his life again, he told himself as he exited the building behind the slim, straight figure striding ahead of him to the parking lot. And no matter what he'd said to her, he was glad she was.

Except that in a day or so he was going to have to arrange things so that she walked away from him again. But this time he'd have to make her hate him enough to stay away, Sullivan thought wearily.

And *this* time it would have to be for good.

IT SEEMED AS THOUGH they'd hit upon a way of being together that didn't lead to a confrontation, Bailey thought—total silence. So far on the drive to Jackson's house neither one of them had said a word. Sullivan had concentrated on avoiding the worst of the traffic snarl-ups, she had stared out of her window, and an edgy peace was prevailing.

She closed her eyes, acutely aware of his presence beside her, and tried to make some sense of the way she'd acted back in his office. She'd walked in there planning to keep her emotions under control whatever the provocation, but within minutes she'd—she'd—

For crying out loud, Flowers, she told herself uncomfortably, *within minutes you practically had your tongue in his mouth. How restrained was that?*

Even so, right up until the second her lips had touched his she'd thought she could handle it, because what she'd told him was true—she was over Terrence Patrick Sullivan. Completely and *totally* over him. So why at the exact moment of contact had she experienced that icily electric thrill, as if she had leaped recklessly out into empty space and was suddenly plunging toward destruction?

Her only consolation was that he'd obviously been hit by the same force that had smashed her detachment to bits. And although she was pretty sure she'd hidden her reaction from him, Bailey thought shakily, there had been no mistaking his response for anything other than pure, immediate desire.

But that meant nothing. She opened her eyes. If all she wanted from the man was another brief physical fling, she could be in his bed within twenty-four hours. She could have those strong, hard hands on whatever part of her body she chose. She could see those blue, blue eyes looking down on her and becoming blindly hazed with passion. She could feel his mouth the way she used to feel it, slowly and unerringly igniting every secret desire she'd ever imagined.

But that would be all she would ever have from him. And *that* was why she was over him.

"The way I hear it, your guy Jackson used to have an alcohol-abuse problem," she said abruptly. "How under control is it?"

A driver in front of them made a typical Boston lane change—no signal and at the last possible minute—and Sullivan jammed on his brakes. He looked over at her. "Hank takes it day by day, just like any other recovering alcoholic. He's got his five-year pin from AA, if that's what you're getting at, and I'd trust him with my life."

"But you're still checking up on him personally," she argued. "You've got some doubts about him, haven't you?"

"No." His tone was flat and uncompromising. "If he hasn't been at work for the past few days then something's the matter. I should have known about this sooner." He geared the Jaguar down as they entered a rotary, merging seamlessly with the flow of traffic. "You were right about one thing. I've let myself slack off these last few months."

There was a hard edge to his voice, but Bailey knew instinctively it wasn't directed at her. It was directed at himself, she thought curiously, darting a look at him through her lashes, but self-chastisement was something that the Terry Sullivan she knew didn't indulge in.

His jaw was set and his expression was unreadable. Maybe she'd imagined that tone of disgust in his voice, she thought hesitantly, but now that she was studying him, she realized there were other changes she hadn't noticed earlier. They were subtle, but they were there.

There was a steel-wire tenseness about him that betrayed itself in the grim lines that bracketed his mouth. His face was leaner somehow, his cheekbones harder looking. He drove with the same casual competence he'd always had, but on closer inspection she could see that the knuckles of the hand wrapped carelessly around the steering wheel were held tightly enough that they were whiter than the rest of his skin.

At first glance he still gave the impression of a big, lazily sexy man with not much more on his mind than the nearest attractive female. He gave that impression because he wanted to give that impression, she thought slowly. Had it always been a facade? Had it been a facade even when she'd known him a year ago?

"Sully? The man was a maniac—always volunteering for suicide missions, always with that incredibly charming but quite mad grin on his face. It got worse after the Salazar woman was killed."

The gray-haired British officer's words came back to her, and so did the feeling of frustration she'd felt when the man had refused to elaborate any further on what he'd told her. The name of Maria Salazar had had that effect on others who had known Sullivan, too. One of his closest friends, a pale-eyed, grimly silent mercenary named Quinn McGuire, had simply gotten up from the table and walked away when she'd asked him what he knew about the woman.

But right now wasn't the time to go into the subject of Maria Salazar. She cleared her throat awkwardly.

"You run a different kind of operation than Triple-A. With the dozens of case files that Sullivan Investigations must be working on at any given time, it's not possible for you to be familiar with each one personally. I was out of line saying that."

"Yeah, but that's what I liked about you, honey." Like magic, the grim look had disappeared from his face. One corner of his mouth lifted wryly as he briefly switched his attention from the traffic to her. "You were always out of line. I've missed that."

He didn't know it, but he couldn't have said anything

more calculated to wipe out the fragile détente she'd been about to embark on. Bailey stiffened.

"If you missed anything at all about me, it was nobody's fault but your own. You had me. You got bored. End of story." Her tone was barbed. "But since you like it when I cross the line, I'll oblige. Tell me, Sullivan, why did you have to destroy me? When you were talking on the phone to your newest plaything that morning, you knew I was right behind you and hearing every word you were saying, didn't you?"

"I knew." His admission took her aback for a moment, but his next words floored her. "I planned it that way." He shrugged. "You had a concept of me that wasn't real. A clean break seemed best."

His words were completely uninflected. Unhurriedly he swung the Jaguar down a smaller side street lined with older, slightly dilapidated homes, as Bailey scrambled to cope with his unwelcome revelation.

She'd lied to herself, she thought. She'd *never* gotten over him—not totally. It had taken this latest admission of his to open her eyes, but this time she wanted to be absolutely sure she understood him.

"You say my concept of you wasn't real. What do you mean?" she asked carefully.

"You were beginning to think of me as someone you could build a future with." He could have been talking about the weather, there was so little emotion in his voice. "Your faith in me was all wrong, but you couldn't seem to see that. I did you a favor, Bailey. I let you see what kind of man I really was before it was too late."

"Your timing could have been a little better," she said, still not looking at him. There was a far-off roaring in her ears that made it hard for her to hear her own voice. It was as if she were holding a conch shell and listening to imaginary waves crashing against an imaginary shore, she thought foolishly—as if she was standing in the middle of a desert, longing for a sea that didn't exist.

"My timing could have been a lot better," Sullivan said harshly. Pulling in to the curb in front of a small bungalow, he switched off the ignition and turned to her. "I never should have gotten involved with you at all."

"So why did you?" she rasped, amazed to find that her voice still worked in any fashion at all. "If going out with me in the first place was such a big mistake on your part, why did you?"

His eyes darkened as he looked at her. "For God's sake, do you think I had any choice?" he said tightly. "You came into my life. I took one look at you and I was lost. I didn't care if it was the smart thing to do, the responsible thing to do, or the right thing to do—I wanted you. Even knowing that I was going to have to make you walk away in a day or two didn't matter, honey." He rubbed the heel of his hand against his mouth in frustration. "You don't get it, do you?"

"What's there to *get*, for God's sake?" Her eyes, wide and uncomprehending, were fixed on his. "You haven't told me anything yet! I'm a pretty simple girl, Sullivan, so why don't you give it to me in words of one syllable, so I can finally grasp it and get *on* with my life?"

Her voice had risen, and in the close confines of the Jaguar's interior they sounded shockingly loud. He looked away.

"Hell, I've said too much already. I'm a bastard, honey, and you're better off without me. There's your simple answer, so let's just leave it at that." He reached for the door. "Come on, let's see if Jackson's here and get some answers from him."

Without waiting to see if she was following him, in one

swiftly fluid movement he got out of the car and started up the cracked walk to the bungalow.

Bailey didn't move. She'd told him she'd come to get some answers about her sister's whereabouts, and that was true. But if she was honest with herself, after they found out where Angelica was, there was still another mystery she needed to find some answers to, another woman she wanted to ask him about.

Maria Salazar was dead. If she existed at all, it was as a ghost. There was no reason why she should still have any power over Sullivan.

But she did, Bailey thought fearfully. She didn't know why she was so certain about that, but she was. Maria Salazar had taken Sullivan away from her, and she was going to find out why.

She looked up. His hands in his pockets, he was waiting at the bungalow's front door, and with sudden resolve she got out of the car. Her determination wavered for a moment, but then she set her shoulders and started up the concrete walk. Even as she did, she saw him slip something out of his pocket.

He was breaking in, she thought in faint shock. She quickened her pace and reached him just as the door swung open.

"What are you doing?" she hissed, nervousness overlaying the jumble of conflicting emotions she'd just been experiencing. "That's breaking and entering, Sullivan—we could both lose our licenses!"

"This was stuck in the mail slot."

His voice was curt. He handed her a business card and she took it from him reluctantly. It bore the name of an S. Wilkes, who was apparently a regional sales director for some unknown company, and a phone number. Flipping it over impatiently, she saw a scrawled message.

"Hank—missed you at the last two meetings. Call me."

"Wilkes is a friend from AA," Sullivan said. "Hank's mentioned him once or twice." He frowned. "Those meetings are his lifeline, Bailey. He doesn't miss them. There's something wrong here."

She met his eyes. "I agree, but it's pretty obvious what it is," she said, trying not to sound brusque. "He's fallen off the wagon, Sullivan. Your boy Jackson's probably out on a bender."

He turned from her abruptly, his expression unreadable. "I don't believe that. I'm going in."

Before she could say another word, he stepped across the threshold, and without even having seen him reach for it, she saw that his gun was in his hand. She looked apprehensively over her shoulder. It was midafternoon, and apart from an old man a few houses down dozing on his porch, the street was deserted. Stifling her annoyance, she slipped quickly in after him and closed the door quietly behind her.

The minuscule front hall opened immediately onto a cramped, untidy kitchen. On the counter an empty bottle lay on its side, and the broken shards of a smashed glass were strewn nearby on the linoleum floor.

"Hell." In front of her, Sullivan slowly holstered his gun. He turned to her, his mouth tight. "Looks like you were right, doesn't it? I'll check the bedroom in case he's sleeping it off in there."

Shrugging in resignation, he started to step across the broken glass, but then he stopped, his glance sharpening on the fallen bottle on the counter. He set it upright, turning it so that the label faced them. She looked at him, confused, and saw the broad shoulders stiffen under the impeccably cut jacket.

"Hank's not a rye drinker. Somebody didn't do their homework," he said grimly.

His hand went to his holster again, and all of a sudden the Armani suit might just as well have been fatigues, and the small, untidy kitchen an ominously silent jungle. He hadn't put his former profession behind him at all, Bailey thought with quick insight. He reacted like a soldier. Just below the casually lazy surface of the man was a tense alertness, and at the first sign of trouble his military instincts took over.

Except she couldn't see what had aroused his suspicions.

"He's an alcoholic," she said dismissively. "If he wanted a drink badly enough he'd break into the cooking sherry."

"Maybe he would, at that. But he still wouldn't choose a grain-based alcohol, and if he had, he'd be lying on the floor with that glass, his throat swollen closed," Sullivan snapped. "He's even allergic to bread, for God's sake. This is some kind of setup."

"A setup for what? To make it look like the man fell off the wagon?" She stared at him in frustration. "For crying out loud, Sully, it doesn't make sense. For one thing, who knew we were coming here today? Who would have expected you to barge in illegally the way you just did?" A strand of hair had escaped from her clip, and she blew it away from her eyes with an impatient breath. "Let's check out the rest of the house before we jump to any conclusions. Maybe he's in the bedroom with an empty bottle of vodka, sleeping it off. Maybe the rye was for a friend."

Without waiting for him to respond, she pushed past him with more annoyance than the situation warranted. With a muttered oath, he grabbed her arm and stopped her.

"I'm armed. You're not. I'll take point position and you bring up the rear," he said tightly. "In fact, I'd prefer it if you stayed right here."

"Forget it. I'm a real woman, not one of your bimbos," she retorted. "If you're going to lead, lead, but I'm coming with you."

He wasn't happy about it, she knew. Too bad, she thought as she shadowed him from room to room, hanging back a little as he cautiously entered each one. She wasn't happy with the situation, either, but her reasons were harder to figure out. Why did his loyalty to the man who worked for him, however misguided she might see it as, irritate her so? They entered the bathroom, and she was jolted out of her thoughts.

"Wait a minute," she said as Sullivan turned to leave. "There's something odd here."

"What?" He shrugged and looked around. "There's nothing out of place."

"That's just it," Bailey said slowly. "Hank's a single guy, and the rest of the house is as untidy as you'd expect it to be. But this bathroom's immaculate. The taps actually sparkle, for heaven's sake."

"And the floor's been washed." He looked down, and then over at the towel rack. She followed his glance.

"Not even a facecloth," she said, frowning. "What does he use to dry himself with?"

"A towel, like everyone else does." His eyes darkened. "But towels can be used to mop up blood, too."

She felt an icy chill settle over her as his words sank in, and it was all she could do to stop herself from backing instinctively out of the small room. Had a man been killed here? Had he been killed so violently that his murderer had had to get down on his hands and knees after the deed and scrub every square inch of the floor to remove all traces of his blood? The bath was a combination shower, she noted. There were plastic rings on the rod, but no curtain. Had it been pressed into grisly service as a makeshift shroud by someone desperate to dispose of a body?

She was letting her imagination run away with her, Bailey told herself sharply. What they had here was an empty house, an empty bottle and an empty bathroom. Combined with Jackson's absence from work and the little she knew about him, her first guess had to be the right one.

But Sullivan wouldn't accept that. He seemed willing to stand by the missing Jackson no matter what.

And that was what stung, she realized. His loyalty to a man who worked for him was unshakable. His loyalty to her had been limited to three days, at most.

"I'm checking out that last room," she said shortly, turning from him back into the small hallway. "What is it, some kind of den?"

He was right behind her, but the door was only a few feet away, and before he could stop her she'd opened it and stepped into the room impatiently. That was as far as she got.

Her eyes widened in shock as she surveyed her surroundings, and behind her she heard Sullivan swear under his breath as his arm went around her and he pulled her closer to him.

It had once been an office, but now it was a disaster area. A computer lay smashed on the floor, and a filing cabinet was tipped over on its side, its drawers removed and upside down nearby. Drifts of paper covered every available surface, obviously ripped from the empty file folders that were scattered about. Whoever had done this had been in a murderous rage, Bailey thought shakily. He'd been looking for something, and either he hadn't found it or the fact that he'd had to search for it in the first place had prompted him to trash everything in sight. She took a hesitant step forward, and then looked down.

She was standing on one of the few file folders that still seemed to contain something. Moving her foot, she bent down and picked it up.

"Plowright," Sullivan said tersely, reading the typed label out loud. "Angelica's case. Is his report all there?"

Bailey flipped open the folder and leafed through the neatly numbered pages. "It seems to be," she said slowly. "Whoever did this, he couldn't have been searching for Angel's file. We'd better call the police."

"Not yet." He hunkered down, sifting through papers, scanning them quickly and then letting them fall to the floor again. He straightened and looked at her. "They're what I thought," he said briefly. "Hank normally wouldn't keep confidential files here—this is his research for a book he's writing on famous crimes of the last century. The Plowright file is the only one here that anyone could have been looking for, so why the hell didn't they take it?"

"Because they didn't want the report itself," she said slowly, her mind racing. "They wanted the photos that went with it—the photos of the woman that Aaron was with last weekend. That's what this is all about, Sullivan. Someone's trying to conceal her identity, and it looks like they'll go to any lengths to do so."

She swallowed, her mouth suddenly dry. "Maybe even murder," she added shakily, her eyes meeting his.

Chapter Three

"Let's take it from the top again. Why the hell did you and your lady here break into the house anyway?"

They were back at Sullivan Investigations, where Sullivan had told the police they would be when he'd contacted them from the trashed bungalow on his cell phone. Bailey could guess why he hadn't wanted to hang around waiting for the authorities to show up, and as soon as the two of them returned to the office her guess had been proved right. Giving a quick rundown of the situation to three of his top operatives, he'd grimly instructed them to drop whatever other cases they were on and start looking for their missing comrade.

His haste in getting a search under way was justified. Within minutes of the briefing session, two police detectives had showed up asking for him and Bailey, and it was clear from the attitude of the younger man of the pair that he was prepared to grill them all night if he didn't get the answers he wanted. So far he'd concentrated his attention on Sullivan, but at this last query Bailey couldn't keep silent any longer.

"Hold it right there, Detective Straub." She pushed herself from the edge of the gleamingly polished conference table that she'd been leaning against and took a step nearer the man. He was fair skinned, with sandy hair that was already starting to recede, and at her interruption he turned a blank look upon her, as if he'd forgotten she was in the room. His partner, a man about Sullivan's age, burly and solid, swiftly hid the flash of amusement that momentarily lightened his somber expression.

"I'm not anyone's *lady,* Detective." She bit the words off curtly. "I run an investigative agency of my own— Triple-A Acme Investigations. Perhaps you've heard of it?"

"It's the first one in the phone book," Sullivan added blandly.

She shot him an annoyed look. "I dropped by this afternoon to discuss an unrelated business matter with Mr. Sullivan. When he learned that one of his employees hadn't been in to work for a few days and couldn't be contacted, I suggested we continue our talk on the way to Jackson's place so he could check the situation out." She didn't meet Sullivan's alert gaze. "Frankly, I think he acted entirely appropriately. Our first thought was that the man had been taken ill and possibly needed assistance. It wasn't until we saw that his house had obviously been searched that we knew the matter was anything more than just an employee laid low by a flu bug."

She was lying through her teeth, Bailey thought in faint surprise, and until the words had actually come out of her mouth, she hadn't known that she had no intention of telling the truth—the whole truth, she fudged weakly to herself. After all, she *had* come here originally to discuss business with Sullivan, not realizing initially that it would have any connection to the absence from work of one of his operatives.

If it did, she added mentally. Finding her sister's case file at the man's house wasn't proof positive that the two disappearances were linked. It could mean quite the contrary, but that didn't alter the fact that there was one other detail that she—and Sullivan, too, she now realized—hadn't bothered to mention to the two detectives. She resisted the impulse to glance guiltily at her oversize shoulder bag, only a few feet away from her on a chair, but when Straub's partner finally spoke, she wondered at first whether he'd somehow been able to read her mind.

"Seems strange that someone would go to so much trouble to empty filing cabinets when all they contained were historical research for a book," he mused, propping one polyester-clad thigh on the conference table and fishing in the pocket of his disreputable sport coat for something. His hand withdrew, and in it was a paper-wrapped toothpick. With the same fascination that a mouse would give a snake, Bailey watched him as he slowly peeled the paper away, wadding it up into a tiny ball and looking around the room as if there was nothing more important on his mind right now than to find a wastebasket in which to throw his minuscule piece of trash. Not seeing one, he sighed and dropped the wadded-up ball into his pocket. Then he inserted the toothpick between his lips and gave it a thoughtful chew.

Straub looked as if he was about to burst into impatient speech again, but the man that Sully had called Fitzgerald gave him a glance and, with obvious difficulty, Straub bit back whatever he'd been about to say.

Fitzgerald was the bulldog to Straub's high-strung fox terrier, she thought suddenly. With his big build running slightly to fat and his slow, deliberate movements, he gave the impression of being the stereotypical plodding cop.

But he was the one she had to worry about. His next comment, although it was phrased as an afterthought, made that abundantly clear.

"I know I don't have to ask if you left the scene exactly as you found it, Sullivan. You've been in this business long enough not to be removing evidence, haven't you?"

There was the faintest of brogues in his inquiry, and when Sullivan spoke his voice held an echo of it.

"Sure, Fitz, and you were right the first time. You don't have to ask." His attitude was as lazily unconcerned as the other man's, but Bailey had the unsettling feeling that the real conversation between the two was as antagonistic as it was unspoken.

"I've changed, Fitz," Sullivan went on, pulling out a chair from the table and straddling it backward. He folded his arms along its back and shook his head ruefully. "You still see me as that crazy lad I used to be, but those days are behind me. I've learned to play by the rules, now."

"Is that so?" There was a harder note in Fitzgerald's voice, but his expression was one of mild interest, no more. "The way I heard it, it took you entirely too long to learn that lesson, and it was an expensive one. But you seem to have come through unscathed."

"The same way you came through that unpleasantness at that godforsaken little desert town unscathed," Sullivan said softly. "Who the hell were we fighting that time, anyway, Fitz? I forget."

His arms were still folded casually along the back of his chair, and his posture was easy and relaxed, but glancing sharply at his face, Bailey saw a muscle at the side of his jaw tense. Puzzled, she flicked her gaze back to Fitzgerald. There was a rigid stillness on his expression, and she saw that Sullivan's words had meant something to him.

"The enemy," the detective said shortly. "That's all we ever had to know, Sully. But maybe we were always really fighting ourselves. You saved my life that night—except we never should have been so far away from backup in the first place, Terry, and you know it.''

Their eyes locked, and for a moment Bailey had the uncomfortable feeling that if she dared to step between the burly police detective and the big man lounging in the chair, it would be like intercepting twin laser beams. She'd known from Sullivan's greeting of Fitzgerald that there was some level of familiarity between them, but now she realized that that familiarity ran much deeper than she had first suspected.

Fitzgerald had obviously served with Sullivan as a soldier of fortune. Unlike the graying Englishman she'd spoken with that day on the Common, it seemed he hadn't approved of his methods.

''What the hell has this trip down memory lane got to do with anything, Donny?'' Straub burst out, his limited supply of patience obviously depleted. ''Whatever wars you two fought together in are long over, so why don't we get back to the matter at hand here?'' He turned to Sullivan. ''I think we should go over your story one more time, mister. Maybe you'll remember a few more details down at the station.''

He'd done what she had known instinctively would be foolish, Bailey thought. He'd interfered in whatever private battle was going on between Sullivan and Fitz, and suddenly the two ex-comrades were once again on the same side, united against him.

''Wars are never over, Petey boy,'' his partner said in a deceptively silky tone. ''Not that you'd know about that, since you never fought in one. If you had, you might have learned something about reading men. Sully here is lying about something, I'm sure of it—but I'd bet my next paycheck that he's telling the truth when he says he doesn't know what happened to his man Jackson.''

"Yeah? Well, any lie is grounds to take him in as far as I'm concerned," Straub said tightly, his fair skin coloring. "Once we get him into an interrogation room, I'm willing to bet *my* paycheck that I can hold out longer than he can. I want some answers from your foxhole buddy, and I'm going to get them."

Sullivan finally spoke. The edge of amusement in his voice was deliberate, Bailey knew. "I don't think so, boyo. Wearing you down would be so easy it wouldn't even be fun. You might be hell on grilling petty thieves and hookers, but you're way out of your league with me. Your partner here will back me up on that one." He glanced over at Fitzgerald, and the burly detective allowed a ghost of a grin to cross his features. He shifted the toothpick in his mouth and nodded.

"Thirty-seven hours of questioning by the leader of that insane rebel faction in the mountains, wasn't it, Sully?"

"Thirty-eight," Sullivan said, frowning slightly. "Or maybe thirty-nine. That last hour was pretty much a blur. I was beginning to think you and the boys had taken a vote and decided to wash your hands of me."

"When we finally showed up, I seem to recollect you were going through Al-Hamid's family tree for him. It was hard to make out exactly what you were saying through a broken jaw and with the side of your face the approximate size of a football, but it appeared as though he was getting the gist. Something about a sheep, or was it a goat?"

Sullivan grinned wryly. "Hell, all I was trying to do by then was make him mad enough to get careless. It would have worked, too, if you and McGuire hadn't barged in just when I was getting to the good part." He glanced over at Fitzgerald. "Anyway, it all worked out in the end. I got the troop strength and materiel figures we needed, didn't I?"

"Yeah, you did." The faint amusement left the other man's face, and his tone was quiet. "And you nearly got what you really wanted. Of course, that didn't stop you from trying again."

"I don't know what you're talking about, Fitz." Watching him, Bailey saw the blue eyes become instantly opaque, although there was no change in the easy good humor of his expression. "I got out alive—that time with Al-Hamid, and every other time."

The detective's gaze was steady and unwavering, and under it Sullivan looked suddenly away. "Don't lie to yourself, Sully." There was an odd intensity in his tone. "Lie to everyone else if you have to, but not to yourself. You did get what you wanted in the end, didn't you? You're a dead man walking," he said softly, his voice pitched so low that Bailey had to strain to hear him.

The conference room was well lit and spacious, but all of a sudden she felt as if the walls were closing in on her and the lights had flickered and powered down. *Dead man walking*. What did Fitzgerald mean by that? Even as the question came into her mind, she knew it was unnecessary to voice it. The heavyset ex-soldier, with his deceptively stolid demeanor and his prosaically unimaginative manner, had simply put into words the impression that she had always told herself was too fanciful and melodramatic to consider. Fitz saw the same thing in Terrence Patrick Sullivan that she'd subconsciously seen the first time she'd laid eyes on him.

He was good-looking, charming and seemingly invulnerable, Bailey thought. But something had a claim on his soul, and eventually that something would call in its claim.

"Your Irish imagination is running away with you, boyo."

Sullivan's wry grin looked so natural that Bailey felt a

momentary doubt. Maybe both she and Fitzgerald were wrong. Maybe Sully was exactly what he appeared to be on the surface, and what he insisted he was—a risktaker, yes, but with no more ulterior motivation behind his actions than an innate tendency to push situations to their limits, simply for the thrill of it.

"Next you'll be taking a leaf from Quinn McGuire's book of fairy tales and telling me that the wild geese have laid their mark on me. Is that what you think, Fitz—that they're waiting to take me with them from some battlefield that still lies ahead? Because if you do, then you're forgetting one thing." His brogue thickened. "I've got no intention entirely of joining them in eternity. That's why I walked away from the profession, isn't it now? They can't take me if I never go back, Fitz."

His words were gently mocking, but, glancing surreptitiously at the man he was directing them at, Bailey didn't see an answering smile on Fitzgerald's face. Instead his eyes closed for an instant, as if in pain. Then he opened them again and fixed Sullivan with an unwavering gaze.

"They don't have to. You're already up there with them, Sully."

"I thought we were here on an investigation, Donny." Straub's interjection was harsh. "What's all this crap about freakin' geese and battlefields and fairy tales got to do with anything?"

"Nothing at all, Detective." Sullivan's answer was just as harsh, but although he was apparently answering Straub, he didn't take his eyes off Fitzgerald. "It's a legend, that's all. Your partner here likes to trot out his Irish fatalism once in a while. It's all part of it, like the wearing of the green on St. Paddy's Day, getting into drunken arguments with strangers over the Troubles and insisting that one day you're going back to the old country for good. Like you so eloquently phrase it, it's crap.''

His grin was tight. ''And to be sure, I'd love to get together and lift a pint to *Erin go Bragh* sometime with you, Fitz, but right now I've got a business to run. If your baby pit bull intends to take me in for questioning, let's go. I'll call my lawyer and tell him to meet us down at the station. If not, then let me get back to work. Jackson was supposed to be looking into a case of industrial espionage this week, and I'm going to have to get another operative to take over the file.''

''All right, that's it.'' Straub's fair skin was mottled with anger. He took a step toward the chair that Sullivan was lounging in. ''Call your lawyer now, mister, because you're under arrest—''

''For God's sake, Pete, put the cuffs away,'' his partner cut in tiredly. ''Until we know what he lied about, it's hands off.'' The big man looked at the toothpick he was holding with sudden distaste, and then he sighed. ''You know, Straub, I'm just counting the days until Tarranova comes back from maternity leave and you get assigned as temporary partner to some other hapless soul.''

''When she does, Fitz, come back and pay me another visit.'' Rising easily from the chair he'd been straddling, Sullivan shoved it in under the table, the innocuous gesture clearly signifying that the meeting was over. ''She's a sweetheart, besides being a damn good cop, and I wouldn't mind seeing Jennifer again. But from now on keep this rookie away from me and my people, understand?''

''I understand, Sully.'' Fitzgerald's voice lost its weary tone and took on a harder edge. ''Don't worry, I won't return unless I have to.'' He stood in front of Sullivan, as if sizing him up. ''Just seeing me brings it all back, and you can't live with that, can you? You never could.''

"See you around, Fitz," Sullivan said shortly, walking to the doorway of the conference room and ignoring the other detective. "You know the way out."

"Yeah, I do." As Straub shot a black glance at Sullivan and stalked out of the room, Fitz hesitated. For the first time his attention focused on Bailey, and she felt oddly off balance under his intent scrutiny.

"You lied, too, Ms. Flowers," he said softly. "You didn't just come here on business. Take my advice and let him go, lady. He's gone already." The blue eyes narrowed on her searchingly. "But maybe you already knew that," he said, so quietly that Bailey realized Sullivan, a few feet away, wouldn't have heard him. "You can't save him, you know. No one ever could."

"Maybe no one ever tried." The words came from her mouth unthinkingly, and in just as low a tone as his. "Or maybe they just didn't try hard enough."

The big detective shook his head slowly. "You're as doomed as he is if you let yourself believe that. He can't change the road he's on. Don't go down it with him."

As Sullivan glanced over impatiently from the doorway, Fitzgerald gave Bailey one last look, and then turned from her. Without another word, he strode past his ex-comrade and was gone, leaving behind him a sudden silence.

Very carefully, Bailey walked over to the conference table. Pulling out a chair, she lowered herself into it, her movements slow and deliberate. The atmosphere in the room seemed close and heavy, but despite that she felt oddly chilled. She hugged herself for warmth and realized with a small shock that the fine hairs on her skin were standing up.

She didn't blame Straub for being confused. She had no idea what that conversation had been about. She didn't even know what her part in it had meant.

Why hadn't she laughed off Fitzgerald's cryptic warning, or at least asked him to explain what he'd meant by it? Why had she answered him the way she had, and so promptly?

Maybe they didn't try hard enough... Her lips pressed together in a line and she sat up straighter in the chair, feeling a flicker of anger catch somewhere deep inside her. She wasn't here to save Terrence Sullivan, dammit. She'd come here to get some answers about what had happened to Angelica. Admittedly, she'd also hoped to gain some closure on her former relationship with him by finally learning the truth about why he'd needed to tear her life apart so completely a year ago, but that had been for her own sake, not his.

She looked up as he moved from the doorway and met her eyes, his own as unclouded as if he'd already forgotten the scene that had just taken place with the two detectives.

"He knew we took the file." He perched on the edge of the long mahogany table and looked down at her, one corner of his mouth lifting. "Well, maybe he didn't know *what* we took, but he knew we had something from Jackson's house. Fitz doesn't miss much."

"I'd already come to that conclusion." She didn't match his light tone. "What was the legend he was talking about? What are the wild geese?"

"*Who* are the wild geese, darlin'," he corrected her, shrugging. "They're the souls of mercenaries who die in battle, if you're inclined to believe in that sort of thing. I'm not. Fitz and Quinn McGuire, another of my old comrades, are."

Despite his wry smile, his tone was clipped, and Bailey knew he was about to change the subject. Before he could, she went on, frowning. "Where are they supposed to be flying to?"

He gave an impatient sigh. "Fitz and his old wives' tales, for God's sake. The story goes that they're fated to fly for eternity, searching the world over for the homes they never had." Without seeming to realize what he was doing, his hand went to his pants pocket and pulled out a small object. He continued, his manner verging on brusqueness. "But he can't have it both ways. If his damned legend were true, then it'd be easy enough to escape fate. All a poor Irish boy like myself would have to do is turn his back on that life and take up another profession, and he'd be out of their reach. All my wars are behind me, honey. I'm safe from Fitz's ghosts now."

The small object was a shell. Bailey watched it flash and reappear as he unthinkingly maneuvered it between his fingers, like a gambler with one last coin. He saw her watching him, and his fingers stilled.

"That's pretty. Can I see it?"

She held out her hand, and after an almost imperceptible hesitation he dropped it into her palm. She looked at it more closely. It was fan shaped, with a perfectly round hole in the exact middle of the fan. It was smooth, as if its ridges had been worn down over the years, and instead of being cool, as she had expected, it felt oddly warm in her hand.

She looked up at Sullivan. "How did you drill such a tiny hole—" She halted abruptly, shocked at the expression on his face.

His eyes were dark with pain, and the skin over his cheekbones seemed to have tightened, sharpening the hard angles of his face. His lips were a tautly compressed line, and when he spoke they barely moved.

"I didn't drill it. It was formed that way, or at least that's what my father told me. He carried it on him for years. After he died, it was sent to me along with the rest of his final effects, and now I keep it on me, just like he did. He said it was his talisman."

As if he couldn't help himself, he held out his hand for the shell and she handed it back. As soon as his fingers wrapped around it, he seemed to relax, and carefully he dropped it into his pocket again.

"Psalm 91," he said, his voice once more edged with rueful humor. " 'The arrow that flieth by day, the pestilence that walketh in darkness.' Thomas Sullivan believed that as long as he carried it, he would be protected from them, and now his son's carrying on the tradition. I guess there's a little superstition in me after all."

Superstition hadn't been the cause of that terrible bleakness she'd seen on his face, Bailey thought, shaken. But she knew the man well enough to realize that if that was what he wanted her to believe, nothing she could say would get anything more out of him. Needing suddenly to bring some semblance of normalcy back to the conversation, she reached for her purse on the chair beside her and pulled out the file.

"I guess this is called withholding evidence," she said, hoping that her voice sounded steadier than she felt. As if he was just as eager to seize upon a new topic as she was, Sullivan took the slim sheaf of papers she handed him.

"Obstructing the police in the commission of their duties, at least." He flipped through the first few pages of Jackson's report, scanning them rapidly. "Nothing here that you didn't already know, is there?"

"Just details." She lifted her shoulders. "But they'll help. He mentions the name of the hotel, for example, and the number of the room Plowright and his playmate were staying in."

"And the photos he took." Sullivan was on the last page of the report. "This is a list of them, with a description of where and when each one was taken. Listen to this. 'Roll 2, frame 16: Subject Plowright beside bed. Unidentified female companion on bed, wearing negligee. Blinds on hotel suite's French doors fully open.' He must have been using a telephoto lens to get that shot.''

He handed the report to her. After a moment she looked up from it in disappointment. ''That was the spiciest one he got. Before Plowright got down to business he closed the blinds.''

''Yeah, I noticed that. Frame 19 is him, shirtless, closing them, according to Hank's list.'' Sullivan shrugged. ''Still, it's pretty conclusive, even if they weren't caught on film actually doing the wild thing with each—''

''Little pitchers have big ears, Terry,'' a brisk voice said from the doorway. ''I know it's asking a lot of you, but try to keep it clean for the next few minutes.''

Bailey looked up swiftly. The woman who had spoken was fixing Sullivan with a glare from blue eyes that looked a lot like his. Her hair was as almost the same midnight shade as his was, too, and not much longer, its urchinlike cut framing an angry, heart-shaped face. Beside her was a young girl with long coltlike legs and a mane of coppery hair tamed into a thick braid that was coming undone.

Sullivan looked at his watch and then swore under his breath. ''I said seven o'clock, didn't I?'' he said weakly. ''I'm sorry, Lee. Something came up and I lost track of the time. But you're here now, so why don't we—''

''Some things just never change, Terry. Not where the Sullivan men are concerned, anyway.'' The dark-haired woman's expression was tight and closed. ''It's way after regular office hours, so I'm guessing this isn't a business appointment.''

She jerked her head stiffly at Bailey, her voice rising.

"Like father, like son. It's obvious that you can't fit into a normal life any more than Thomas could. Why don't you just go back to being a damned *mercenary,* like he did in the end?''

Chapter Four

Swiftly Ainslie turned on her heel. Shooting an agonized look of apology at Sullivan, the young redhead—Tara, Bailey guessed—followed her down the hall. Bailey waited for Sullivan to go after them and work his charm on his sister, but to her surprise he simply stood there, his hands clenched into fists at his sides, his eyes shadowed.

"I screwed up," he said harshly. "And with Lee, of all people. Dammit, I *knew* how fragile this relationship was— how the hell could I have let her down in exactly the same way."

She didn't understand all the ramifications of the scene she'd just witnessed, Bailey thought swiftly, but she knew one thing. For some reason her presence had seemed to be the decisive element for Sullivan's sister, the factor that had turned her anger to pain.

Some things never change—not where the Sullivan men are concerned... There'd been a rawness in Ainslie's voice as she'd made the accusation, and it had been the rawness of a wound that had never fully healed. She'd been there herself, Bailey thought in resignation. She knew what it felt like.

"For heaven's sake," she muttered, getting quickly out of her chair and striding to the doorway. "Covering your butt was the *last* thing I expected to be doing when I came here today, Sullivan.''

She saw them as soon as she stepped into the hallway. Standing by the vacant reception desk—Moira had left for the day just after Fitzgerald and Straub had arrived—they were waiting for the elevator to arrive, and their discussion looked heated. Tara, almost as tall as Ainslie but with the awkward slenderness of a preteen, had her arms crossed tensely in front of her. Despite her antagonistic attitude and the trendy clothes she was wearing—a skinny baby tee that stopped just south of her belly button and jeans that rode low on her nonexistent hips—she only succeeded in looking heartbreakingly young and miserable.

Ainslie, on the other hand, appeared to have regained a little of her composure. She was wearing an outfit that was simply a more mature version of her goddaughter's—jeans and a multicolored sweater—but instead of looking vulnerable, she looked ready to punch in the elevator door. She was probably more than capable of doing so, Bailey thought nervously. Sullivan had mentioned once that Ainslie had boxed professionally in a women's featherweight division for a time, and now she trained her own fighters at the gym that she ran downtown.

But I know karate, Bailey told herself hollowly, advancing on them with a confidence she didn't feel. *Besides, I made it to the finish in the Boston Marathon last year. I can probably outrun her.*

''If you're here to relay an apology from my big brother, tell him to forget it,'' Ainslie snapped. She jabbed at the elevator call button impatiently. ''And tell him his damned elevator's just as unreliable as he is,'' she added with an edge of frustration.

''He's not unreliable, Auntie Lee.'' Tara's bottom lip stuck out pugnaciously. ''What's your problem with Uncle

Sully, anyway? You didn't even let him explain why he hadn't shown up!''

''I didn't need to hear his explanation. The O'Connell women have heard enough explanations from the Sullivan men over the years, and I'm about to end the tradition right here and now. It's her birthday, for crying out loud.'' Ainslie directed this last sentence to Bailey, and her eyes were glittering with unshed tears. ''Maybe you two had a hot date or something, but I would have thought even Terry would consider a young girl's thirteenth birthday dinner a little more important than his latest conquest.''

''I'm not his latest conquest,'' Bailey finally managed to interject. ''I'm last year's,'' she added dryly. ''Which means that whatever you've got against him, I'd normally be on your side, except that this time it really wasn't his fault. One of his men went missing, and the police were here questioning him up until half an hour ago. You're lucky he didn't have to phone you from jail to make bail for him.''

Ainslie's stunned gaze went past her, and Bailey turned to find Sullivan behind her. ''It's true, Lee, but that's no excuse. I should have phoned you. I'm sorry.''

''Who's missing?'' His sister ignored his apology.

''Hank Jackson.'' He grimaced. ''You've heard me speak of him—he's been with the agency since before I took it over from Uncle Sean. We think it might be tied to a case that Bailey was involved with.''

''Bailey?'' The navy gaze, not quite as dark as her brother's, switched back to Bailey and widened. ''As in Flowers?''

''Cut it out, sis.'' Sullivan's tone was sharp, but it softened as he turned to Tara. ''What a babe,'' he said admiringly. ''New jeans, new top...'' He paused and peered closely at the pink-cheeked young face. ''And if I'm not mistaken, my little sister's finally caved in on the no-makeup rule now that you're officially a teenager. Is that eye shadow you're wearing?''

"Eye glimmer." Tara's blush deepened. "And lip gloss, too."

"Only for special occasions, and I'd better not catch you wearing it to school yet, young lady," warned Ainslie with mock gruffness. "The nuns would have my hide."

The elevator chose that moment to open, and on impulse Bailey turned to Sullivan. "I should leave. We can go over the Plowright file tomorrow and decide where we're going to take it from here," she said swiftly. "Why don't you three keep that pizza date you had planned?"

"I've got a better idea." Ainslie looked up at her brother, and before her features assumed their normally wry expression, Bailey saw a flash of loving concern pass across her face. "Why don't we order in here? It'll still be a party, but you and Bailey will have a chance to look over the file and make plans. I know you're worried about Hank, Terry," she added quietly.

"Cool!" Tara's eyes lit up with excitement. "While we're waiting for the pizza, can I log on to the Internet on your computer and e-mail my friends, Uncle Sully?"

"I guess so." Sullivan raised a dubious eyebrow. "But from now on you're going to have to use your own at home, sweetheart. I can't have you on mine all the time."

"But I don't have one at—" The inexpertly glossed mouth dropped open and the green eyes, beautiful despite the smear of shine that decorated each lid, widened. "You got me a computer for my birthday?" she squealed incredulously. "Oh, Uncle Sully, you're the greatest!"

She wrapped her arms around him, almost knocking him backward, and over her head he grinned weakly at his sister. "Don't be mad, Lee. I know you said it was too extravagant, but I wanted to. I'll cover the Internet charges, and I arranged for an extra phone line so yours wouldn't be tied up all the time. I hope you like lime,'' he said to the top of Tara's head. She was still hugging him. ''Because that's the color I got. I thought it would go with those cat's-eyes of yours, sugar.''

''I *love* lime! Is it here? Can we see it?'' Tara turned to Ainslie, her face alight. ''Do you mind phoning for the pizza while Uncle Sully shows me my computer, Auntie Lee? Double cheese, no anchovies, and pineapple on half, okay?''

''Only because it's your birthday.'' Ainslie shuddered, and then flapped her hand at her brother and her goddaughter. ''Go on, Bailey and I can manage to order a pizza, I guess. I'll tell Martin at the security desk downstairs we're expecting a delivery.''

''Order one for him and Mike, too.'' Fishing his wallet out of his pocket with difficulty, since Tara was still clinging to him like a limpet, Sullivan grinned. ''But ask them first if they want pineapple on theirs. Their palates might not be sophisticated enough to handle it.''

''My palate's not sophisticated enough. Or maybe it's just that I'm not a teenager anymore,'' Ainslie said wryly to Bailey as she slipped behind Moira's desk and punched in a number on the phone.

From Sullivan's office a couple of doors down the hall came a series of high-pitched exclamations, interspersed with the deeper tones of Sullivan explaining the features of Tara's new computer to her. Ainslie caught Bailey's amused expression and grinned herself.

''He's a pushover, but then so am I when it comes to her,'' she said ruefully. ''She's a good kid. I just hope I'm raising her the way her mother would have wanted me to.''

Within a matter of minutes, she'd placed the orders. The

more subdued murmurs now coming from Sullivan's office seemed to signify that he and Tara had passed the bells-and-whistles stage of the computer demonstration and were now getting down to exploring its more complicated capabilities. Ainslie tipped her head to one side, listening.

"Nah," she said decisively. "I'm not going in. I might have been able to help them get it out of the box, but that's about where my expertise ends. No need to give them a chance to feel *too* superior to me."

"It sounds like they're getting along fine without us," Bailey agreed with a smile. "Tara's your adopted daughter?"

They entered the conference room and Ainslie pulled out one of the comfortably upholstered chairs that ringed the massive table. With a sigh she sat down, leaning back and propping her crossed legs on the gleaming tabletop. Her pose was almost identical to the one that Sullivan had been assuming when she'd first walked in on him in his office this morning, Bailey noted with amusement. It seemed that the two of them were alike in some ways, at least. She sat down herself, pushing the Plowright file aside for the moment.

"Her mom was my cousin." Ainslie raked back her glossy black bangs and met Bailey's gaze. "She got pregnant when she was a teenager herself, but instead of giving the baby up for adoption she insisted on keeping it. Everybody told her she was crazy, even the teenaged father, who promptly moved with his family out of state. But when Tara was born the whole O'Connell clan fell in love with her." Her smile was touched with sadness. "Seven years later Babs was gone. Leukemia," she said briefly. "It was as if she'd known she only had one chance to be a mother, and she'd made the most of it. Tara was her pride and joy."

"She must have been very close to you to leave her daughter in your care," Bailey said gently.

"Her mother was my mom's sister, and we moved in with them when my father left, so yeah, we were close." Ainslie looked over at her. "Thomas Sullivan was my father, but he just wasn't the type to settle down with one woman and a family, even though he already had a son from his first marriage. He was almost as good-looking as Terry is now, and women just couldn't resist him. He couldn't resist them, either. When my mother realized he was never going to change, she gave him his walking papers and he was gone, taking Terry with him. I was five years old, and I lost my father and my adored big brother in one day," she said softly. "I never saw Thomas again, and I didn't see Terry for years. We don't even share the same last name anymore—Mom changed it back after the divorce."

And that explained much of her reaction half an hour ago, Bailey thought with a rush of compassion. Ainslie O'Connell might be tough enough to deal with the sweat and blood of a boxing ring, but some part of her was still that little five-year-old who only knew that the males in her life had walked out one night and never come back to her. No wonder she was so wary with her brother—half brother, Bailey corrected herself. But how had it been for Sullivan? He would have been around Tara's age when his feckless charmer of a father had uprooted him for the second time in his life, continuing with him on the restless journey that apparently had been Thomas Sullivan's life.

"It sounds like Sully inherited more from his father than just those black Irish good looks," she hazarded.

"From what you said, I guess you've got firsthand knowledge of that." Ainslie put up a hand, frowning. "I'm not prying. But you're the only one of his women he ever mentioned by name.''

"I wouldn't make too much of that if I were you," Bailey said impassively. "Your brother's moved on since last year, and so have I. I really did come here to see him on business today.''

"That's too bad.'' Under straight dark brows, Lee looked appraisingly at her. "I've got a feeling that only the love of a good woman is going to be enough to save the man.''

Bailey felt an uncomfortable prickling sensation run down the length of her spine at Ainslie's words. It was the second time today someone had tried to cast her in the role of Terrence Sullivan's savior, she thought sharply. If that was the impression she was giving out, she wanted to dispel it—and fast.

"I'm sure he'll have no trouble finding plenty of takers for the position," she said. "But right now I've got a more immediate problem to worry about, and so does he. I seem to have mislaid a sister, and his best operative's gone missing.''

She'd just finished sketching out the details of Angelica's disappearance and their discovery of Jackson's trashed home office when Sullivan joined them. He was bearing a large flat box, and under one arm he had three cans of cola that were in danger of falling. Ainslie jumped up and took them from him as he set the pizza box down on the table.

"Where's the birthday girl?" she asked, pulling a wad of paper serviettes from his back pocket and lifting up the pizza box just high enough to slip a nearby telephone book underneath. "Really, Terry, it's mahogany,'' she chided distractedly.

"The little ingrate asked if she could have hers at the computer. I said we'd be glad not to watch her eating her revolting fruit-topped concoction.'' He flipped open the lid of the box. "Pepperoni, tomatoes and onions. Now *that's* the way God intended pizza to be."

"Which is why He invented mouthwash," his sister said dryly. "But as long as we're all on the same garlicky playing field, I guess it doesn't matter."

She lifted a slice from the box and took a bite. Bailey and Sullivan did the same, and for a minute or so all that disturbed the silence of the elegantly appointed conference room were the sounds of chewing and the occasional murmur of appreciation from Ainslie.

"Good pizza," she said, daintily licking her fingers and taking another piece. "Bailey was telling me about her sister's marital woes, Terry. How can you be so sure Angelica's case has anything to do with Hank's disappearance? Come to that, how can you be sure that Angelica's disappearance has got anything to do with what's in that report? After all," she added apologetically to Bailey, "from the way you describe her it sounds as if she might just have taken off for a few days to nurse her wounded pride. Is she the type to do something drastic?"

"I wouldn't have said so if you'd asked me a week ago." Bailey shrugged and took another slice of pizza herself. "And I still don't think she threw herself off the nearest bridge or anything like that. But she was upset when she left that message on my machine—it's entirely possible that she's decided to pay Aaron back in his own coin."

"A little fling?" Ainslie raised an eyebrow. "Isn't that slightly rash, when he's the one with the money? And I presume the money's important to her, since there's a thirty-year gap in their ages."

"Oh, the money's important to my sister." Bailey gave a humorless smile. "She was determined to hold out for a millionaire."

"You don't sound like the two of you are that close,"

Ainslie said cautiously. Sullivan shot her a warning look, but after a moment's hesitation Bailey answered her.

"I'd like to have been closer, and maybe it was my fault we weren't," she said slowly. "I know that since our parents were killed in a car accident six years ago, Angelica made it clear that she was going to live her own life, with no interference from me. At seventeen she quit school, found a job and rented an apartment with a couple of other girls. It wasn't until a lot later that I learned she was working underage in a bar, thanks to some fake ID an obliging boyfriend had obtained for her. But even from the day she became part of the family, I felt as if she saw me as competition. It wasn't hard to figure out where that came from, though," Bailey added fairly. "Her mother had been an addict, and from the little I know about the first five years of Angel's life, love was a pretty scarce commodity. It's no wonder she went for something she could actually be sure of when she married."

"How sure?" Sullivan said suddenly. "Aaron Plowright, as determined as he must have been to get his new little eighteen-year-old plaything into his bed one way or another, certainly wasn't a lovesick boy when it came to his fourth marriage. Did he get her to sign a prenuptial agreement?"

Bailey looked at him, startled. Slowly she dabbed at her lips with the serviette, her gaze thoughtful. "I seem to remember she did, although she wasn't happy about it. Like I said, Angelica's blond and she puts on that dumb act when it suits her, but she's not stupid when it comes to money."

"Which means it's also unlikely she'd be impulsive enough to jeopardize her marital status by fooling around." Ainslie eyed the last slice of pizza in the box and then shook her head. "You take it, big guy."

"I hadn't thought of that, but you're right," Bailey said, her gaze darkening. "Dammit, if my little drama queen of a sister staged that phone message just for effect, I'm going to wring her neck when I see her!"

"I'd say go for it, except for one thing," Sullivan said with a frown. "Hank's missing, too."

Ainslie fiddled unnecessarily with the lid of the pizza box, and Bailey looked down at her hands. Neither of them spoke, and Sullivan's jaw tightened.

"I thought you agreed with me on this." His tense comment was directed at Bailey, and reluctantly she met his gaze.

"I'll admit, back at his house I was halfway convinced. The fact that you say he can't drink rye, the missing towels, the wrecked computer, the files all over the floor." She bit her bottom lip. "But to be honest, I think it was the atmosphere that really got to me. For some reason I had the creeps the whole time we were there."

She shrugged helplessly. "But don't you see, Sully, there was nothing there that couldn't be explained away, if only you'd accept that Jackson—" She broke off, not wanting to complete the sentence. Ainslie did it for her.

"He's a friend, and you're loyal to a fault to your friends, bro," she said brusquely. "But he likes the bottle, and when he's gone off the wagon in the past he's been a mean drunk. He even trashed the office of Sullivan Investigations when it was just a two-man operation in that seedy location in the South End years ago. Uncle Sean almost fired him over that, remember?"

"Sean liked the bottle a little too well himself, and his stories always got embellished in the telling," Sullivan said tightly. "Hank never tried to hide the fact that he had a problem, but in the past few years he's gotten it under control. What are you saying—that he trashed those files himself?''

He sounded incredulous, and Bailey saw Ainslie's eyes spark with anger. ''At least admit it's a possibility,'' she snapped. ''For God's sake, loyalty is one thing, but there comes a point where you have to turn your back and walk away.''

''I did that once.'' Her brother's voice was ice. ''I promised myself I'd never do it again. Jackson's one of my men, Lee, and I won't let him down. I'm going to find him, and if anything's happened to him I'm going to find the person who did it.''

He sounded nothing like the indulgent man who only an hour ago had been bantering with Tara. His tone was implacable, and his expression was bleakly remote.

He was sitting here beside her, Bailey thought suddenly, but in reality Terrence Patrick Sullivan was so far away he was out of her reach. He was somewhere in the past, reliving it over and over again.

''I did that once.'' There had been cold self-condemnation in his words, and she realized that she'd gained another tiny fragment of the puzzle she'd been trying to piece together for the past year. He obviously felt that he'd let someone down, with tragic consequences—but who?

There was only one person it could have been. There was only one person from his past that Sullivan still mourned, one person whose death had nearly destroyed him, according to all accounts.

Maria Salazar.

''...just show up at the Harris Hotel and start snooping around asking questions about Aaron Plowright, for heaven's sake. You'll look like what you are—a damn gumshoe on an investigation!'' Ainslie's voice was annoyed enough to break into Bailey's thoughts, and she looked up in surprise.

"You're planning on taking a room at the Harris? Ainslie's right, Sullivan, it's a small, very exclusive bijou hotel. That's probably why Aaron took his honey there, because the staff is the last word in discretion. There's no way they're going to spill confidential information about a guest to you."

"Not even if hotel security is headed by an old buddy of mine?" His smile was tight. "And besides, I'm not going alone to the Harris, you're coming with me. I figure we'll attract less attention as a couple."

"I don't think so." Bailey's reply was immediate. She met his hard gaze with one of her own. "You and me in a hotel room together, Sully? That phase of our relationship is over."

"It's business, darlin'." Something flickered at the back of his eyes, and just as swiftly was hidden again. He went on, his tone losing its edge. "You came to me, Bailey, and even though you're obviously not convinced that anything's happened to Hank, you've got to admit that two missing people connected to the same case bears investigating. All we have to go on is Plowright's weekend at the Harris and the mystery woman he took there. It can't hurt to find out who she was."

He made it sound so reasonable, she thought. And he was right. Individually, Hank's disappearance and Angelica's unknown whereabouts weren't grounds for panic, but together they were more disturbing than she wanted to admit. But spending today with him had brought back too many conflicting emotions for her to contemplate anything more intimate, even if it was under the guise of business.

"For crying out loud, Terry, how dense can you get?" Ainslie snorted inelegantly. "I don't know a lot about what went on between you two, but I know that it didn't end pretty. Do you blame the woman for not wanting to get up close and personal again with you? If I was Bailey, I'd be scared of history repeating itself, too!''

"I'm not scared, Ainslie," Bailey said tartly. "Your brother's not *that* irresistible. I think I can work with him on a case without going all weak at the knees at the thought of spending a night with him in a hotel room." She looked sharply over at Sullivan. "Separate beds, though, Sully. That's not negotiable."

He looked uncomfortable. "Well, that could be a problem. See, the Harris only had one room available for tomorrow night, and it was the—"

"You booked it already?" She narrowed her eyes at him in outrage. "You took it for granted that I'd agree, Sullivan?"

He met her eyes directly. "I hoped you would," he said, his manner suddenly uncertain. "Ainslie's right—a single man stands out at a place like the Harris, especially a single man asking questions. John Steiner's a friend of mine, but he's not about to lose his security position there just to help me out on a case. I need to know if Hank saw something last weekend that put him in danger, Bailey. I can't just leave it in the hands of the police. I have to look into this myself, and for that I need your help."

If he'd tried to charm her into agreeing, she would have been able to turn him down flat, Bailey thought in resignation. But the one thing that Sullivan had never done before was to ask her for her help.

For a job, Flowers, she told herself sharply. *That's all this is—a job. You're going undercover with the man on an investigation, and your cover just happens to be as a pair of lovers. It's not as if you're going on your honeymoon or anything.*

She looked suddenly up at him, her thoughts screeching to a halt as a thought occurred to her. "Don't tell me." Her tone was flat with certainty. "The only room available at the Harris was the—"

"—the bridal suite," Sullivan finished for her. "So pack some rice, honey."

Chapter Five

When he'd been told that the honeymoon suite was the only room available, Sullivan hadn't expected anything too out-of-the-ordinary. Maybe more pink in the decor than normal. Maybe the odd heart-shaped pillow scattered here and there on the furniture.

Not this.

"I've never *seen* a bed so ridiculous," Bailey snapped. She plopped down on the edge of the satin spread and struggled with the oversize corsage that he'd pinned on her dress's matching jacket earlier. Her voice was muffled as she went on, her head bent over the spray of orchids.

"What's with this canopy and these lace bed curtains, for Pete's sake? Does the Harris have a mosquito problem?" Her tone grew more querulous, but all he could see was the top of her head and the orchids shaking violently as she wrestled with them. "And all this damn white velvet and satin—it looks like the world's biggest casket!"

With a muttered oath, she suddenly stood up and shrugged out of her jacket before he could help her. Swiftly she freed the recalcitrant pin that was securing the corsage, and then she tossed jacket and orchids onto the despised bed. With both hands she scooped back her hair from her face and took a deep breath.

"Sorry about that," she said shortly, exhaling. She met his eyes and took another, shakier breath. "Once upon a time I thought there was a possibility that someday we'd be doing this for real," she said simply. "Even though I got over that particular fantasy a long time ago, it still felt a little odd watching you sign the register Mr. and Mrs. and tipping the rice out of my shoes in the elevator."

She gave him a lopsided smile. "I think I'll go change out of my going-away outfit into slacks and a top."

Quickly unzipping the suitcase the bellhop had set on a low table near the bed, she pulled out some clothing and headed for the bathroom. As she closed the door behind her, Sullivan heard her muttering something in an irritated undertone about the size of the bath.

He sat down heavily on the edge of the bed. Then he let himself fall back into a prone position. Above his head where the canopy came together in lacy gathers was a gilded cupid.

He'd stood there and said nothing to her just now, because there'd been nothing to say, he thought, closing his eyes and still seeing her face. He couldn't tell her anything like the truth, because the truth was something he'd lost the right to give her long before he'd met her. His currency was counterfeit—counterfeit emotions, false loyalties and a lie of a life. It had been that way up until that day in the jungle seven years ago. It had continued in that way ever since, because on that day he had learned that he'd left it too late to change.

Fitz had been right. Slowly Sullivan sat up and rubbed the heel of his hand across his forehead. What had he called him—a dead man walking? However he'd put it, he'd been right.

But what Fitz hadn't known was that he was getting tired of walking. And what Bailey could never know was that when he took that last step, her face would still be the one he saw when he closed his eyes for the final time.

He stood up, peeling off his jacket and slinging it onto a nearby chair, catching a glimpse of himself in the mirrored closet doors that stretched the length of the room as he did so. On an impulse, he drew closer and stared at his own reflection as if the man in the mirror were a stranger.

Black hair, blue eyes, rangy build. Big wrist bones, that when he'd been a boy had stuck out awkwardly from the cuffs of all his shirts. Thomas had always been pleased at how much his son had resembled him, and Sullivan could still remember how that handsome, tanned face had broken into a grin when anyone had commented on the resemblance.

His father had loved him, that had been the problem. He'd loved him right up until the end, when the legend had come true for him. That had been eight years ago, on some disputed border between two countries that Sully had only vaguely heard of. Amazingly, his personal effects had been carefully gathered up and sent back to the address he'd provided when he'd signed on that last time, and that address had been his son's. They hadn't amounted to much. When the battered package had arrived on his doorstep, Sullivan remembered, at first he'd thought it was empty, it was so light. By then he'd been notified, and the official notification had been confirmed by a friend of his father's who'd seen him killed, so he'd opened the package with a jumble of conflicting emotions, none of them good.

It had contained a woman's silk scarf with the unknown charmer's perfume still clinging faintly to it, a watch with a shattered glass and a dog-eared snapshot. He'd sat there beside the open box, holding the photo of himself as a boy in his hand, and he'd cried.

Sullivan blinked at his reflection in the mirror. He hadn't

cried for his father's death. Death had simply been the release that Thomas Sullivan had been searching for during all those years of restless wandering and relentless philandering, and had never found. No, he'd cried for his father's life, he thought dully. It had been a wasted one and a destructive one, and at the end Thomas himself must have known that.

It had been the way he was. He'd failed everyone who'd ever put their faith in him. And his son was just like him, Sullivan thought, except that he knew himself for what he was.

"You tell yourself sometimes that you could make it work, but you know it never could," he told the man in the mirror softly. "A woman like Bailey deserves a whole man, not a ghost who left his soul in a jungle hellhole. You don't have the right to want her, not when you know that sooner or later you're going to have to go back."

He fell silent, gazing into the unreadable blue eyes that gazed back at him. From the bathroom he heard the sound of running water stop, and he knew that at any minute she would rejoin him. There was one thing he could do during these next few days with Bailey, and no one was going to stop him, he thought. He was going to stockpile memories—as many as he could, from the way she smiled to the way she frowned and everything in between. He was going to try to make her laugh, and he intended to hoard that image, too. And when this case was finally over and they went their separate ways again, she would never have to know that some part of her would be with him always.

"I WISH I COULD HELP YOU more, Sully, but you know how it is. This job comes with a pension and benefits, and I've got a family to worry about now."

John Steiner was a small, wiry man with skin the color

of rawhide. He looked as tough as rawhide, too, Bailey thought, and it was obvious that not much got by him in his capacity as head of security for the Harris.

"This telephone log is more than I'd expected, Rocky." Sullivan ran his gaze down the computer printout of numbers that the other man had just handed him. "Plowright and his little friend placed and received a lot of calls from Room 201 in the couple of days they were here."

Steiner grinned. "God, no one's called me that since the old days. I'm more used to being called Da-Da now, since my youngest started learning to talk." He shook his head, but Bailey could see the pride in his expression.

Sullivan smiled. "One day I'd like to come by and meet Diane and those two little girls of yours." He started to fold up the printout, but then paused.

"You're looking at the time of that first incoming call," Steiner said, frowning. "I caught that, too, and I'm still looking into it. It's a little harder to get the numbers for the calls that came in, but not impossible."

"Almost an hour before Plowright and his guest arrived," mused Sullivan. "Let me know if you find out where it was placed from." He clapped the hotel detective on the shoulder. "I appreciate it, John. I know you're sticking your neck out on this."

"Yeah, well…" Steiner shrugged. "Hey, I worked with Hank Jackson on a couple of divorce cases when I was still freelancing. He was an okay guy when he wasn't drinking. I hope you find out what's happened to him, Sully." He turned to Bailey. "You took over Jane McLaughlin's agency, didn't you? Acme Investigations?"

"I've put a few more *A*s in front of the Acme, but yes, it's the same one that Jane used to run." Bailey's gaze softened in affectionate amusement. "She retired down to Florida a few years ago, but we keep in touch. She still thinks of me as that painfully inexperienced young book-keeping graduate she hired to keep track of her expenses—the one who found out within two weeks that it was a whole lot more fun to tail erring husbands around Boston than to sit at a desk adding up figures.''

Steiner chuckled. ''I'll second that. And this time it's your brother-in-law who's the erring husband, right? Well, as long as my name never comes up in the divorce documentation, I'll help you out as much as I can. You've got my pager number, and the front desk usually knows where I am, Sullivan.''

As they left his office on the ground floor of the hotel and made their way to the lobby, Bailey glanced over at the man beside her. She was dressed in one of the few pairs of dressy slacks that she owned—a pale beige pair in linen—and she'd topped them with a sleeveless white vest-cut blouse. The Harris was no place for her Pearl Jam tee, she thought dryly. But although she knew she blended in well enough with the other guests at the Harris, that didn't alter the fact that Sullivan was attracting attention.

It wasn't the suit he was wearing. Silver-gray and conservatively styled, there was nothing about it that immediately drew the eye unless it was the faultless way it was tailored to his height and the breadth of his shoulders. No, the suit wasn't the problem, she sighed. It was the man inside it, and Sullivan couldn't really help that, either.

Casually he took her by the elbow and steered her toward the flower-banked entrance to the hotel's restaurant as if, Bailey thought, they were what they were pretending to be: a couple so newly married that they still seized every opportunity to touch each other as often as possible. She gave him an inquiring glance.

''It's lunchtime,'' he said lightly. ''We'll work out a plan of action while we eat.''

The Harris was famed for its cuisine, as well as its impeccable service, and their waiter appeared a little taken aback when they both ordered without looking at the menu. Sullivan requested cold poached salmon, and Bailey followed suit, her mind not really on what she was going to eat. She leaned across the linen-draped table, impatiently shoving aside the small crystal bowl of sweet peas and pansies that sat there.

"I think I know who was in Room 201 before Plowright arrived." Abstractedly she took a bread stick from the wicker basket that their waiter had brought them, and bit off one end. "It had to have been Hank himself," she said, chewing thoughtfully. "He must have been trying to set up the hidden mikes."

"How do you figure that?" Sullivan frowned. "If he'd bugged the room there'd be a transcript included along with his report. I didn't see one."

"I know, but he mentions somewhere in there that the audio wasn't working." Bailey sat back, taking another bite from the crisp bread stick and brandishing it like a lecturer's baton. "He intended to bug the room—he *did* bug it—but when he got back to the van or whatever he was using for his listening post, he found out it wasn't transmitting. By then it was too late to go back and replace it."

"Where'd you see that?" When she took the report from her purse and handed it to him, he scanned it rapidly, stopping on the third page. He looked up at her with sharp annoyance. "I missed that. What the hell else am I missing, dammit?"

"Probably nothing." She shrugged, brushing crumbs from her lap. "It's a pretty run-of-the-mill report on a cheating husband. The only other thing that struck me at all were the descriptions of the photos, but I could be reading too much into them."

Before he could reply, their salmon came, and while their waiter refilled their wineglasses with the light German Riesling Sullivan had chosen to go with their meal, Bailey studied him covertly.

He had skipped over a small detail in an exhaustive report, a detail that he would have noticed sooner or later. But he was beating himself up over it as if he had carelessly endangered the whole investigation. It just didn't jibe with the man that Fitz had described, the man who ran crazy risks and took insane chances. It didn't jibe with what the Englishman had called him—a maniac, whose missions were almost suicidal.

From what she'd learned of him secondhand, that old Sullivan had been a dangerous man to know, she thought reluctantly. Tough and competent, yes, but with a penchant for cutting corners that might well have jeopardized those around him. It was obvious that he had changed.

Last night she had thought his guilt stemmed from his belief that he hadn't been there for someone who'd relied on him, and she'd wondered if that someone had been Maria Salazar, the woman he'd loved once and lost. Now that possibility appeared more likely than ever. Her death must have affected him so deeply that he could no longer tolerate even the smallest carelessness from himself.

But how had Maria died, and in what way did he hold himself responsible?

It wasn't hard to guess the answer to that one, Bailey thought heavily. Where Sullivan and women were concerned, it was never hard to guess how things would play out. He loved them and left them, but, although as a soldier of fortune he would have moved on to the next assignment, the woman he had left behind would have still been in a war-torn country, where lives could be snuffed out suddenly and the casualty count included the innocent. When he'd learned of her death he would have known that he could have saved her, if only he'd committed himself fully to her.

He'd been reckless in love as well as in war. Now he overlooked nothing where his work was concerned—and he made sure that no woman ever got close enough to him to depend on him again.

She felt a sudden sorrow engulf her. Without surprise, she realized that her pain was as much for him as it was for her.

"You'd have to see the photos themselves to be sure, but from the way Jackson described the shots he took, Plowright seemed to be a pretty passive participant in the action."

Sullivan's voice broke into her thoughts, and she realized that he was looking at her over the rim of his glass. Hoping desperately that she had betrayed nothing of what was going through her mind, she took the sheet of paper he was passing across the table to her and looked down at it blankly.

"That's the addendum with the photo descriptions, and you're right—there is something odd there." He frowned. "Read them yourself. Mystery woman with her arms around his neck, kissing him. Mystery woman lying on bed while he's sitting on a nearby chair. Mystery woman obviously wearing a robe and nothing else, opening the blinds in the morning while Plowright appears to be still asleep in the bed behind her. She ran the whole damn show, for God's sake."

At his words something stirred in the depths of Bailey's subconscious, but even as she tried to identify it, it was gone. She lifted a forkful of salmon, buttery tender, to her mouth, forcing herself to concentrate on the matter at hand.

Later, and in solitude, she would examine what she had

pieced together about Sullivan's past and come to a decision on what, if anything, she would do about it. But right now she had to get herself under control and start thinking like the investigator she was. He'd picked up on the same impression about Aaron and his companion that she had. Bailey wrinkled her forehead dubiously.

"I don't know much about these things, but could it be something...well, kinky?" She felt her face flush. "Apparently some of those high-powered types like being ...being..." She floundered to a stop, feeling like a fool.

"A dominatrix type of deal?" Sullivan was watching her with amusement, and it was obvious he was trying not to smile. "Triple-A's gotta get a better class of clientele, Flowers. You're far too familiar with the sordid side of life." He sobered. "I don't buy that. Hank would have mentioned it if it had occurred to him, and he obviously didn't read the situation that way. Anyway, it gives us a clue to her character. Whoever she is, she's not your ordinary bimbo."

"I still think our best lead is trying to find out who phoned into the room when Jackson might have been there. Maybe he was working with a partner on this case." Bailey sat back, dabbing at her mouth with the linen napkin. She set it aside as their waiter appeared like magic to whisk away her plate, and shook her head to the suggestion of coffee.

"Not officially, or I'd know about it. And Hank wouldn't have hired anyone freelance to help him out without clearing it through me first." Sullivan gave her a direct look. "I know him, Bailey. He's a straight shooter, no matter what you think. The incoming call's worth following up on, but I don't think it was meant for Hank."

"You're probably right." Her shoulders lifted in an ironic gesture of resignation. "Which means that now it's time for the fun part of this job—methodical legwork. What is it they say about investigation—that it's ninety percent boredom and ten percent sheer terror?''

''No, that's what they say about soldiering,'' Sullivan said shortly, signing their bill and pushing his chair back from the table. ''Although sometimes the two professions don't seem that different to me. Look for the bad guy. Deal with the bad guy. Go on to the next assignment and hope that you don't start turning into the bad guy.'' His smile was brief as he stood, his attitude suddenly restless. ''But right now we'll concentrate on the first part. Let's go look for the bad guy, honey.''

THEY'D PUT IN the boredom part—well, maybe not boredom, but definitely futile, Bailey thought a few hours later as she and Sullivan reentered the elegant reception area of the Harris. They'd spent the afternoon wandering around the hotel, striking up casual conversation with everyone from the doorman to the bellhops. At one point they'd sauntered out to an enclosed courtyard that led off from the main restaurant, where they'd ordered drinks, pretended to watch the other guests and had seized the opportunity to pump the attractive young woman who did double duty as both bartender and server about the previous weekend.

Despite the warmth of the afternoon, the little patio had been quiet, with only a few other couples relaxing at the nearby tables. Their waitress had been inclined to talk, especially when Bailey had mentioned that she and Sullivan were on their honeymoon and that Aaron Plowright had been a guest at their wedding.

She'd remembered Aaron, as Bailey had hoped she would. Her brother-in-law was attractive, in a distinguishedly silver-templed kind of way, but the Harris was full of men with those kind of moneyed good looks. However,

Aaron had an invisible but almost palpable aura of power that insured he stood out in any crowd. On the few occasions she'd joined him and Angelica at a social gathering, she'd seen herself how effortlessly he commanded attention.

Unfortunately, his companion apparently hadn't left such an indelible impression.

"We're really here because Aaron recommended the Harris so highly to us," Bailey had gushed, sipping at the kiwi and mango juice concoction she'd ordered. "We said we had a few days between the wedding and when our cruise ship departs, and he suggested we spend them here. So this is really a kind of prehoneymoon honeymoon, isn't it, honey-bunny?"

"That's right, pumpkin." Sullivan had reached over for her hand adoringly, but that hadn't stopped him from giving their waitress a slow, sexy grin. "I figured if the Harris was good enough for our friend Aaron and his sweetie, then we'd like it, too. Isn't he seeing that gorgeous blonde we met at the VanKellars' about a month ago?" This last had been directed at Bailey, and she'd wrinkled her nose.

"Ermegard? The Norwegian one who always reminded me of a Viking? I think he's moved on since then."

"He seems to have switched to brunettes," their waitress had said, and laughed. "But gorgeous still described her, although I've got to admit, I was really concentrating on the ring she was wearing. So was she," she added with a touch of envy in her tone. "It was enormous—platinum and the biggest darn diamond I've ever seen, even in a dinner ring."

A brunette with a rock on her finger, Bailey thought sourly now as they headed to Steiner's office. She'd seen at least a dozen women this afternoon who could fit that description, and of all the staff members they'd engaged in conversation, the waitress had been the only one who'd given them even that much to go on.

But Sullivan had been right in one thing, she admitted reluctantly. In their roles as newlyweds, they'd aroused no suspicion at all. *Everybody loves a lover, Flowers,* she told herself, looking down at the band of gold on her finger that was a slimmer version of the one he himself was wearing, and wishing suddenly that Sullivan hadn't gone to such lengths to make their disguises so complete. She would take it off as soon as they were alone in their room, she decided, quailing inwardly at the thought of returning to that lace-festooned bower. It was going to be hard enough spending a night in the Harris Hotel's honeymoon suite with the man she still loved, without having to wear a pretend—

She froze just as they reached Steiner's open office door, but luckily Sullivan didn't notice her sudden stiffness. He was greeting his friend, and numbly Bailey fixed a smile on her face, sitting abruptly down in a chair while the house detective closed his door and shifted through a pile of papers on his desk.

He and Sullivan were talking, but their voices seemed to be coming from far away.

She'd gone and done it, she thought hopelessly, her hands clenched tightly together in her lap and the shiny gold wedding ring glinting up at her. She'd done what she'd told herself there was no possibility of her doing—no possibility at all. She'd let herself fall for the man again.

Oh, who was she trying to kid? Bailey's eyes felt hot and burning, and the wedding ring blurred in front of them. She'd never fallen *out* of love with Terrence Sullivan. She hadn't wanted closure from him—she'd wanted to reopen their relationship, as if it were an unsolved file that she'd never been able to put aside completely, as if she'd hoped that by going over it again she would find some detail, some clue as to why she had failed the first time.

Except she hadn't failed. Bailey blinked once, hard, and the wedding ring came into focus again. She hadn't failed; she'd never even been in the running. Sullivan had felt some kind of attraction toward her, he'd admitted as much yesterday. But as soon as he'd realized that she wasn't just looking for a purely recreational affair, he'd deliberately sabotaged what she'd thought they had together.

Maria Salazar's tragic death was what had held him back. *She took him from me,* Bailey thought, a tiny flicker of anger burning away some of the numbness that surrounded her. *A real live woman I could understand—but I was beaten by a damn ghost.*

"That's him. Freeze that frame, Rocky." Sullivan was leaning forward, his gaze fixed on the video monitor that stood a few feet away, and as he spoke he lightly grasped her arm. "And that must be his bimbo beside him, admiring her latest payment for services rendered."

His touch, as casual as it was, was too much to bear. Under the pretext of leaning closer to the monitor herself, Bailey pulled her arm away. Out of the corner of her eye she saw the quick glance that Sullivan shot her way, but she pretended to be studying the grainy black-and-white picture on the screen in front of them.

"You're lucky. In twenty-four hours this particular tape would have been rerecorded. They just run them in a loop, you know." Steiner was squinting at the monitor. "The concourse shops aren't really part of the hotel, but I spun the owner some tale about being alerted that a con man had been staying at the Harris last weekend, possibly with an eye to picking up a rich widow. He was only too glad to cooperate."

Sullivan had left a message at the front desk for Steiner

an hour or so earlier, after they'd talked to the waitress on the patio, Bailey recalled. She had assumed at the time that he'd been simply touching base with the man, but she realized now that he'd obviously been alerted by the mention of Aaron's companion's ring and had played a long shot, hoping that the expensive bauble had been purchased at the concourse's jewelry store.

It seemed his long shot had paid off. Steiner hit a button on the television's remote and the surveillance tape ran backward for a few seconds. He pushed another button, and the elegantly spare figure of Aaron Plowright could be seen again, entering the store and approaching the display cases with an obviously much younger woman on his arm. She wore a summery wide-brimmed hat, and her face was obscured.

"Wait for it," murmured Sullivan beside her. "She points to something in the case, the clerk brings out the ring and puts it on her finger, and then she throws her arms around her doting sugar daddy and her hat falls off. Her face is plainly visible."

It was as he said. Bailey sat, her thoughts not fully focused on the flickering images in front of her, and saw a slim, braceleted arm gesture toward the jewelry case as she and Plowright bent over it. The store clerk took a key from the cash register and unlocked the case from his side, sliding open the glass door nearest him. He looked up, a finger tapped impatiently on the top of the case again, and Aaron Plowright glanced away with an air of boredom. The clerk drew out an object—presumably the platinum-and-diamond ring, Bailey thought, getting caught up in the silent tableau in spite of herself—and placed it on a square of velvet in front of the woman. She slipped it on to her finger, held her hand out admiringly and then flung her arms around Plowright's neck.

Her hat fell off, tumbling to the floor behind her out of the surveillance camera's view just as Steiner froze the tape again.

"Thanking her sugar daddy like I told you," Sullivan said, nodding at the screen and frowning.

"No, she's not."

Bailey got up on legs that felt strangely weak, and got to within a few feet of the monitor. She bent down, taking in the details of the brunette's classically beautiful face, recognizable despite the poor quality of the video.

"She's thanking her daddy," she said flatly. "That's Tracy Weiss—Aaron's illegitimate and unacknowledged daughter. And no matter what else I think of my brother-in-law, I don't think he's capable of doing anything as heinous as Jackson described to my sister, since she's his own daughter."

She turned to Sullivan and met his shuttered expression. "Which means that your man's report is a complete lie, Sully. He had to be running some kind of scam on Angelica. Unless—" She stopped, her gaze darkening.

"Unless what, Bailey?"

Sullivan's voice was harsh, and when she spoke again her own sounded even quieter in comparison. "Unless he and Angelica are running some kind of scam on Aaron Plowright," she said slowly. "And if that's true, then for some reason my sister's been playing me for a fool all along."

Chapter Six

"Plowright's in Washington till tomorrow. He's at the White House, for God's sake."

Bailey walked over to the bed and sat, forcing a control over her features that she didn't feel. Sullivan was doing something by the delicate white-and-gold antique dresser on the other side of the room, and she spoke to his back, her tone abrasive with annoyance. "But the word is still that Angelica's probably taken off on one of her impulsive shopping sprees. Marta, his housekeeper, said she'll ask Aaron to phone me—"

"Here, hold these."

Crossing the distance between them and interrupting her without ceremony, he handed her a pair of champagne flutes, their stems tied with gold ribbon. In his other hand he held a bottle of champagne. She gave him an incredulous look.

"What the hell do we have to celebrate, Sully?"

"*Nada.*" He reached into his back pocket and pulled out a small folding knife. Using his teeth, he pried open a miniature corkscrew from the assortment of implements it contained. "I wasn't thinking of celebrating, I was thinking of getting drunk. Besides, we either drink this up like the happy newlyweds the hotel obviously thinks we are, or we pour it down the drain so we don't blow our cover."

"It's Cristal," Bailey said thoughtfully, glancing up at the label as he inserted the corkscrew. "I guess it would be unprofessional to blow our cover."

"Yeah, that's what I thought, too." Holding the bottle at waist level, Sullivan grasped it by the neck and gingerly nudged the almost freed cork with his thumbs. The next moment it exploded out of the bottle with a loud pop, ricocheting off the mirrored ceiling above the bed, a froth of champagne cascading like a fountain from the bottle.

"Hold out the glasses or open wide, honey." With a grin he directed the stream of champagne into the flutes she quickly thrust out, and Bailey couldn't resist laughing with him. As the froth subsided, he topped up the two glasses until they were brimming with what looked like liquid gold.

"We're fools," she said as her giggles finally subsided. "We have absolutely no reason to laugh, Sullivan, especially after the fax that came through to Steiner before we left. I wish I could say that someone else might have used her cell phone, but that thing's never out of her reach. That number is Angelica's, and she had to have made that call to Room 201."

"It doesn't look good, does it?" He swallowed the last of his champagne and reached for the nearby bottle, refilling her glass as well as his own. "Hank obviously used some pretext or another to find out what room Plowright and his daughter were going to be staying in before they got there, but how the hell did Angelica know?"

Bailey stared at him. "She obviously found out from him. The two of them are in this together."

"You're wrong. Hank wouldn't be a party to any kind of a scam. I know him and I'm telling you you're wrong." His jaw set stubbornly. "No, somehow Angelica set him

up, but how and why I don't know. And what worries me
most is that since she did no one's seen him.''

"For God's sake, listen to yourself, Sullivan!" Bailey
drained her glass and reached for the bottle herself. She
divided the last of it between the two flutes, scowling at
the tiny festive bubbles that danced through the pale liquid.
"You may think you know Jackson, but I've lived with
Angelica most of my life. Trust me, the woman's not a
mastermind. What are you saying—that she somehow
conned him into falsifying a surveillance report on her husband, overpowered him at his own home, searched his files
until she found the report that he was about to give her the
next day anyway, and then took the photos and disposed
of Jackson's body? And that she did all this *alone?*" She
snorted inelegantly. "Yeah, that flies for me. Get real—she
wore a low-cut blouse to her appointment with your guy,
batted her baby blues at him and told him that if he could
figure out a way to help her she'd do anything at all to
thank him. *That's* how Angelica operates.''

"First he's a destructive drunk, then he's a crook, and
now you're saying he's a sap and your sister used him,"
Sullivan said tightly. "Pick one and stick with it, Bailey,
so I know what I've got to defend him against.''

His gaze was almost navy, it was so dark with anger.
Looking at him, she felt her own temper draining away, to
be replaced by impotent frustration.

He could make her laugh, even when she didn't want to,
even when only a few hours ago she had faced the most
wrenching truth about herself—that she had never gotten
over him, and probably never would. But maybe that was
why it was so easy to let herself forget reality when she
was with him, Bailey thought helplessly. She wanted to.
She wanted to pretend that they were the two people they
had once been, even if she knew that she was lying to

herself, and even if she knew that their relationship had always been a lie.

She set her wineglass aside and took a deep breath. But they weren't lovers, they were partners on a case. And he was refusing to look at the facts.

"A lot of men have fallen for Angelica, Sully," she said, leaning forward a little and meeting his eyes. "Aaron Plowright did, and he's about as hard as they come."

He stared at her, his gaze still unreadable.

"Tracy's his daughter, but the report and the photo descriptions make it seem like she's his lover, so the report's a blatant lie," Bailey went on quietly. "That's a given. Hank prepared that report, but since he'd have no reason to falsify it on his own behalf, he had to have been doing it for Angelica. What I think happened is that he took this assignment, got here and realized that whatever the relationship was between Aaron and the woman he was with, it certainly wasn't a sexual one, and phoned Angelica to let her know. After all, he wouldn't have wanted to waste his time and her money over a job he already knew wasn't going to pan out." She hesitated, and he nodded curtly.

"Go on."

At least he was listening, she thought. She gave a small shrug. "I'm guessing that's when Angelica poured on the waterworks, telling Hank that even if Aaron wasn't cheating on her this particular weekend, she still knew that he was running around on her and she wanted something that would show him she wouldn't stand for it. Maybe Hank thought of her as a damsel in distress, or he just couldn't resist her, or he thought fudging a report a little couldn't harm anyone. But then he got home Sunday night and started thinking about what he'd done, and the guilt set in."

"And he went off the wagon with a vengeance, is that how the rest of it goes?" Sullivan stood up and looked down at her. "He trashed his own office, he planted a liquor bottle that he couldn't have drunk out of, and he disappeared into the night, taking his photos with him but leaving his report in plain sight for anyone to find. Honey, that one doesn't fly for *me*."

"There never were any photos, there were just the descriptions and they were fake," she said, holding on to her patience with an effort. "And like I said before, the bottle could have belonged to one of his old drinking buddies."

"But that still doesn't explain away the phone call. Jackson would have had to watch Plowright and Weiss for an hour or so before he figured out that their relationship was completely innocuous. You saw that jewelry store video yourself. Would you have been able to tell right off the bat that those two were father and daughter?" He shook his head. "Even if your theory was true, Hank wouldn't have gotten in touch with Angelica until long after they'd checked in and he'd been watching them for a while. So who was Angelica phoning in Room 201 *before* it was occupied?"

"For crying out loud, I didn't say I had all the answers!"

Bailey stood, too, needing suddenly to address him on a more equal basis rather than tipping her head back to look at him. Faint hope, she thought in irritation as she faced him. He was still close to a foot taller, and she felt as if he was deliberately looming over her. She planted her hands on her hips.

"For all I know, Angelica could have found out the room number herself and phoned there hoping to talk to Jackson before her husband arrived. Maybe she had some last-minute instructions for him. It's a *detail*, Sullivan—and the only reason you're hanging on to it is because you won't admit that the rest of it makes sense!"

"Details are what keep innocent men from being convicted, dammit!"

He *was* looming over her, she thought angrily. He was using every advantage he had to win this one—his height, his nearness to her, the way his lashes fanned so thickly down on his cheekbones when he narrowed his eyes. She could even smell the scent of the *soap* he used. She felt herself wavering.

She pulled herself up sharply and came back at him with the sharpest weapon she had available.

"Sully, this isn't the *past!* Whatever you did back then, you can't make it right by sticking blindly to Jackson now!" Her voice was a decibel or two short of a shout, and with an effort she lowered it, but that didn't affect its intensity. "Your loyalty's misplaced, but you just can't see it because you won't walk away from whatever battlefield you're still fighting on!"

In the sudden silence that followed her rush of words she heard him take in a harsh breath. His face was a mask and, without moving a muscle, he seemed somehow to have withdrawn from her. A moment ago his nearness had been overwhelming her senses, Bailey thought, already regretting her outburst. Now he was a stranger, and a remote one at that.

"First Fitz and now you." He barely moved his lips as he spoke. "It seems everyone has their own theory. I'm getting a little tired of it, honey."

She'd been about to turn away from this confrontation, which had ballooned into something much more personal than she had ever intended, but at this she stiffened. Her hands clenched into fists at her sides and deliberately she pressed her nails even harder into her palms, trying to use the small physical pain to overlay the much more acute one that had bloomed deep inside her at his words.

"Come on, Sullivan, you don't have to put on your party manners for me. Face it—the phrase you'd really like to use is a lot shorter and a lot more basic. Two words, right?" She smiled tightly at him. "I get the picture, though. Fitz got the picture, too. You don't walk away from the people you care about. You just do everything to make sure that they walk away from you. What an unpleasant little shock it must have been yesterday when I came back into your life again."

His mouth was set. "That's not—" he began, but Bailey didn't let him finish.

"I'm going to take your advice, Sully." She crossed over to the dresser and picked up the room key, feeling his eyes on her as she did. Lifting her gaze, she met his in the mirror, and for a moment she thought there was something wrong with the reflective qualities of the glass, because the man looking back at her seemed eerily insubstantial. He was standing in front of the bed and Bailey could almost swear that the lace hangings behind him were faintly visible.

Sullivan shifted slightly. His reflection was once again solidly normal, and Bailey broke eye contact, dropping the room key into her pants pocket. She turned from the door and faced him directly, for some reason not wanting to look at him in the mirror again.

"I think we should take a time-out." She managed a small smile. "I was going to say before we both said something we might regret, but it's too late for that."

"I'll leave." His response was immediate, but already her hand was on the doorknob, and she shook her head.

"No, I will. Don't worry, I just want to be alone for a while. I'm not planning to play the part of the frightened bride running away from her husband, or anything, Sullivan."

A ghost of a grin touched his features, and even at that inappropriate moment Bailey felt something in her stir in response to the man. She opened the door.

"I'll walk around the concourse for an hour or so, do some window-shopping. There was a linens shop that I saw earlier today—maybe I'll pick up a lace pillow for my apartment. This place is beginning to grow on me."

She stepped out into the hall, but before she could close the door behind her, he said her name and she looked back.

"Bailey?" He was still standing by the bed. He hadn't moved. "What you thought I said to you a few minutes ago. You're wrong." His eyes met hers. "Never, honey. I could never even think that." He held her gaze for a second longer, and then he smiled faintly. "Go on, go buy a canopy bed or something. I'll be here when you get back."

He didn't have any idea what he did to her, Bailey told herself numbly as she made her way down the lushly carpeted hallway to the elevators. He didn't know how just one smile, one quick glance could make her forget every resolution she'd ever made to herself. She looked at his eyes and saw midnight and velvet and the way she'd once made them glaze over with pleasure, and telling herself that she was playing with fire was no use at all. She *wanted* to play with fire. She wanted to strike the match, drop it into the gasoline and feel the conflagration engulf her.

Even if it only blazed for one night, it would be worth it.

She'd reached the lobby, mechanically letting her steps take her to the entrance of the elegant concourse of boutiques that adjoined it. Staring unseeingly at the strikingly arranged window displays and hardly aware of the well-dressed shoppers around her, Bailey found herself moving slower and slower, until finally she stopped in front of one of the boutiques. She was in real trouble, she thought shakily. She was in as much danger as if she were poised on top of the ledge of a high-rise and considering throwing herself off just for the thrill of the fall.

Don't forget what happened last time, Flowers, she told herself desperately. *Eventually you'll hit the ground. Eventually you'll end up getting smashed to bits again. When you try to tell yourself it's worth it, make yourself remember how it ended.*

But what if this time it didn't end? What if this time it lasted, this time he fell with her, this time it *worked?*

What if this time she made him forget Maria?

Her vision came back into focus, and dimly she realized what she was staring at. The small display window held a frothy set of lingerie—cream-and coffee-colored wisps of panties, a garter belt trimmed in coffee and—most daring of all—a low-cut bustier that laced up in the front. It was a ridiculously sexy outfit. It would take a woman much more confident than she was to wear it, Bailey thought dismissively. It wasn't her at all.

And once she'd added the cream-colored seamed stockings that she'd had to have to go with the garter belt, it had been *way* too expensive, she thought shakily a few minutes later, speeding away from the shop and heading back to the lobby with the minuscule pink-and-gold shopping bag tucked furtively under her arm. She saw the elevator doors closing ahead of her and put on a further burst of speed, making it just in time and almost losing her shoe in the effort.

There were two older couples in the elevator and, as it ascended, out of the corner of her eye Bailey saw one of the matrons discreetly nudge the other, smiling. She frowned, wondering if the tag was sticking out of the back of her blouse, or if she had a smudge of something on her face. Thankful that she was getting off on the second floor, she stared down at the floor silently.

The last of the confetti had spilled out of her shoe. And dangling demurely from the bag under her arm was a scrap of pink wrapping tissue and one creamily beribboned garter.

"I've got a black Pearl Jam tee," she muttered to herself as she stalked down the hall to the honeymoon suite. Her jaw clenched. "I've been thinking about getting a tattoo— and *not* a wimpy little rose on my butt, either. I'm a freakin' private *investigator,* for crying out loud. They thought I was some dewy-eyed bride going all out to knock the socks off her *man,* for heaven's sake!"

She unlocked the door clumsily, all of a sudden feeling close to tears. She blinked them back, her lips firming to a determined line.

"For the rest of the month it's going to be macaroni and cheese, and for what? A stupid outfit that you're never going to wear. I can't believe you were actually thinking of trying to lure back a man who's already jerked you around once, Flowers!"

She shoved open the door with more force than necessary, and stopped on the threshold, feeling obscurely let down. Sullivan had obviously gone out himself. The silk-shaded sconces that flanked the bed filled the room with enough soft light to see by, but the main lamps had been switched off and the place was silent.

All the better, she told herself. With any luck, she would be asleep by the time he came back, and tomorrow this excruciatingly forced intimacy would be over. There was a massive damask-upholstered sofa against the far wall that she could use as a bed for tonight, and Sullivan could have that football field of lace and satin all to himself.

She'd come so close to making the biggest mistake of

her life, Bailey thought, stripping down to her panties and bra. She padded over to her suitcase in her bare feet, jammed the boutique bag under the rest of her clothes and started to pull out the sleep shirt she'd packed.

She froze.

From around the rim of the slightly open bathroom door came a faint glow. It seemed oddly unsteady, as if whatever light was causing it was moving, and all of a sudden she felt a terrible chill settle into the pit of her stomach.

It could be a flashlight. But if it was, what would an intruder be doing in *there,* of all places? Before she could stop it, the image of Hank Jackson's scrubbed and gleaming bathroom flooded into her mind, along with the horrific and irrational dread that had gripped her while she had been in the man's house.

She'd told herself that she'd been letting her imagination run away with her, that all that had happened to Jackson was that he'd slipped back into the bottle again. The logical part of her brain still believed that, Bailey insisted hollowly to herself.

Except the logical part of her brain wasn't working right now. It had been taken over by something much more basic and primitive.

What if Sullivan hadn't gone out after she had? What if he'd answered the door, thinking it was her, and had been taken by surprise by whoever was in that bathroom right now?

She didn't have her gun with her. She'd figured a Glock wouldn't normally be part of a trousseau, and besides, she didn't really like carrying it anyway. Her gaze darted quickly around the dimly lit room, and fixed on a table lamp only a few feet away on a low table. Without hesitation she went to it, jerking the lamp's cord out of the wall and swiftly pulling off the rose-pink shade. The base was heavy and solid, and in the shape of a cherub. Bailey gripped the cherub's protruding belly firmly and advanced to the bathroom door.

She stopped only inches away from it, listening, but she heard nothing. She tensed. No, that wasn't true, she thought—she *could* hear something, but at first she couldn't identify the sound. It was oddly liquid, like water slapping gently against the sides of a boat. It *was* the sound of water lapping gently, she realized in confusion a split second later. Even as the thought went through her mind, she was nudging the door open and peering into the room.

Yeah, it was water, all right. Bailey closed her eyes in shaky relief and then opened them again. It was water lapping against the black marble sides of that enormous tub.

She pushed the door fully open and leaned against the jamb, her arms crossed and the cherub lamp clutched in her hand. She still felt a little unsteady, but there was no way she was going to let *him* see that, she thought.

Sullivan lay back in a cloud of bubbles up to his chin. There was an overpowering scent of lily of the valley in the air, and all around the massive black marble rim of the bath flickered candles in small pebbled-glass holders. His eyes were shut, and there was a line of miniature liquor bottles crowding the candles beside him.

"Honey, I'm home," Bailey said dryly, still leaning against the doorjamb. "What the hell are you doing, Sully?"

"What does it look like? I'm taking a bath and working my way through the minibar." He opened one eye and squinted up at her. "These were on the vanity. I thought it would be romantic if I lit them and put them around the tub. It *is* romantic, admit it."

"I guess." Bailey uncrossed her arms and set the lamp base on the floor beside her. "But you know what might have been even more romantic, in an ironic kind of way? Getting brained by a cherub while you were in your bubble bath with your candles all around you. Ask me someday to tell you how close you came to that, Sullivan.''

"You'd never hurt me, honey.'' His hair was a wet tangle obscuring that one-eyed gaze. He gave her a sweet, slightly unfocused smile. "You're an angel yourself, Bails. You're *my* angel.''

She stared at him. Then she looked down at the tiny bottles lined up on the rim of the bath and did a rapid count. Her eyes met his again.

"Are you *drunk*, Sullivan?'' she said in disbelief.

"Not really,'' he said thoughtfully. "They were all liqueurs—I guess because this is the honeymoon suite and having the groom knock back a few belts of hard liquor to loosen him up might make for a less than memorable wedding night. They were more like candy, really. But when that sugar rush kicks in, honey, watch out.''

"Okay, so you're stone-cold sober. Then why the bubble bath?'' She wrinkled her nose. "For the love of Mike, Sully, you must have dumped in a *quart* of that stuff. You're going to be smelling it on yourself all night long.''

"That was the plan.'' His arms had been on the rim of the marble tub. Now one tanned hand slowly moved to the billow of foam and scooped some up. "You used to wear lily of the valley once, didn't you, honey? I always think of it as your scent.''

With a sudden breath, he blew the bubbles from his hand into the air. A few of them broke free and floated lightly toward her, shimmering in the light from the candles. She saw him watching them with a concentrated effort, and as they touched her bare leg and burst he blinked, very slowly. Then he looked up at her again.

"I want to see you wet, Bails. Get in and let me scrub your back,'' he said softly.

Chapter Seven

Bailey had read books in which Victorian females swooned when some dandy verbally accosted them. Whenever she'd come across that phrase, she'd lifted one eyebrow in disbelief, given a derisive little grunt and told herself that women had never been that weak.

She felt like swooning now.

So *this* is what those Victorians had really been talking about when they'd used the word, she thought in shock—this immediate heat that was spreading through her body, this heavy languor that suddenly made her feel like she had to cling to something just to stay upright. She wanted to fall into a pair of strong arms. She wanted to let her eyes flutter closed, her lips part, and let herself…well, *swoon*.

He was lying there in that enormous marble bath, the flickering little flames around him throwing gold lights on the tanned angles of his face, and he was looking up at her through those thick black lashes. His arms and wrists were beaded with moisture. For some reason, she thought faintly, the contrast between the broad, heavily muscled shoulders and the froth of bubbles clinging to them was almost overpoweringly sexy.

Carefully she let out the breath she'd been holding. "Get in with you? How smart would that be, Sully?"

He frowned, as if her question was a tricky one. Then he gave her a slow, rueful smile that made him look like a bad choirboy, all grown up. "Not smart of you at all, honey. I didn't really think you'd agree."

The bath was about three feet from the doorway. She moved closer until she was only an inch or two away from the marble rim. "I didn't say no, Sullivan," she said without meeting his eyes. "I just asked you if you thought it was the smart thing to do. I don't think it is, either."

Very deliberately, she stepped into the bath and lowered herself into the mass of bubbles, and immediately she could feel his body against every inch of hers.

Her hands were braced lightly against the hardness of his chest. Her thighs were on either side of the washboard flatness of his stomach, straddling him. Her calves were pressed against the long outer muscles of his legs and she could feel the silky prickle of his hair against the smoothness of her own skin.

She'd lit the match, she thought hazily. She'd tossed it into the pool of gasoline. Tomorrow there would be nothing left of her but the ashes of the woman she once had been, and she would have no one to blame but herself.

But for the next few hours she would walk through fire and let herself be consumed. And she would make sure that after tonight, the man with her now would forever bear the marks of this blaze himself.

She raised her head and met his eyes. He didn't speak. His gaze fixed on hers as if he was waiting for her to make the next move, and his muscles felt rigidly tense. Slowly she scooped up a palmful of water with one hand, and even more slowly she tipped her head to one side, baring the line of her neck, her gaze never leaving his. She opened her fingers, and the water ran down her throat, past her collarbone, soaked into the flimsy material of her bra. The scent of lily of the valley wrapped around her.

"You said you wanted to get me wet," she said huskily. "I'm wet, Sullivan."

His jawline was in shadow, but even so she saw a slight movement as it clenched and then eased. "But not all over, Bails," he said hoarsely.

Up until now his arms had been gripping the wide flat marble surround of the bath, his fingers splayed against the black stone. The next moment they were around her, pulling her down to his chest and dragging her fully into the water with him, and his mouth was covering hers.

He might look like a choirboy, but if he'd ever been one it would have been a long, long time ago, Bailey thought disjointedly, and since then he'd strayed far from the straight and narrow. His kiss was pure sin—distilled, refined, concentrated down to its essence and pouring through her as if she was drinking him in. She could feel his hands spreading wide against the flare of her hips, his thumbs hooking under the thin wet nylon of her panties, but he made no move to push them farther down her thighs.

He made love as if he had all the time in the world, she remembered. His kisses had always been long and slow and wet.

Her mouth felt ripe and soft under his, and when he ran the tip of his tongue along the bow of her top lip and then held it gently between his teeth, she could almost imagine it swelling even fuller from the tiny nip he gave her. She heard a small sound, half sigh, half plaintive cry, coming from the back of her own throat, and through her half-closed lashes she saw his eyes open. He licked the underside of the lip he'd been holding between his teeth, flicked his tongue against the sensitive curve at the top and looked at her.

"How long do you think we can hold our breath underwater?" he murmured. "Come on, honey, let's go skinny-dipping."

In the wavering shadows from the candles she could see the slow smile that lifted one corner of his mouth, and then he was sliding smoothly down the marble sides of the bath, taking her with him.

The water rushed silkenly around her as she followed him down, rising swiftly to her breasts, to her shoulders, and then finally closing over her head, and Bailey immediately had the sensation that she had entered another world. Sullivan's mouth found hers, and this time he didn't hold back. His tongue was in her, his hands were woven into the floating strands of her hair, and he was taking her deeper.

She no longer was kneeling. Her legs were stretched out behind her, as if she really was swimming with him, and in this even more intimate position it was impossible not to realize that his arousal was complete. She felt one long, leanly muscled leg wrap around hers, trapping them, and something inside her felt as if it was shattering, breaking up into a million tiny pieces.

She no longer had a body, she thought incoherently. That was what had just happened. She'd dissolved into pure feeling, without any physical boundaries at all. She was warm, perfumed water lapping against every inch of him, she was wrapping liquidly around him, she was imprinting her very self on him.

His mouth opened even more greedily against hers, as if he needed everything all at once, and suddenly Bailey felt solid and real again. She let her arms float dreamily up and slowly twined them around his neck, giving herself to his kiss.

She'd been right, she thought, tasting the liquor and hazelnut sweetness of his mouth and feeling the unshaven rasp of his jaw against the corners of her lips. It was worth it. She'd been lying to herself for a year, but she couldn't lie anymore. She'd needed this, *fantasized* about this, every night since she'd walked out of his life.

She felt him run a gentle finger down the side of her cheek to her neck, and then he was rising toward the surface of the water, with her riding him as if he was some mythical creature returning her to her own element.

Bailey opened her eyes as she felt the air touch her skin. Drops of water hung on her lashes, and the tiny lights around the bath spangled and glowed like prisms. She was still firmly snuggled up against Sullivan's chest, and his mouth was only inches from hers. His eyes were shadowed deep blue, and his lips were slightly parted as he looked down at her.

"You look like a mermaid," he whispered, pushing her wet hair from her face. "Like the one in the fairy tale. There's a statue of her in Copenhagen harbor, and you look just like her, Bails."

One of the candles nearby guttered and went out, and Bailey felt the ghost of a draft on her bare skin. She blinked the water from her eyes.

"What does she look like, this mermaid of yours?" she asked softly, wanting only to hear him talk. She'd always loved the sound of his voice in bed, she remembered. In the dark it was huskier than it normally was, and the cadence of his sentences changed subtly, hinting at the Gaelic of his forebears. He was the last of a long line of warrior-poets, he'd told her once. Which only meant that the men in his family had always been brawlers and liars, he'd added wryly, making her laugh.

"She's delicate." His arms tightened around her. "Her head is bent and turned away, looking over her shoulder at the water. She looks sad, because she gave up everything for the man she loved, and in the end she found it was impossible for her to live in his world.''

There was an unidentifiable tone in his voice, and suddenly she realized that the arms around her were taut with tension. The draft on her skin became a chill, and her gaze widened in the flickering light. She drew slightly away from him and looked into his eyes, but even that small movement splashed some water onto the bath's marble rim, and two more of the candles went out, making it harder to see.

''She didn't find it impossible to live in his world, Sully.'' Her throat felt raspy and dry, which was strange, she thought, considering she was immersed in water. ''I remember the story, too. In the original version she gladly exchanged her world for his. But in the end he didn't want her.''

''Someone should have stopped her.'' His voice was no longer velvety, but harshly edged. The light from the last few candles burning made pinpoint reflections in his pupils. ''He obviously wasn't worth it.''

She wasn't just chilled, Bailey thought. She was cold—as cold as ice, and that deadly cold was spreading from the pit of her stomach through her body, her limbs, her face. Her lips felt numb and her fingertips, although they were spread open on his chest, couldn't seem to feel his skin.

''We're not talking about fairy tales anymore, are we, Sullivan?'' she said carefully and clearly. ''We're talking about—''

A muted buzzing noise came abruptly from a few feet away, cutting across her question. She halted, startled.

''It's my damn cell phone over there on the vanity.'' He had been tense before, but now his words were almost bitten off. ''Let it ring. Listen, Bailey—''

The buzzing came again, sounding obtrusively loud in the almost dark room. She felt edgy enough already, she thought. She didn't need this. She pushed herself away from him jerkily and stood up before he could protest.

"It could be important," she said stiffly, not looking at him. Water streamed down her as she stepped out of the bath, molding her bra and panties revealingly to her body, and she grabbed at one of the thick towels stacked up on a glass shelf by the sink. Snatching up the phone and handing it to Sullivan, she wrapped the oversize towel around her shoulders like a cloak before getting another one and blotting the water from her face.

Déjà vu all over again, she told herself tightly, bending slightly forward and roughly toweling her wet hair. He had been a sentence away from letting her know in plain English that it would never work between them. She rubbed at her hair harder, grateful for the dark, the concealing towel and Sullivan's low-voiced, obviously intent conversation on the phone.

She'd left out one last part of the story, she thought, fiercely swallowing back the aching lump in her throat. When the mermaid had exchanged her tail for legs, every step she'd taken had felt like she was being pierced by knives. She'd born the pain because she'd loved her prince so much.

She was a fool, Bailey thought angrily. *But she was only a character in a fairy tale, so maybe she had a right to expect a happy ending. This is real life, and you knew going into this that it wasn't going to—*

"That was Moira."

Sullivan's voice came from beside her and she jerked her head up. Dropping the towel she'd been using onto the counter, she flung her damp hair back from her face and combed the last stray strands out of her eyes with her fingers. He was standing less than a foot away, and a skimpier towel than the one draped over her shoulders was wrapped low on his hips. He raked his own hair back with an unsteady hand, and she stared at him, feeling a nebulous dread taking shape.

"The police found a body in a Dumpster." The last candle on the rim of the bath flared up in one final dying flame, lighting up his face and revealing the bleakness in his eyes. "They think it could be Hank, Bailey. They want me to go and make a positive identification."

"STAY BEHIND THE TAPE, Ms. Flowers. Believe me, you don't want to get any closer."

Moving like an automaton, Bailey took a step backward, away from the impromptu boundary the police had set up in the alleyway. The Belmont-Wallace Hotel, despite its impressive-sounding name, was a flophouse where rooms were rented by the hour rather than the night. It was a world away from the Harris. This alleyway behind it was a world away from *everything* civilized.

It had been Detective Straub who had spoken to her, and faintly she realized that his voice held none of the antagonism he had shown the previous day in Sullivan's office. Correction—two days ago, she thought dully. It was well after midnight, and the date had changed, although not for whomever it was in the Dumpster. For that poor soul, time had stopped permanently.

She could see Sullivan, his face drawn into lines of strain, his skin washed out under the harshly brilliant crime scene illumination. He was standing by the Dumpster with Fitzgerald. Even as she watched, two husky police technicians who had been standing in the garbage bin itself bent down and lifted up the corners of a heavy, clear plastic tarp. Their faces were obscured by respirator masks, and they both wore clumsy oiled-rubber gauntlets. It looked like a scene from a bad horror movie, Bailey thought suddenly, turning away.

"Crappy place to end up dead, no matter who it was." Straub grimaced. "The hell of it is, somebody actually lives here. That's the only reason the body was found tonight instead of next week when they come around to dump that thing."

"Lives where? In this alley, you mean?"

She looked around her at the garbage-strewn pavement. There was a smashed bottle by the graffiti-scrawled brick wall that was the back of the hotel, and she'd already seen the glint of a hypodermic needle nearer the taped-off Dumpster.

"Carl the Cat." Straub jerked his head at a police cruiser a few feet away. A uniformed female officer with a patiently soothing look on her face was speaking with a wildly gesticulating man who looked to Bailey as if he was clothed in some kind of moth-eaten fur. She squinted. He *was* wearing a moth-eaten fur.

"He lives in a cardboard box just the other side of the Dumpster," Straub said quietly. "He's a schizophrenic, and he's under the impression that he's an alley cat. He booked himself into the hospital earlier this week because he was starting to lose it, and the one thing you can say about Carl is that he knows enough to get off the streets before he gets violent. Anyway, he was under observation for a few days while they adjusted his meds, and when he came back home—" He jerked a thumb at the cardboard box just visible past the Dumpster, and hesitated before he went on. "Well, let's just say it didn't take long for him to notice that something was wrong," he finished lamely.

Bailey's eyes darkened as she looked back at Sullivan and Fitzgerald, both squatting by the tarpaulin. Mercifully, the heavy plastic had been arranged in such a way that its occupant was hidden from the view of onlookers.

"Tough on him if it is his friend." Straub followed her glance. "I wouldn't want to ID a buddy under these circumstances." He cleared his throat awkwardly. "I owe the both of you an apology, I guess. I was a little hot under the collar yesterday when Fitz and I interviewed you and Sullivan."

"I don't recall you bothering to address me at all," Bailey said dismissively. "But it looked to me like you walked in there with a grudge against Sully."

"Maybe I did." His admission was the last thing she'd expected, and she looked over at him.

"Hell, it's not the first time he's investigated a matter where the police were involved," Straub said with sudden heat. "I'd heard about him from some of the guys down at the station. He's got a rep for playing a lone hand and not letting the authorities in on his cases. It didn't help that on the way over Fitz kept telling me that Sullivan was the one man he'd want beside him in a tight situation, and that I should handle the guy with kid gloves."

"Fitz said Sully was the one he'd want beside him in a situation?" Bailey darted a quick look over at the burly detective hunkered over the tarpaulin. "That wasn't the impression he was giving yesterday," she said softly.

"They've got a history, and I gather they don't always see eye to eye." Straub looked over at his partner, too. "But on the way back to the station Fitz reamed me out good, and he let slip a few things. I began to think that maybe that big Irish mercenary would be the guy *I'd* want beside me in a fight."

"His fighting days are over," Bailey said curtly. "He's put it all behind him, Detective."

He gave a short laugh. "He might say that. He might

even believe that. But I've known men like him before, and I've seen the same look in their eyes that your Irishman has. He's got one last battle in him, and sooner or later he'll have to fight it.''

Bailey was about to reply when out of the corner of her eye she saw Sullivan abruptly straighten up from his position by the tarpaulin. She saw Fitzgerald wave a weary hand at the two police technicians and then heave himself to his feet.

''Aw hell, it doesn't look good,'' Straub said in a low tone. ''I should get over there. Listen, if I haven't completely blown it, would you take a word of advice from me?''

His tone was suddenly serious, and she nodded, finding herself liking him more than she had previously. ''I might,'' she said cautiously. ''What is it?''

''If you care about the Irishman at all, don't let him go home alone.'' The pale skin flushed, but he continued doggedly. ''Don't get me wrong. It's just that I saw that body before you arrived. If it was his buddy Jackson, Sullivan's going to have a rough night of it. He's going to need someone to keep the ghosts away.''

''I don't think he'll want company tonight.'' Bailey bit her lip and looked over at Sullivan's grim figure. As she watched, he rubbed his mouth wearily and looked down at the ground, while Fitz snapped out some order to a young cop nearby.

And you're the last person he'd want, even if he was looking for company, she told herself hopelessly. *The man was trying to find a polite way to let you know that earlier tonight, even before all this.*

''He probably won't. But he should have it.'' Straub met her eyes with a direct look. ''Stay with him tonight, if he's any kind of friend of yours at all.''

She watched him unseeingly as he ducked under the police tape and picked his way through the filth and the garbage to his partner's side, inclining his head in greeting at the silent man standing with Fitzgerald and receiving the slightest of nods in reply.

It was Jackson's body that Sullivan had just identified, Bailey thought with dull certainty. What he had feared all along had proved to be true—he'd lost one of his men. He would feel that he'd failed him.

She'd never known Jackson. So although she mourned the man's death and felt horrified pity at the sordid circumstances in which he'd been found, her grief was far less personal than Sullivan's, Bailey told herself—and that meant it was up to her to see if she could make any sense of this latest development.

Her gaze clouded in thought, and abstractedly she pulled the thin sweater she was wearing more tightly around her. The night was cool and her hair was still damp, but she paid little attention to her physical discomfort, her mind more occupied with trying to assemble what little she knew of Jackson into some kind of coherent pattern.

To her, fact number one had always been that the man had once had a problem with alcohol. Fact number two was that he'd deliberately falsified a surveillance report. There was no way he'd simply misread the relationship between Plowright and his daughter. True, that relationship was a well-kept secret—Aaron had been married at the time he'd fathered Tracy, and he'd never publicly acknowledged her as his, mainly to avoid any possible claim she might have on his wealth—but it still would be impossible to mistake it for a sexual entanglement.

But Jackson's report described gestures and scenes that only fit the scenario of a mistress with her lover. He'd lied.

And that meant that he wasn't the man Sullivan had thought he was.

The only theory that worked was the one Sullivan had already rejected—Hank had been played for a fool by the lovely Angelica and had felt ashamed enough of his actions when he'd had time to consider them that he'd taken a drink or two to numb the guilt. But that drink had reawakened the demon in him. By all accounts, alcohol had inclined him toward violence, and in this dingy alleyway he'd met his death, probably as a result of some drunken confrontation.

"It was Hank. Come on, let's get the hell out of here."

Sullivan was beside her, his hands thrust deep into the pockets of his pants, his shoulders set. The suit jacket he was wearing was open, and sometime in the past half hour he'd obviously loosened his tie and impatiently pulled open the collar of his shirt. He needed a shave and he looked exhausted.

Handsome, tough and dangerous, Bailey thought. It was a potent mix, as she knew.

"I'm staying with you at your place tonight," he said shortly, avoiding her eyes.

He was everything he appeared to be, she thought. But right now he was also a man who had just identified the body of a friend. His expression was closed off, his eyes unreadable, but obviously Straub had been right. She felt a quick compassion that she was careful not to let him see. As hard as it was for him to admit it, Sullivan wanted the company of another human being to help him get through the next few hours.

She could give him that. Maybe it was all he would ever need from her, but she could give him that.

"But as of tomorrow, I don't want you anywhere near

this case,'' he added tersely, holding the door of the Jaguar open for her.

She stiffened and shot a look of disbelief at him, but his face revealed no more than it had a moment ago. Not that it would have made a difference if it had, she thought with a quick flicker of anger. It seemed that no matter what, she kept reading the man wrong.

"Maybe this didn't turn out to be much of a case, but it *is* my case, Sullivan. I still intend to track down Angelica and get the details out of her,'' she said coldly. She looked past him down the alleyway and her tone softened slightly. "I'm sorry about Hank. This was no place for him to die.''

"He didn't.'' His answer was delivered in a terse undertone. "He died in his own home.''

She looked at him, stunned. Then she recovered. "You don't know that, Sully. The body's going to have to be examined before anyone can know exactly how and where he died.''

"How he died wasn't hard to figure out. He was shot at close range in the face.'' Sullivan's jaw tightened. "And I don't need a pathologist to tell me where he was killed, either.''

"I don't understand.'' Suddenly her legs felt unsteady, and blindly she clutched at the open car door for support, her eyes wide with unspoken horror. "What do you mean, you know where he was killed?''

She felt his hands on her shoulders, and despite everything that had happened between them in the past few hours, she found herself wanting to lean closer into his embrace. She didn't have to. With a muttered oath, Sullivan pulled her to him, pressing her head into the hollow of his shoulder as if to shield her from some terrible sight.

"That piece of plastic he was wrapped in, Bailey,'' he said softly against her hair. "It wasn't a tarpaulin. It was a shower curtain—the one missing from his house.''

Chapter Eight

"I don't need protection, Sullivan. Watch your head on the lintel—I lost a paying customer that way once," Bailey added sharply, unlocking the door of her second-floor office and preceding him in. "I admit I usually don't carry a gun, but if it makes you feel better, I'll get it out of the safe right now, okay?"

"Not okay. Where do you want this?" Not waiting for her reply, Sullivan walked past the scarred oak desk with her overnight case in his hand, pushing open the door at the back of the office marked Private.

Bailey's lips tightened as she followed him into the small apartment that came with the office space. "Put it anywhere."

She flicked on the light switch, but even as she did she exhaled in sharp frustration. Though the rice-paper shade that hung over the unmade bed immediately gave off a warm glow, it faded into nothingness compared to the garish red and blue neon that was flashing on and off outside the window. Sullivan frowned as she hurried over to the matchstick blinds and released them to cover the worst of the neon.

"That's right, you've never been here at night," she said briefly, taking the three steps that in the cramped room meant she'd entered the area of the kitchen. It consisted of a sink and a counter, a hot plate and a microwave. "The sign's for the restaurant next door."

"It's not the greatest neighborhood to live in."

His tone was neutral. Her back to him, Bailey lifted a small painted tin down from the single shelf above the sink and pulled out the tiny utensil drawer beside her with a jerk.

"You take sugar in your tea, right?" Plugging in an electric kettle and dumping several spoonfuls of loose tea leaves from the painted tin into a squat brown teapot, she turned to face him. "No, it's not the greatest neighborhood. But I've lived here since I took the business over from Jane, and she'd lived here for twenty years before that. There's a German shepherd that sleeps in the rug store downstairs all night, so if anyone tried to get up the stairs Max would raise a ruckus. I'm perfectly safe here. You don't need to appoint yourself as my bodyguard, Sullivan."

"Hank could take care of himself, too. He was lying dead in an alleyway tonight." He met her gaze. "I don't give a good goddamn what you say, I'm not leaving you here alone. A man's been killed, Bailey."

"I know a man's been killed." She turned back to the kettle and unplugged it just as it started to whistle. Carefully she poured the boiling water into the teapot, brought down a couple of mugs from the shelf and clattered spoons into the mugs. As she reached across them for the canister of sugar, the sleeve of her sweater caught on one of the spoons, and the mug it was protruding from was knocked to the floor.

She looked down at the shattered crockery without moving. Then she looked up.

"I won't be your duty, Sully." Her voice was uneven, but with an effort she controlled it. "I'm not an annoying detail you have to take care of before you can get back to the job at hand. I thought you might need someone to talk to tonight. You don't. I can handle that.''

She smoothed her palms on the fabric of her pants. ''But I won't let the only connection between us be one of *obligation*,'' she said with sudden intensity.

She bent to pick up the broken crockery, but he was quicker than she was. Stooping swiftly, he scooped up the chunks of thick china, opened the cupboard door under the sink and dropped them into the small waste bin that was wedged by the water pipe there. He straightened and met her eyes. When he spoke his voice was low.

''Since when did you start buying loose tea like a civilized person, instead of those disgusting bags you used to use, Bails?''

Her gaze wavered, but held on his. ''Since you told me that was the kind you liked,'' she said steadily.

''And I've got a package of those teabags that you like in my kitchen. Still unopened.'' His voice was quiet. ''Sure and if that's not a coincidence, I don't know what you'd call it, would you?''

He was close enough to her that she could feel the warmth of his breath as he spoke and see the undefinable shadow that darkened those blue eyes nearly to black.

''No, Sully,'' Bailey said quietly. ''I wouldn't know what to call it, either. It probably is just a coincidence. The world's full of them, or so I hear.''

Slowly she turned away, and as she reached for another mug on the small shelf she heard him inhale, as if he was about to speak. She brought down the mug and lined it up with precise care next to the one on the counter, turning its handle so that it faced exactly the same way as the other one. He walked over to the window, and out of the corner of her eye she saw him just standing there. The sign from the restaurant glowed red and then blue through the slits in the bamboo blinds, looking like flashes from far-off detonations and reflecting onto his face.

"He had his five-year pin from AA in his pocket. He once told me that if he managed to beat the drinking he would feel his life had been worth something." Sullivan's features tightened. "I told Fitz that when they were through with the body at the morgue I'd take care of the funeral arrangements. I want Hank to be buried with that pin."

Bailey crossed over to a small table by the window. She set the two mugs and the teapot down, and then got the sugar canister from the counter. She pulled out one of the pair of plain wooden chairs by the table and sat.

"His death wasn't your fault, Sullivan. This case turned into something uglier than anyone could have foreseen." She folded her hands carefully in her lap, wondering with detached annoyance why they were trembling. "If anyone's responsible, it's me. Angelica wanted me to tail Aaron last weekend."

"Do you think that hasn't been in my mind from the start?" Swinging abruptly away from the window, he turned to her, his expression hard. "God, Bailey—it could have been *you* there tonight."

"But it wasn't. And maybe if I'd taken on the job when Angelica asked me, this whole thing would have turned out differently." Her hands had stopped trembling, Bailey noted with relief. "But trying to second-guess what might have been isn't going to get us very far. We have to find out who killed Hank, and why."

"He was my man. It's my job to go after his killer," Sullivan said. His jaw was tight. "Ainslie's got a cousin in Vermont. I'll call her first thing in the morning and arrange for you to stay there for a few days."

"With the cows." Her tone was flat. "Sorry, Sully. I don't do rustic."

"Then learn. The country's a lot healthier than the city." Folding his arms across his chest, he leaned back against the window, flattening the flimsy matchstick blinds behind him. The fingers of his left hand were relaxed, but his right hand was closed in a fist. "I should have been on top of things with Jackson, Bailey. I should have known what case he was on, and I should have known that he hadn't shown up for work on Monday. Maybe it would have been too late to do anything, but I should have *known*, dammit. I'm not about to let anything happen to you."

"Good, because I'm not about to let anything happen to you. You're my partner on this investigation, and I'll watch your back while you watch mine. Either that or we both leave for Vermont tomorrow." Bailey gave him a brief smile that didn't reach her eyes. "Which one is it, Sullivan?"

She saw his right hand tighten. Stiffly he pushed himself away from the window. "I guess I don't have a choice," he said shortly. "You've got every intention of working on this case whether we're partners or not, haven't you?"

He hesitated and then tossed something onto the table. "Keep this." He pulled out a chair and sat down, reaching for the sugar canister. "It can be your good-luck charm while we're working together."

Bailey looked down at the object and then her gaze flew to his. "I can't take that," she protested. "That was your father's—you said you never let it leave your person." She started to push the small shell back across the table at him, but he reached over and clasped her wrist.

"Take it, okay? Humor a poor superstitious Irish boy for once."

"But if I have it, what are you going to do for luck?"

She'd tried to match the lightness of his tone, but even to her own ears her voice sounded foolishly fearful. It was only a *shell*, Bailey told herself, and she'd never been superstitious. So why was she reacting like this? Sullivan folded her fingers around it and gently held them closed.

"You've got the shell. I'll stick close to you." He gave her a wry grin. "You can be my charm, honey. As long as we don't let each other out of our sight we're both protected."

He let go of her hand and sat back. "Pour the damn tea, Bails, and let's try to figure out what our next move is. We're agreed now that Hank was killed because of his involvement in your sister's matter?"

He was all business once again, and she found herself feeling obscurely grateful for that. Slipping the shell carefully into her own pocket, she positioned a tea strainer over Sullivan's mug and poured his tea. The mundane task gave her a moment to collect herself, and when she answered him her voice was as brisk as his had been.

"My sister's gone into hiding. Aaron Plowright's supposed mistress has turned out to be his daughter. And the man who was the link between those two facts is dead." She took a sip of her own tea and watched him spooning too much sugar into his. "I don't think there's any doubt he was killed because of Angelica's case, but for the life of me I can't figure out what's behind all this. God, Sully— three sugars?" Over the rim of her mug she raised a distracted eyebrow.

"I need the energy." He shot a sardonic glance at her and went on. "Let's start with what we have—the surveillance report that Hank prepared. What does it tell us?"

"It tells us that Aaron Plowright spent the weekend with his mistress," Bailey said promptly. "But we saw the jewelry store video, so we know that's not true."

"And I can't accept that Hank would have falsified that report." Sullivan set his mug down on the table and leaned forward. "But that's because I knew the man, Bailey. Do you still think he was playing some kind of double game?"

"You're right, I didn't share your faith in him," she said slowly. "But I do now. Murder raises questions, Sully. People aren't killed if they can be bought. Except that leaves us with two completely contradictory facts."

"The report isn't true, but the report can't be a lie." Restlessly he shoved his chair back and stood up, his hands jammed into his pockets. "Yeah, I've been trying to reconcile those myself, ever since we learned that the brunette Aaron was with was his daughter, not his lover." Quick distaste flashed across his features and he looked at her. "I'm not naive. I realize that the unthinkable isn't impossible, but I'm not ready to accuse Aaron Plowright of *that* yet."

"Neither am I." Bailey frowned. "A report that's a lie and the truth at the same time. It sounds like a riddle." She raked her hair back from her face and scowled. "Even when I was a kid I hated riddle books."

Sullivan had started pacing the floor, and he flashed her a wry grin. "Me, too. I'd always give in and turn to the back page for the answers. It beats me why we both became investigators."

She shrugged. "I told Steiner I became one almost by accident, but that wasn't strictly true. Growing up with Angelica, it was important to me to choose a life as different from hers as possible, and I just couldn't compete with her in anything girly."

"Don't forget, I've met Angelica," Sullivan said briefly. "You and I ran into her at a restaurant one night, remember? I can see how she would have made sure the spotlight was on her when the two of you were kids."

"But that's just it. Angelica never stopped being a child." She grimaced. "It wasn't until I was older that I learned what her life had been like before she'd been put up for adoption. At the time that she was taken into care by the authorities, she'd been found abandoned in the motel room where her crack-addicted mother had left her two days earlier."

"It explains a lot." Sullivan frowned. "The woman that little girl grew into made sure she would never be abandoned again."

"That's why I thought it was possible that she might have convinced Hank to fake a report, complete with descriptions of photos that never really existed, that she could use to keep Aaron in line with." Bailey massaged her temples tiredly. "I know—it wouldn't have worked. He would have laughed in her face and told her that Tracy herself would confirm it was her at the Harris with him, but Angelica wouldn't have thought it out that far. None of that matters now anyway. The report wasn't faked."

"And the report couldn't be true," reiterated Sullivan. "So we're back to the damn riddle again. When is a lie not a lie?"

Getting up and taking their mugs to the small sink, Bailey glanced at the clock on the wall and mentally added an extra hour, as she'd been doing, she thought guiltily, since everyone else on the continent had set the time forward for spring except her. It wasn't twelve-thirty, it was one-thirty, and she'd been up early in order to get her suitcase packed for their stay at—

She stopped suddenly, her mind racing.

"What is it?" Sullivan looked sharply at her, his own pacing footsteps coming to a halt.

"When is a lie not a lie, Sully? Riddle me that," she said, her eyes meeting his.

"I told you, I always looked up the answers to—" He frowned. Then one corner of his mouth lifted in a slow grin. "When the person who tells it thinks it's the truth? Bails, that has to be it. Hank reported exactly what he saw, but what he saw was a damned con job!"

"It was a performance put on for him, just so he'd make the report that he did. We both thought that the descriptions of the photos made it seem like the brunette was calling the shots, Sully. What if she *was?* What if Tracy was putting on a performance, and Plowright didn't even know it?"

"How the hell could he not have known? Where's the damn report?" Sullivan muttered, his hand going to the breast pocket of his jacket. Bailey's shoulder bag was by the door where she'd left it when they'd arrived, and swiftly she ran over and got it, pulling out the stapled and folded sheets of paper and handing them to him.

"Once you know what you're looking for, it jumps right out at you," she insisted. "She's got her arms around his neck, giving him a kiss—probably a daughterly kiss as far as Plowright was concerned, but posed in such a way that it would give quite another impression in a photo. He's on a chair, she poses herself on the bed. When he *is* in bed asleep, where's she? Standing right where she knows Hank can get a good shot, apparently naked beneath a skimpy robe."

"Tracy sleeps in the adjoining room that Plowright booked, but makes sure she's awake before him and parading around in front of doors leading out to *his* balcony." He slammed the report down on the table with an oath. "But *why,* dammit? What did she have to gain by this? More important, how does any of this tie in with Jackson's murder?"

"That's where I run into a brick wall, too."

Yanking the noose of his tie down even farther and slinging his jacket over the back of a chair, Sullivan rubbed the back of his neck tiredly. "We're beat and we're not thinking clearly anymore. Tomorrow morning I'll fill Fitz in on what we've come up with and see what he says, but for now I think we should call it a night."

"I didn't want to be the first to suggest it, but that sounds good to me, too." With a weary sigh, Bailey slumped down on the edge of her bed. The purple velvet spread that she'd run up herself from a remnant had been hastily pulled over the sheets this morning just before she'd dashed out of the apartment to meet Sullivan, and now she gave it a half-hearted tug. She caught his eye and flushed.

"I wasn't expecting a gentleman caller." She gave a self-deprecating little laugh. "My social life isn't exactly on a par with yours, I guess."

"Mine's been dead in the water for quite some time, honey." A corner of his mouth lifted at her sceptical look. "Hey, last Saturday I went bowling with Moira and her new boyfriend—the guy carries a bottle of nasal spray in his pocket, if you can believe it. The next day I was telling Ainslie what a tool he was and how I couldn't figure out what Moira saw in him, and all of a sudden I realized that at least he'd been the one with the girl."

"Cute, Sully." Bailey slanted a cynical gaze up at him. "But see, the only kind of man who could tell a story like that against himself and laugh is someone like you. It's like Cindy Crawford saying that she's having a bad hair day, when even at her worst she makes every other woman around look like a sack of potatoes. The girl's just not going to get any sympathy. For crying out loud," she added acerbically. "Don't you ever look in a mirror?"

"Not if I can help it." His muttered response was automatic, and she had the feeling it had been unintended. He recovered swiftly. "But let's talk about something more important, like where I'm going to sleep tonight. The bed's out, I take it?"

"You take it correctly," she said with a trace of self-consciousness. "The bed's no-man's-land, Sully."

"All the time, or just tonight with me?"

His question was casual, but she couldn't help the quick color that rose to her cheeks. Flustered, and annoyed that she was, she was about to brush off his inquiry with a noncommittal answer when she saw him watching her with an intentness that belied his light tone. She hesitated, confused.

The last time he'd been in her life she'd had a few heady, glorious weeks and three nights so perfect she'd thought she'd found heaven. Then in the space of a couple of minutes everything had been turned upside-down, and she'd been tipped into a world of pain and blackness. It had taken her the best part of a year to climb even a little way out of that pit, but she had, she told herself. She'd finally reached a level of emotional flatness that had been bearable.

But for the last thirty-six hours—ever since she'd walked into his office, she thought with a spark of sudden anger—her internal barometer had been swinging wildly back and forth again. The man blew hot and cold. One moment he was giving her that slow, heart-turning smile and notching up the temperature between them so high that the humidity in the air around her seemed almost saunalike. The next moment he would have so completely withdrawn into himself that she felt as if she'd just been caught unawares in a rainstorm, and had been chilled to the bone.

She'd never really known how to play games, Bailey thought frustratedly. And like she'd told him, she'd never been good at riddles. He had the answer to this one, and she didn't want to guess anymore.

With deliberate slowness she let herself lean back onto one elbow, looking up at him and smoothing the velvet spread with her fingertips. She shook her head and gave him a small, rueful smile.

"Oh, who am I kidding, Sullivan? We started something in that bath tonight that we never got to finish." Her laugh was low and breathy. "Of course I want you in my bed tonight."

Deer in the headlights, she thought, concealing her sharp glance under downcast lashes but not missing the quick disconcertion that crossed his features. He was standing only a foot or so away, and she reached over and hooked a finger in one of the belt loops of his pants before he could realize what she was doing.

"It's not as if we haven't done this before with each other, and it's not as if we don't both remember how good we were together." She injected a husky note into her voice and gave a little tug on the belt loop, bringing him an inch closer. "I'm willing to play it your way, Sully—no promises, no regrets. There's no reason for us to fight this anymore."

She felt him move infinitesimally toward her of his own accord. Then he stopped.

"Maybe we both want it, but we both know it's not such a good idea," he said. His voice had a hoarse edge to it. He cleared his throat. "I'll bunk down on the sofa with a blanket, Bails."

"I've got a better plan." She'd had no idea she could purr, Bailey thought in faint surprise. She went on, punctuating each phrase with another gentle pull on the loop. "You go into the bathroom and get out of that suit." *Tug.* "Turn the shower on until the mirrors steam up and the water's almost too hot to stand." *Tug.* "When you think you're hot enough and you think you're steamy enough,

Sullivan, I'll get in with you and give you my opinion.'' *Tug, tug.*

She widened her eyes at him, letting her gaze flick down to where her fingers were, and then back up again. ''I know you're not carrying a gun, Sully, so this must mean you like this plan better, too,'' she said softly.

She gave one last tug, and this time he didn't resist. He brought one knee onto the bed and braced his arms on either side of her, his face only inches from hers.

''Yeah, I like the plan,'' he said huskily. ''And you're right, honey, I'm not carrying a gun.''

His eyes were as she'd seen them a million times in her broken dreams over the past year—dark, dark blue and glazed with an overriding need. Bailey caught her breath as they stared into hers.

''Any minute I'm going to wake up alone in my own bed,'' he muttered. ''This time, don't disappear before we're through, darlin'.''

His mouth came down on hers, hard and urgent, and with none of the slowly mounting pleasure that he'd always been capable of before. Still leaning back on her elbows, through the thin knit of her sweater Bailey felt his bicep tighten against the side of her breast as his arm went around her, lifting her up to meet his kiss. She felt her head tip back on her neck, felt her hair slide past her shoulders to hang free behind her, felt him shift slightly, still supporting himself with one arm, his knee on one side of her and the thigh muscles of his other leg taut against hers.

Except his tongue was inside her and his mouth was covering hers and she really couldn't concentrate on anything else at all.

He kissed as if he was on the edge of losing all control, and wanted to get as much of her as he could before he did. He was *licking* the inside of her mouth, she thought in heated shock. He was licking her as if she was ice cream. She felt a liquefying desire cascade through her, and blindly her own hands came up and her fingers sank into the rough silk of his hair.

He moved his mouth just enough to the corner of hers that she could hear his whisper. "More, honey. Open *up* to me, sweetheart." Even as he spoke he moved farther onto the bed, lifting her with him as he did. He was still half kneeling, half standing, his body bent down to her and hers arched so closely to him that the heat emanating from his skin seemed like a palpable force. His hand slipped up under her sweater and impatiently pushed past the soft cotton of her bra, cupping one breast and then spreading wide to take in the other.

He was so *bad,* Bailey thought, dark pleasure staining whatever coherent thoughts were left to her. And he made her feel sinful, too, as if nothing he needed from her was out of the question, as if he could take her any way he wanted and she would do the same with him. Without conscious volition, she let her hands move down the sides of his jaw, the muscles of his neck, his open collar. His tie was crushed between them and she felt it slip past her fingers as she fumbled with the bottom buttons of his shirt, finally freeing them and sliding her palms against the smooth hardness of his stomach. She pulled his shirt a little way out of his pants, her fingers trembling now with urgency, and then let one fingertip trace a light trail downward from his belt.

It wasn't *really* sinful, she told herself disjointedly. The man was fully dressed, even if she'd managed to dishevel him slightly. And she was keeping her hands on the outside, wasn't she? Could she help it if he'd chosen a summer-weight suit to wear today, and that it was made of wool so fine it felt like no barrier at all? She just wanted to *feel* him, she thought. She just needed to know how much he really wanted—

He wanted her.

With immense effort, Bailey dragged her mouth from his, slowly opening her eyes. His were still closed, those inky black lashes like tiny brushes on his cheekbones. He looked like a man who had passed the point of no return, she thought. He looked like a man who couldn't say no anymore. And that was all she'd needed to be sure of, because she'd known from the start that she wouldn't be able to say no to him.

He opened his eyes and drew in a ragged breath, blue-black strands of hair partially obscuring an unfocused gaze. The high, tanned ridge of cheekbone was flushed with heated color. His gaze locked and held on to hers, and she felt her breath catch in her throat.

She'd wanted everything from him once. He hadn't been able to give that to her, and she'd walked away from him. Now she was one year older and one year more knowledgeable about herself, and she'd come to realize that she was willing to have any part of Terrence Patrick Sullivan that she could get. She had this moment, she thought, drinking in the blueness of those eyes so close to hers. If this alone was all she would ever be allowed of the man, it would still be the image she would be holding in her mind years from now, when everything else had faded.

This moment and the night ahead of them, Bailey thought tremulously. She felt him exhale, his breath warm against her parted lips, and with a soft sigh she closed her eyes as he gently lowered her to the velvet spread.

"I can't do this, Bails. Not tonight, not ever."

Her eyes flew open. He was still leaning over her, but the distance between them had widened. His features were a mask of pain and his voice was cracked and harsh. A moment ago his eyes had stared into hers with the drugged, unseeing gaze of a man who had let go of all restraints. Now they were shadowed with a terrible regret.

The weather had changed, the temperature was dropping, and Bailey felt as if a cruel east wind was starting to slice through her heart, frosting it with a crystalline skin of ice. She stared up at him, trying to hold on to her disbelief and knowing that it had already been replaced with a piercing certainty.

"But you want this, I *know* you do," she whispered, holding his gaze. "You want *me*."

Abruptly he stood, as if he needed to put even more space between them, and fast. His movements jerky and mechanical, he tucked in that part of his shirt that she'd disarranged only minutes ago, and started to tighten the knot of his tie. Then he stopped. Slowly his hands fell to his sides.

"Yeah, I want you." His tone was shockingly raw. "I want you as badly as I've wanted you every night for the past year, honey. I want to have you all over me—your sweetness, your scent, your hair in my eyes and your taste in my mouth. Once upon a time that would have been enough, because what I wanted I took. I even did that with you, and I've hated myself for it ever since."

One corner of his mouth lifted, but there was no hint of humor in his smile. "I'll want you for the rest of my life," he said simply. "And for the rest of my life I'll know I can't have you, Bailey."

Chapter Nine

He didn't want to look into her eyes because he knew what he would see there, Sullivan thought dully. Incomprehension. Pain. The death of anything she'd ever thought she'd felt for him. He could make it fractionally easier on himself if he didn't look. If he didn't, he wouldn't have to carry the picture of what he knew he'd see in his heart for the rest of his life.

But he wasn't the man he'd once been. The easy way had taken his soul and left him with nothing but iron-hard resolve. Bailey had been the one thing in his world that had weakened that resolve—not only last year, but tonight—and Bailey would be the one his weakness would destroy, if he gave in to it.

He needed to look into her eyes. Her pain would be like a knife thrust in his gut, sharp enough and searing enough to force him to back away before he did her more damage. He forced himself to meet her gaze.

As he'd known, the light hazel irises were sheened with silver. He'd caused those tears, Sullivan told himself harshly. He'd hurt her again, just as he'd vowed he never would. The only thing in his favor was that he hadn't put her through it as thoroughly as he'd done before, but that wasn't much of a consolation. The fact that his own pain was tearing him apart made absolutely no difference to how he judged himself. He wanted her, not just for tonight and not just physically, and knowing he couldn't have her was a wound that would never heal. That was tough, he thought grimly. And he was going to have to learn how to endure it, because the man he'd once been had brought this fate upon himself.

But right now he was looking into the eyes of the woman he would always love, and those eyes were filled with—

"I don't *believe* you!"

A moment ago those lips had been as soft as the velvet she'd been lying on. Now as she jerked herself bolt upright on the bed, they were thinned to an incredulous line. He felt a familiar flash of self-loathing, and tiredly he started to turn away from her.

"I don't believe myself, either, Bails. I never meant to let things go—"

"Don't you *dare* walk away from me, you—you—" Out of the corner of his eye he saw her bounce up onto her feet, and before he could react, she'd covered the space between them in one quick stride and had grabbed his arm. She spun him around to face her. "You know what you are, Sullivan?" she hissed in a low, deadly tone.

"Yeah, I know what I am," he said tonelessly. "Believe me, Bailey, I'm under no illusions as to my character." The hand gripping his sleeve tightened, and her unspoken anguish tore through him like a blade. "I'm not worth it," he said softly, fighting the overwhelming compulsion to take her in his arms, kiss that trembling mouth, stroke that glossy hair and never, *never* let her go.

He reined his thoughts in abruptly, hating himself even more. "I'm not worth one single tear of yours, honey."

He started to turn away again, but this time when she jerked him back she brought her face up to his.

He'd been wrong, he realized in swift confusion. Those hazel eyes weren't filled with pain, they were filled with outrage. The glitter he'd seen in them was pure, unadulterated *fury*.

"No one's *crying,* Sully," she ground out between clenched teeth, searing him with that angry stare. It was as if she had turned an arc welder's torch his way, and was directing the spray of sizzling sparks straight at him, he thought disjointedly. "What I'm doing is wondering just what the hell you get out of throwing these buckets of cold water on me every so often. Is it some kind of power trip for you, is that it? Or are you just a natural-born *tease?*"

Despite himself, he stiffened. She had a right to call him just about anything she wanted, he thought. But somehow the word she'd chosen stung.

"I don't think that term's in use much anymore, Bails." He attempted to notch down the tension between them with a wry smile. "And the only people I ever heard use it in the first place were randy boys who needed someone to blame for their nonexistent sex lives."

"So it fits, then." She narrowed her gaze. "I'm not feeling particularly politically correct right now, Sullivan. In fact, I feel an awful lot like one of those randy teenagers you're talking about. After flirting with me, after raising my blood pressure with your damn candles and your damn bath, after driving me out of my mind right here on my own bed—now you've got the nerve to turn around and tell me you aren't that kind of *guy?*

"I mean it, Sully." Her voice was quieter but no less intense. "I want to know what happened here tonight, what happened earlier at the hotel, and what happened between us last year. Because you've never really given me any kind of explanation that makes sense."

She hesitated. Her teeth caught at her bottom lip, and the

impact of that tiny action slammed into him with the force of a blow.

"You told me that my faith in you was all wrong, and you've tried your best to prove that to me. I'm close to believing you, Sully. I don't want to, but you're very— you're very convincing." Her voice cracked on the last few words, but her gaze didn't waver. She stood in front of him, pinning him with that clear, direct look of hers that had always made him wonder how far into him she could see.

He didn't have much with her anymore, Sullivan thought. After tonight he would have less than the little he'd survived on for the past twelve months. But if he gave her the explanation she was asking for, he would have to stand here and watch those clear eyes turn away from him forever. Or maybe it would be worse. Maybe those eyes would lose their directness, would try not to meet his, would look anywhere but at him if they ever met again.

All of a sudden he felt a twinge of irrational anger. He'd done his best to protect her from himself, and all right— maybe his best was one hell of a poor effort, but he'd *tried,* dammit. He'd never said he was a saint. That was why he'd stayed away from her since the last time—because he knew his limitations when it came to Bailey Flowers.

But then she'd come back into his life. And now she was asking him to destroy the last scrap of feeling she might have for him.

He kept his voice even, but he could feel a muscle twitching at the side of his jaw. "You shouldn't have come back, Bailey. I told you how it would turn out."

Her eyes widened. For a moment he felt her grip on his arm slip. Then it tightened again, and this time he could feel the small half-moons of her nails digging into him through the fabric of his shirtsleeve.

"In bed together, or at each other's throats," she said flatly. "And I told you that the second scenario was the more likely one. It seems I was right."

She stared into his eyes for a long second, and then she released his arm abruptly. Walking past him, she went to the window and jerked the blinds.

Immediately the room took on a bluish hue. Then the blue turned to red, and her face was suddenly bathed in crimson.

Sullivan found himself fighting to drag in a breath. The blood was pounding in his ears, and all at once he was certain he could discern the acrid sting of cordite in the air. His hands closed into fists at his sides, and the tendons tightened in his neck as he waited for the moment to pass.

It did. It always did. The neon sign outside buzzed and flickered, and then the room and Bailey turned blue again. He felt the steel wire edge of tension that had bound him loosen its garotte-like grip, and he willed himself to relax.

The next moment it had jerked so tightly around him that his lungs stopped working completely.

"It's got something to do with the Salazar woman, hasn't it, Sully? The Salazar woman...and the deaths that you witnessed back there in the jungle."

He couldn't speak. He couldn't even breathe. All he could do was stare at her and feel his world cave in around him.

Her face was partially turned away from him, and she was still looking out of the window into the night. Slowly she brought one hand up to the glass, pressing her palm against its blackly reflective surface in an odd gesture of surrender. The neon flickered to crimson. Her eyes closed. Sullivan found his voice.

"Where did you hear that name?"

IN THE SILENCE of the small room his whisper was explosive. Shocked, Bailey turned fully toward him, and at the sight of him she felt a terrible fear.

Her fear wasn't for herself. It was for him.

His eyes were a blazing blue in the tan of his face, and a muscle jumped at the side of his jaw. The corners of his mouth were white with tension. "How did you find out about Maria? What do you *know* about her, dammit?"

She'd been right, she thought in dull stupefaction. It had been based on guesswork and rumors from the start, but however she'd hit upon it, it seemed she'd stumbled upon the truth. *"…suicide missions…incredibly charming but quite mad…worse after the Salazar woman was killed…"* Everything the Englishman had said now made terrible sense.

"I know you loved her and lost her. I know she's dead," she said tersely. "I dug into your past, Sully. I'm not proud of it, but I'd do it again if I had to. I needed to know why you—why you acted the way you did," she finished unevenly.

"Hell, why not?" The muscle at the side of his cheek jumped again, and he set his jaw. "You're a detective. That's what you do. So tell me, honey, did you find out what made little Terry Patrick tick?"

"Not until now." She looked down at her hands, clenched together in front of her. "I didn't have the last piece of the puzzle until tonight. For a whole year I've thought I'd been one of your whims, that I'd meant nothing to you at all, but the man who kissed me on that bed a while ago wasn't feeling nothing, Sullivan. That kiss was real."

"But you've said it yourself, Bails. I deliberately pushed you away a year ago." His smile was briefly ironic. "So how does that fit in with what you think you felt in my kiss?''

He was trying hard, she thought. He was trying as hard as he could to turn her from him, as he'd done once before. But now she saw through it. She kept her eyes steady on him.

''You pushed me away because you were afraid of losing me, just like you lost Maria,'' she said quietly. ''I think you were starting to fall in love with me, and I think that terrified you.''

For a moment she saw pain flare up behind his gaze. Then his features hardened.

''No one told you how she died, did they?'' He grinned humorlessly. ''You know, I like your version, honey. I come off as the tragic hero. Let's say we go with that one, okay?''

''No, let's say we go with the truth.'' She looked up, her eyes clouded. ''Are you telling me you didn't love her? Are you saying her death didn't tear you apart?''

''I was crazy about her.'' He smiled tightly. ''I couldn't eat, sleep or function for thinking about her. And when she died, I think I went a little insane.''

''Then I don't understand.'' Bailey shook her head, hoping that the sudden pang that had shot through her heart at his declaration didn't show on her face. ''That *is* tragic. But you can't let it overshadow the rest of your life, Sullivan. She must have loved you as much as you loved her. She would have wanted you to find someone else eventually.''

His gaze held hers for a long moment, the blue of his eyes so bright they almost glittered. ''Maria didn't love me. She hated me. She died cursing me, and I guess I don't blame her.'' He smiled down at her, but the expression didn't match the bleakness in his voice.

"We don't ever talk about this again, honey," he said softly. "But yeah, you're right in a way. Maria's the reason why I wanted you out of my life before it was too late. Ask me how she died, Detective."

"All right. How did she die, Sully?" There was a faint buzzing noise in her ears, as if she was listening in on a bad telephone line and the connection was about to fade out for good. Suddenly she wished that the buzzing was louder, so she didn't have to hear his answer.

She didn't want to hear it, she thought fearfully.

"I killed her. She died because of me," Sullivan said. "Maria and five good men died that night, honey, and I made it happen. I didn't lose my heart with her. I lost my soul."

The glittering eyes held hers for a long moment. Then abruptly he turned from her and went over to the table, his shoulders set rigidly.

Maybe he had been starting to fall in love with her, just a little, a year ago. But that didn't matter now. Whether she'd stayed or not, it never would have gone much further than that. He would have made sure of it. He'd said it himself just now—he had no soul. He had nothing to give anyone, including himself.

She turned and looked out at the street below, needing all at once to make some connection with the outside world—the world that she lived in, the world that she understood. The pavement was dark and shiny, and with a detached part of her mind she realized that it had just rained. The air outside would be clean and cool, she thought, wishing suddenly that she could go out into the night, walk down the rain-slick pavement and never look back.

Bailey pressed her lips together and turned back to the window. Unsnapping the twin latches at the sides, with a small grunt she heaved it up and open, and immediately the rain-cleansed air from outside poured into the room. She reached up and released the cord of the blinds.

She walked over to the bed and sat down. Smoothing her palms carefully on her pants, she looked over at the silent man sitting motionless at the table nearby.

"I want to hear it all, Sully," she said harshly. "Five men died and you say you made it happen. I want to know how."

He raised his head and met her eyes, his own shadowed in the soft glow from the light over the bed. "Maybe I owe you that," he said tonelessly. "Maybe it's time I told you."

He passed his hand across his eyes, as if he was scrubbing away the memory of something he'd seen—or trying to, she thought. When he began to speak, his voice was almost inaudible.

"It wasn't even a war. They called it an action, and we were hired on by the leader of the rebel forces to show peasants and farmers and grade-school teachers how to fight." His head was still bowed, but she saw the corner of his mouth lift in a mirthless parody of his trademark grin. "They were hopeless at first. Most of them had never handled a gun in their lives, and I wondered why they just didn't give it up as a lost cause and go back to their safe, everyday lives. I was in it for the money, but I couldn't figure out why someone would throw away everything for a damned idea."

"This was in South America?" she hazarded tentatively.

He shook his head. "Where it was doesn't matter. I learned a long time ago that it's always the same war." He fell silent for a moment, and then he resumed, his voice still a monotone, his eyes still staring unseeingly down. "You don't eat and sleep and drill twenty-four hours a day with a group of soldiers without getting to know them pretty well, and after a while I began to see that even though they had no experience, most of them had something more valuable—conviction. They really believed in what they were fighting for. I couldn't understand the concept.''

''I don't believe that.'' Her voice came out louder than she'd intended, and he glanced over at her. ''You must have chosen certain jobs and declined others on more than just a monetary basis, Sully. I know it was a job to you— for heaven's sakes, your father was a soldier for hire, too, so it was what you grew up with—but there *must* have been something more.''

''Look up the meaning of the word *mercenary* sometime, honey.'' His face was expressionless. ''And Thomas himself brought me up to believe that nothing was worth giving your heart to.''

He seldom mentioned his father, Bailey realized. Ainslie had revealed more of the man who had deserted her mother and herself, but for at least the first half of his life Thomas would have been the main figure in his son's life. And until tonight Sullivan had carried his father's talisman on him constantly, so despite his offhanded comment, there had to have been some kind of bond between them. She frowned, realizing that he had taken up his story again.

''Enrique had been a surgeon—one of the best until he'd been arrested and taken in for questioning a few months before. He told me that it had been his misfortune to be a totally innocent man, because in his innocence he didn't have the answers they were looking for. They knew what he did for a living, of course, and over the next ten days they broke all of his fingers, one each day. Then they let him go.'' Sullivan shrugged. ''Except he had nothing to go back to. His young wife had been pregnant when they'd arrested her, and she'd gone into premature labor in the prison where she was being held. Enrique came home to find himself arranging a funeral for both his wife and the baby he'd never even seen.''

''Dear God,'' Bailey breathed, her eyes stricken with horror. ''How could anyone go on after having their whole life ripped away from them in such a terrible way?''

''Most of the others in our camp had gone through the same, or even worse,'' Sullivan said briefly. ''There were women who were just as determined as the men to fight. Maybe more so,'' he added, his gaze darkening. ''Maria was one of them.''

Just speaking her name tore him apart, Bailey saw. His jaw tightened, as if he were riding out a wave of pain, and his hands, clasped lightly on the table in front of him, clenched until the knuckles whitened. She'd had no right to ask him to relive this. But maybe he'd been right. Maybe it was time he talked about the pain and the apparent guilt he had carried for so long.

I just wish it wasn't me who was hearing it. I don't want to know how much she meant to him, how much she still must mean to him. As soon as the thought came into her mind she was ashamed of it, but if he had noticed anything, Sullivan gave no sign.

''She was different from the rest. Her father was one of the generals who had the country by the throat, and it took a long time to convince the others that she had turned her back on the decadent, monied lifestyle she was used to. But gradually she won them over, doing every dirty chore that needed to be done without complaint, although before then she'd had servants for those things, and learning how to become a guerilla fighter along with the best of them. Of course, it didn't hurt that she became the favored pupil of one of their instructors. Quinn warned me to break off my liaison with Maria. I told him to go to hell.''

"Quinn McGuire?" The big silent mercenary who had walked away from her when she'd started to ask questions, Bailey thought. Sullivan nodded curtly.

"Yeah. He could see I was heading for trouble. But I blew him off because I was bored, and she was beautiful and willing. That had been the pattern of my life up until then, dammit." He shrugged tightly. "I didn't see any reason to change just because there was a chance the woman might start taking me seriously."

He didn't sound like a man talking about the lost love of his life, she thought, disconcerted. He went on, his features so grim they looked carved.

"By the time she told me she'd fallen in love with me it was too late. Quinn and I and the other mercenaries had only been hired on to train the rebels, and our job there was coming to an end. Enrique, with his fingers that no longer had the skill and delicacy to save a life, had proved to be more than capable of handling a gun and leading men, and he was ready to take over. One night I told her that we would be leaving the next week, and that I hoped she wouldn't forget me too fast."

Bailey blinked. "But I thought you said you were *crazy* about her," she protested. "How could you leave her when you loved her so much?"

Sullivan's head jerked up. He stared at her blankly.

"I never *loved* her, for God's sake. That wasn't my style. For a time I was obsessed with her. For a time I couldn't get enough of her, couldn't concentrate on anything but her. But I never loved her, and Maria knew that. Things might have turned out differently if I had cared for her, just a little."

He gave a short laugh and leaned forward in the chair toward her stiff figure, seemingly not noticing the impact his revelation had had on her. "But I didn't want to care for a woman. I knew that as soon as I did, I'd have to leave, and it was easier to walk away if you didn't let yourself feel anything. I'd learned that lesson so early on it was part of me.''

During her conversation with Ainslie she'd wondered how Thomas Sullivan's tomcatting lifestyle had affected his young son. Now she knew, Bailey thought with a pang of compassion for the boy the big man in front of her had once been. His mother, the stepmother he'd been close to, the baby sister he'd had to leave behind—he'd lost them all. And the only way he'd known how to protect himself was to look upon every arrangement as temporary. Even she'd only been temporary, she knew that now. But hearing that Maria had been in the same category was a shock.

She didn't believe him. If Maria had meant nothing to him, then why did the woman still haunt him so? And what had happened to turn her against him so thoroughly? He'd said she'd died hating him, but surely his ending of their affair hadn't been reason enough to change her feelings for him so violently.

"Anyway, she overestimated my attachment to her, and she underestimated everything else about me," he went on quietly. His gaze shifted to a point past her, and Bailey knew he was no longer seeing the homely little details of the room around him. "The night I told her I would be leaving soon, she put her arms around me and said she'd arranged things so that we could stay together. All I had to do was switch sides, she said, and she knew that a man with few loyalties would have no trouble turning his back on a ragtag group of radicals that had been doomed to defeat from the start. Her father wanted me to head up the army. She'd convinced him that if he paid me enough, I could be bought.''

"She *never* could have loved you, Sully!" The words

tumbled out of her in an impulsive rush, and she went on, her voice edged with anger. "She didn't even *know* you if she thought that. How did she take it when you told her no?"

"I didn't. I told her yes," Sullivan said, standing up from the chair he'd been sitting in. Walking over to the counter by the sink, he leaned against it with his back to her, his hands gripping its edge and his arms braced stiffly. His head was bowed, the broad shoulders tense.

"The surprise attack on the rebel camp was to occur within the hour. I told her yes, and as soon as I could get away from her without arousing her suspicions, I found Quinn and we tried to get our people out of there. They were guerillas," he said, his voice low and his back still to her. "They'd been trained to strike swiftly and unexpectedly and then melt back into the jungle, but they had no chance against a concerted attack by a massive force. Before we could spread the word, it had begun. Enrique was the first one down, and when I saw him take the bullet something inside me snapped."

He pushed himself away from the counter and turned to face her, his features expressionless. "There were two things I knew how to do well—bed a woman and fight an enemy. I'd let myself be distracted by the first, and maybe if I hadn't been thinking of Maria as my latest diversion I might have seen something in her that would have alerted me. But I'd been criminally careless, and now a decent man was dead because of me. All that was left was to make sure he hadn't died in vain, and the only way to do that was to take out as many of the general's men as I could. Quinn was beside me for a while, and we must have made quite a pair—him coolly firing off round after round, me with a knife between my teeth and one of the clapped-out assault rifles that the rebels had been equipped with on my shoulder.''

He raked his hair back with a restless gesture and shrugged. ''We were pouring on covering fire to give our people time to get away into the jungle, and when there were only a few left, we started retreating ourselves. At one point Quinn and I got separated, and that's when I ran straight into Maria. She knew I'd betrayed her, of course.'' He shook his head, his eyes dark with memory. ''I'd never seen so much hatred on a person's face before. I'd just run out of ammo and I was trying to reload when she brought up her own weapon, screaming at me all the while.''

''What was she screaming?'' Bailey asked through frozen lips, but even before he answered her she remembered what he'd told her earlier. The woman had died cursing him. The tale was nearly told.

''She said she would send me to hell,'' he said simply. ''And then she did—just as Quinn's bullet took her down. Weeks later, when I came to in the hospital, they told me I'd actually been clinically dead for a minute or so, before they managed to get my heart started again, but I'd already known that. I could remember seeing the whole scene from somewhere just slightly above my body—Maria falling, and Quinn frantically bending over a man who was covered in blood. I knew that man was me. And then through all the shouting and the explosions and the gunfire I heard the rush of wings, and I knew they were coming for me.''

He didn't have to explain. She knew what he was talking about, and though he'd insisted he didn't believe in them, she knew now that he did.

''The wild geese—the souls of mercenaries who die in battle and are fated to fly for eternity, looking for the home they never had,'' she said woodenly. ''But it's only a legend, Sully. Whatever you thought you experienced during that minute or so, it wasn't that. It *couldn't* have been that," she added with sudden force. "In the end you survived. They *didn't* take you."

"Didn't they?" He looked over at her and smiled faintly. "Fitz thinks they did. Quinn won't talk about it. And I know what I saw and heard that day, honey." He shook his head, the small smile fading from his lips. "She sent me to hell and they came and took away my soul. When I met you I thought maybe I could get to heaven without one, but then I realized I couldn't do that to you. For the first time in my life I did the right thing—I made you leave."

"Except I came back, Sullivan. I came back and I don't believe in ghosts or fairy tales, and unless you can show me some proof I *won't* believe in them," Bailey said sharply. "You don't have proof, do you? So how can you let—"

"Oh, I've got proof, all right."

For the first time since he'd started talking, he came over to where she was still sitting rigidly on the bed. Taking one of her hands in his, he pulled her to her feet, and, looking up into his face, Bailey saw the emptiness behind that navy gaze.

"I gave you the proof tonight. It's in your pocket. Go on, take it out, Bails."

Her eyes never leaving his, slowly she slipped her free hand into her pocket and pulled out the small shell he had given her earlier—the perfectly formed fan with a hole through the exact center of it. She kept her palm wrapped tightly around it, suddenly not wanting to look at it.

"Your father's shell," she said, her voice foolishly uneven. "You said it was sent to you after his death."

"I lied. He wrote to me a couple of days before he was killed and told me he'd lost it during a skirmish. He was afraid that was an omen, and the way things turned out for him, I guess it was," he said softly. "It wasn't sent to me with the rest of his things, because it wasn't on him when he died."

"I don't understand." She searched his face apprehensively, a nameless fear stirring in her. Still holding her one hand, Sullivan lightly grasped the other as well, gently prying open her fingers to reveal the pierced shell sitting there on her palm.

"Neither do I. But when they were trying to bring me back from the dead, they found it in my hand, Bailey."

Chapter Ten

"Fitz is saying his hands are tied because of Plowright's political connections. He'll look into the Tracy Weiss aspect, but he's not going to rock her boat just yet in case it causes a ripple in Aaron's pond." Exhaling in sharp irritation, Sullivan snapped on his seat belt, pulled away from the curb with a squawk of the Jaguar's tires and continued with a frown.

"His pet theory seems to be that Jackson was whacked by the mob boss he testified against last year. Hell, Hank was on the stand ten minutes and his evidence consisted of saying he'd seen Pirelli outside of a downtown bar when the man was supposedly at home with his wife. He wasn't even tailing Pirelli at the time and the sighting was pure coincidence, but Fitz likes that scenario and he's going to run with it first."

"Did you tell him we were on our way to Plowright's estate right now?" There was no real interest in Bailey's tone. Too late she saw the exit sign for Dedham coming up, but already he was making the lane change to get onto the off-ramp.

She had to get focused, she thought. They were investigating a man's death, and all she could think about was what had happened between her and Sullivan last night. *Let it go, Flowers,* she told herself bleakly. *There's nothing you can do to change the man's past and there's no place for you in his future. Like he said himself last night, after this investigation is over the two of you will go your separate ways and it's unlikely you'll ever meet again.*

She'd seen him as haunted. What she hadn't realized was that there were two ghosts he couldn't exorcise—the woman whose bullet had nearly destroyed him and the man whose flawed legacy had come close to tearing him apart. But Thomas's hold over him was the more powerful because it was rooted in love.

Whether or not Sullivan really believed that the shell he'd given her last night had been mystically transferred to him during a near-death experience, the small talisman proved that he'd never made his peace with the man who had raised him. He obviously saw himself as following the same destructive path as his father, and she had to admit that the similarities between the two of them might give rise to that comparison at first glance. From what Ainslie had said, Thomas had been irresistible to women, and Sullivan certainly had that in common with him. They'd both been professional soldiers. Neither had shown any inclination to settle down permanently with one woman, and like his son, Thomas had apparently had a belief in omens and signs—although how deep-rooted Sullivan's faith in them was, she wasn't sure. He'd scoffed at the legend that Fitz had referred to, but it seemed that on some level he didn't entirely dismiss it.

The wild geese. Her lips thinned to a line. Last night when Sullivan had related the story to her she'd felt a chill run down her spine at the eerie myth of doomed souls of dead mercenaries laying claim to one of their own. But in the cold light of day she felt annoyed with herself for letting it get to her. Sullivan blamed himself for what had happened at the rebel encampment, and that guilt had translated into a belief that he could never be absolved of his actions. No wonder that at the moment of death he had heard a rush of wings, seen a shadowy flight of lost comrades in his imagination. The geese were symbolic of his own inability to forgive himself, but that was all they were.

Except that was enough, she thought somberly. The wounds of childhood never really healed, she knew that herself. Angelica, with her need for total security and adoration, was proof of it. So probably was Aaron's daughter, Tracy, whom he'd refused to legitimatize or formally acknowledge, and who seemed now to be playing some puzzling game against him. Sullivan was no different. He had been the only person his father had cared for enough to never leave, and as a boy he must have loved Thomas with the hero-worshiping adoration that any young son would have for a father. But as a grown man he'd judged him, found him sorely wanting, and then realized that he himself was a mirror image of the man he'd lost respect for.

"Yeah, I told Fitz we were on our way to talk to Plowright," Sullivan said as they left the interstate behind.

At his reply to her question she wrenched her thoughts back to the present with an effort, but he went on, saving her from the need to formulate an immediate comment.

"He said he didn't want us interfering in police business, and I reminded him that you were family and had a right to drop in on your brother-in-law whenever you wanted to."

Sullivan slowed to turn off onto a secondary road. "Then I told him that I was calling from a pay phone only a couple of miles from the estate anyway, and when he started swearing at me I guess we somehow got disconnected."

"I was hoping he'd insist on questioning Angelica right away," Bailey said. "Someone must have some way of getting in contact with her, wherever she is, even though she's not answering her cell phone. I'd feel easier if I knew for sure she was okay.'' She shrugged. ''Of course, after that I'd wring her neck for putting me through all this worry and then I'd do whatever I had to, to get the truth out of her.''

''Have you considered the possibility that she was in on this with Tracy?'' Sullivan's question was carefully uninflected, but immediately she jerked her attention from the passing scenery to him.

''Angelica? Are you crazy?'' She gave her head a firm shake and then frowned. ''I think the entrance to the grounds is somewhere around here. Slow down, it's easy to miss.''

It was easy to miss because it had been designed that way, she thought a moment later as Sullivan swung the car into a small, badly rutted lane that, after about twenty feet, opened abruptly into a wide, well-paved road.

''When we get to the gates we'll have to buzz for admittance,'' she said abstractedly. ''What are you saying— that the two of them are partners, for crying out loud? There's just no way. Aaron's trophy wife and his legal eagle of a daughter have absolutely nothing in common, believe me.''

''Without even trying hard I can think of one thing they've got in common,'' Sullivan said dryly. ''His money.''

''Not really.'' Her voice was beginning to take on a tinge of irritation. ''Neither of them have any claim on it. Angelica's barred by the prenup, and Tracy's always known she's not a legal heir.''

''That's right.'' They had come to the massively ornate gates of the estate, and he let the Jaguar roll to a stop just feet from them. He turned to her, his expression serious.

"Can you imagine how that must eat away at them—to be so close to so much money, and to know that they'll never get any closer? If Aaron runs true to form, sooner or later he'll start looking around for wife number five and Angelica will be out in the cold. Then again, he's not a young man anymore—in twenty or so years he'll die and Tracy won't get a penny."

"Exactly. So why would my sister and his daughter jeopardize what they have now with him by framing him for an affair he wasn't having, for heaven's sake?" Despite her earlier lack of concentration, Bailey's rejoinder held a spark of animation. "And how do you tie any of this to Hank's murder? He wasn't killed for the photos, although since we've concluded that he didn't lie in his report I'll accept that they must have existed. But they simply could have been stolen, which they were." She reached for the door handle. "I'll buzz up to the main house and get them to let us in."

She was halfway out of the car when his next words checked her.

"The photos were stolen, and after that they weren't a threat to anyone anymore. But Hank still was," he said abruptly. "He was the only one who could positively identify Tracy Weiss as the mystery woman in the report."

Slowly Bailey sank back into her seat. "You're right, of course," she said with slow reluctance. "Everyone we talked to at the Harris had trouble describing her. All they saw was a brunette with a wide-brimmed hat on, or a slim woman in sunglasses. Whenever she was actually out in public, she made sure she wasn't easily recognizable."

"I'd better phone Steiner and tell him to hang on to that videotape." His eyes narrowed. "With Hank dead and the photos gone, it's the one hard piece of evidence we have."

"But I still don't get it. Why was it so important for

Tracy to establish that her father was having an affair?"
She looked at him in frustration. "Why did she have to
create a mystery woman?"

"Two entirely different questions," Sullivan said after a
pause. "Maybe we've been focusing on the wrong one."
His voice took on a sharper edge. "What if we hadn't stumbled upon the fact that it was Plowright's daughter there
with him last weekend? Who would we be looking for right
now?"

"A woman who didn't exist?" she hazarded vaguely. A
second later her eyes widened. "And a woman who doesn't
exist is invisible—she would *never* have been found," she
said in dawning comprehension. "No photos, no eyewit-
nesses to her identity. Nobody would have even known
what her voice sounded like, since the bugs that Hank
planted in the room were defective."

"They weren't defective, she disabled them," he said
shortly. "She must have searched the room for them before
Aaron showed up, found them and made sure they wouldn't
transmit anything to Hank, especially the phone call she
was expecting from her partner in all this. She *had* to be
the person that Angelica was phoning in 201, Bailey."

"But *why?*" Her voice rose. "What could they possibly
have been planning?"

"Murder comes to mind," Sullivan said slowly. His gaze
met hers. "What better way to commit the perfect murder
than to first create the perfect murderer—a mystery
woman?"

"A mystery woman who can never be found, because
she never existed in the first place?" Bailey's brows drew
together in a frown. She tapped her thumbnail thoughtfully
against her teeth and then went on, thinking out loud. "If
you're right, then this *is* all about the money—it always
would be, with Angelica. She knows it's only a matter of

time before Aaron dumps her, but if he dies now she inherits a fortune. Five years have passed since she's had to scramble for a living,'' she added softly. ''She's still beautiful, but she's five years older…and that would frighten Angelica.'' Falling silent, she looked swiftly down at her hands, her shoulders bowed.

''Tracy could have set it up in such a way that after her partner in crime inherits, half finds its way into some numbered and untraceable account that only she has access to. The woman's a lawyer, after—'' Sullivan stopped. Even as Bailey looked up, his arm went around her slumped shoulders.

''Hell, Bails, we're flying by the seat of our pants here,'' he said forcefully. ''We could be completely offbase on this, and even if our basic theory's correct, your sister might have no idea what Tracy's gotten her involved in.''

Last night he'd asked her if she'd found out what made him tick. She'd told him he'd turned her away because he was terrified of falling in love. She'd been wrong, Bailey thought, feeling the warmth of that strong arm around her and wishing she could lean her head into the hollow of his shoulder and simply forget everything. He'd known that if he allowed her to fall in love with him, all he would be able to give her was heartbreak, and so he'd ended things between them as brutally as he could. Except he'd left it too late.

One day he would go back, she thought with dull pain. Maybe he didn't even realize it himself yet, but Sullivan was just marking time until he returned to the life he'd left behind. Ainslie had inadvertently put her finger on it—he couldn't fit into a normal life anymore, no matter how hard he tried, and some part of him was acutely aware of that.

He would go back to try to earn redemption. In the end

all he would find was death. Nothing she could do or say would change the path he was on.

He'd been lost to her before she'd even met him.

Carefully she allowed herself to lean against him, and knowing he couldn't see her face, she let her eyes close briefly as she inhaled the clean scent of soap that clung faintly to him. After a moment she opened her eyes and sat up, but she didn't move away.

"I know Angelica better than anyone else in the world does, Sully. I care for her, but I think she's capable of doing almost anything to get what she needs." She sighed. "I hope we're wrong on this, but even so, I think we have to tell Plowright what we suspect. The man's life could be in danger."

"But we can't just drop a bombshell like this on him and not expect him to want proof." Sullivan sounded dubious. "And let's face it, Bailey, right now we don't have any."

"Whether Fitz wants to ripple Aaron's pond or not, he's going to have to question Angelica, because it was her case Hank was working on at the time of his death." She reluctantly slid out from under his arm and started once more to get out of the car. "Even if he doesn't buy our theory completely, he'll at least bring up the subject of that cell call to Room 201, and if he handles it right Angelica might spill everything. But we can't wait until then. We have to warn Aaron today."

"Does this place have a circular driveway?" Sullivan asked as she turned to the estate gates to buzz for admittance. She looked back at him, puzzled.

"Yes, why?"

"Because if it didn't I was going to make sure I parked this thing facing back out for a quick getaway," he said wryly. "In about three minutes Aaron Plowright's probably going to want to throw us out of his house."

IT HADN'T TAKEN three minutes; it had taken more like fifteen, Bailey told herself. Aaron was demonstrating more self-control than Sullivan had given the man credit for, but it was obvious that beneath the polite social mask he always wore when he had occasion to speak with his wife's sister, he was sharply annoyed.

"Really, Bailey," he said, a shade too heartily. "Angelica and Tracy conspiring to do me in? It sounds like something out of a cheap detective novel."

He leaned back in a tapestry-covered wing chair, a glass of sherry held negligently in one manicured hand and an expression of amused forbearance on his patrician features. She wasn't sure whether it was the amusement or the forbearance that got under her skin more.

"You're forgetting that I *am* a cheap detective, Aaron." She took a sip of her own sherry and set her glass down with a sharp click on the exquisite inlaid table beside her. "But some people think I'm a pretty good one, and Sullivan here runs the largest agency in the city. Although I'll admit we don't have much to go on yet, what we do know doesn't look good. One man's been killed already. Do you really want to take the risk that you'll be next?"

"Even if we're way off base on this, why not humor us, Plowright?" Sullivan had declined both a seat and a drink, and had been examining with detached interest the hand-painted Italian wallpaper on the study's walls. Now he shrugged and looked over at the man in the wing chair, forcing Aaron to twist his neck in order to meet his gaze. "Take a vacation. Hire a bodyguard. You can afford to do either or both, obviously."

"Obviously."

Plowright's reply was as dry as Sullivan's comment had been, and Bailey realized that the two men had taken an instant dislike to each other. She didn't blame Sullivan. She herself hadn't warmed to her billionaire brother-in-law over the years, although he'd never been anything less than correctly courteous and distantly friendly with her. But underneath the courtesy, she'd always suspected that Aaron found it a trifle embarrassing to have a private investigator in his own family.

Which was probably why she found herself talking like a Dash Hammett character when she was with the man, she thought wryly. She knew it irritated him, and irritating Aaron Plowright was childishly satisfying.

"Angelica's taken a powder, admit it," she drawled. She saw Sullivan's swiftly bemused look, and felt herself flush. "She's disappeared, I mean," she corrected herself. "You assume she's gone off on one of her shopping sprees, but she hasn't been in touch with you since Sunday night, has she?"

"No, she hasn't." Aaron lifted an eyebrow quizzically. "But Bailey, we're not exactly Ozzie and Harriet, you know. For the most part, your sister has her life and I have mine. I expect her to attend certain functions with me, but aside from that she's on a fairly free rein."

"Maybe she decided she didn't like being on a rein at all." Sullivan's tone was curt. "Especially knowing that at any time you might get yourself a new little filly and turn the present one out to pasture to fend for herself. So she hired Jackson, and when his report came back it certainly read like an exposé of an adulterous husband's spicy weekend. But that was because your daughter knew you and she were under surveillance, and Tracy made it seem that way to whoever was watching. I'd say that sounds suspiciously like the two of them were setting you up for something."

"The other possibility might be that your man Jackson had a twisted imagination, and read something into the situation that wasn't there at all," Aaron snapped.

As if realizing that he had betrayed a spark of real emotion, he compressed his lips tightly and set his sherry glass down with more care than the action warranted. When he spoke again, his voice was once more under control.

"Let's not beat around the bush. It's a distasteful enough subject without the allegation of conspiracy to commit murder. Whether I've publicly declared that I'm Tracy's natural father or not, the fact remains that she *is* my daughter. I won't have the tabloids getting wind of this sordid theory of yours and printing snickering innuendos about my relationship with her."

"That sounds like a threat. Is it one?" Sullivan had picked up a fragile-looking blown-glass ball from a carved ebony side table and was idly rolling it from hand to hand. He slanted a curious glance at Aaron. "Because we're doing you a favor, Plowright. Like Bailey said, a man's dead. To my way of thinking, he was worth ten of someone like you, but Bailey felt an obligation to at least warn you that you might be in danger, too. We're not stringers for a tabloid, so if this story gets out it won't be from us."

"The story won't get out. There is no story." Aaron's chilly blue gaze was on the glass ball rolling back and forth in Sullivan's hands, but he went on forcefully. "For God's sake, man, the police have already contacted me, and I've told them the same thing I'm telling you. I have no idea where she is right at this moment, but if it's vital that they talk to her all I need do is cancel her credit cards. She'll be on the phone to me within an hour. And as for her hiring this Jackson person to tail me, well…" His voice trailed off, his bluster suddenly subsiding. Bailey leaned forward in her chair.

"What? Did you know what she was planning, Aaron? Did you suspect she was having you followed?"

He shook his head, not meeting her gaze. "Not anything that specific. But she's been acting oddly lately. One moment I'll see her flirting outrageously with some stranger at a party, and the next she'll be hanging on to my arm, crying and asking me if I still love her. I've got to admit, her having me followed when she knew full well where I was and who I was with doesn't surprise me. Your sister was always mercurial, Bailey. That was part of her charm. But now she's verging on instability." He looked up at her, his still-handsome features drawn. "Lately I've been thinking I should have her see a specialist."

"You mean a psychiatrist." She sat abruptly back in her chair and let out a deep breath. "That would explain a lot," she admitted reluctantly. "She sounded hysterical when she called me Sunday night, but hysterical never was Angelica's style."

"She cries prettily. I don't believe I've ever seen her sob uncontrollably," agreed Aaron somberly. "You see now why I'm hoping to keep a lid on this. It's unfortunate that the man she hired has turned up dead, but that has to be sheer coincidence. The police suspect a possible mob hit, don't they?"

"The police might, but I don't," Sullivan said flatly.

He was still toying with the glass globe, not even watching it as it rolled back and forth between his open palms. Bailey saw Aaron blink as the fragile thing balanced on the edge of Sullivan's right hand and dropped into his left.

"Even if Angel's as crazy as a loon, we still have that report. For some reason your daughter went to great lengths to provide the investigator Angelica hired with a false picture of what was going on in that hotel room, and that means the two of them were working together."

"So it's the report that convinced you." Aaron looked down at his hands, and with a frown he carefully buffed the nails of one hand against the sleeve of the navy blazer he was wearing. He looked up with an oddly crooked smile. "Oh, hell, I guess it's time to come clean. Suppose I told you that Angelica's suspicions were correct—that it wasn't my daughter who was my escort at the Harris last weekend?"

"But we—" Bailey checked what she'd been about to say as Sullivan shot her a barely perceptible warning glance. "We were sure it had to be Tracy," she ended weakly.

"I guess we jumped to a conclusion, Plowright, and everything else just seemed to fall into place after that." Sullivan held the ball securely between his two hands, as if Aaron's nervousness had finally communicated itself to him. "We're certainly not about to pry into your private life, and if you say you were with a lady friend and not your daughter, then we'll regard the matter as closed."

He hadn't mentioned the video that proved Tracy had been the woman with her father, and he hadn't wanted her to mention it, either, Bailey realized. Aaron had lied, and Sullivan wanted to see just how far he would take that lie. But why was the man implicating himself in the first place?

He was protecting someone, she thought suddenly. And that someone had to be either Tracy or Angelica or both, except, for the life of her, she couldn't figure out why he would feel any obligation to shield either of them.

"I told Angelica I would be with Tracy, and I asked my daughter to cover for me if Angel checked up on me." Aaron looked slightly abashed. "It was nothing serious. The lady was lovely, we spent an interesting weekend together, and I expected the matter to end there. Unfortunately, a man's been killed and now it looks as if my little secret will have to come out, if only to reassure the authorities that the two incidents can't possibly be related.''

"We may be able to help you.'' Holding the globe in one palm, Sullivan lightly traced the fine gold veining on it with a casual finger. "This must be valuable,'' he added, his manner offhand.

"It is. It's Venetian, with a provenance that documents back to one of the Borgias.'' Aaron frowned. "But what are you saying? Is there some way you can insure that my privacy's protected?''

"Detective Fitzgerald's going to need to know.'' Sullivan shrugged carelessly, and Bailey caught her breath as the globe rocked slightly. "But Fitz is a friend of mine. I'll explain your situation to him and ask him to be as discreet as possible. Besides, he's of the same opinion as you—he thinks it's unlikely that Angelica can tell him much. Questioning her was only going to be a formality.''

"I'd appreciate whatever you can do, Sullivan. You, too, Bailey.'' Aaron's smile was strained. "I know I've put myself in a bad light.''

"We're all sophisticated people here. Sometimes these things just get out of hand.'' Sullivan held the globe up admiringly. "The Borgias?'' he mused. "I'll bet this little bauble's seen more than its share of chicanery and double-dealing, wouldn't you say?''

With a quick movement, he tossed it up into the air. Bailey gasped and, across from her, she saw Aaron's fingers tighten convulsively on the arms of the wing chair. The ball spun like a child's toy, the flecks of gold in it catching the muted sunlight that streamed through the enormous Tiffany window at the far end of the room.

Then it dropped lightly back into Sullivan's palm.

"*Dammit,* man—'' Aaron was out of his seat, his face pale, but as Sullivan turned inquiringly to him, he bit back the rest of his angry expostulation. "Dear God, what in the world are you playing at? Please be a little more careful, Sullivan. That globe is irreplaceable."

"So was Hank Jackson."

As Sullivan spoke, he threw the ball to Aaron. Scrambling frantically for the thing, the older man caught it just before it hit the polished granite slabs of the floor, but Sullivan didn't give him time to draw breath before he went on, his voice flat and deadly.

"I'm not playing at anything, Plowright, and this isn't a game. This is murder, and for some reason you've been trying to make a fool out of me. I want the truth and I want it now, do you understand?"

Bailey had risen from her chair, and now she moved away from Plowright and closer to Sullivan. "It was Tracy who was with you last weekend. We've got the two of you on a store surveillance video, so it's no use lying, Aaron."

He was still pale beneath his usual healthy tan, but as he carefully set the Venetian bauble back on its stand his movements steadied. He turned back to her with a thin smile.

"You're mistaken. I don't know what else I can do to—"

"She's right, Aaron. It's time to tell them the truth." The low, clear voice came from the open doorway to the study. "I know you were hoping to keep me out of this, but even you can't protect me now."

The woman who had spoken didn't move from where she stood. Perfectly posed as if for a portrait, for a moment she remained framed by the heavy oaken doorway. She was dressed in a slim dove-gray skirt and a plain white blouse, but the somberness of her outfit only served to emphasize the classical beauty of the pale oval face, the raven-dark richness of the swath of shining hair clipped neatly at the nape of her neck with an unadorned silver clasp. Tracy Weiss belonged here, Bailey thought suddenly. How hard had it been for her to accept that she would never be anything more than a privileged visitor to this setting of quiet wealth and taste that suited her so well?

"You and your partner are right, Bailey." Lips that were free of any artificial color curved into a small, regretful smile. "I was the woman at the Harris with my father last weekend, and I knew Angelica had someone watching us. It was just as you guessed. I deliberately let that Jackson man get shots of me that could be construed as being evidence of an illicit meeting between Aaron and a mystery woman."

"Tracy, *enough*." Her father moved forward, his tone urgent. "Don't tell them anything more, for God's sake!"

"They suspect most of it anyway, Aaron." Finally stepping into the room with unhurried grace, she touched him briefly on the arm and then turned to Bailey and Sullivan. "It was almost exactly the way you outlined it. Angelica and I wanted to create a woman who didn't exist."

She paused, and for the first time Bailey could see a spark of emotion in those clear gray eyes. Before she could go on, Sullivan spoke, his voice harsh.

"It was murder, then?"

Tracy nodded slowly, her gaze meeting his. "Yes, Mr. Sullivan, the crime our mystery woman was to be framed for was murder. And you were right—it was my father we intended to kill."

Chapter Eleven

"You're a lawyer, Ms. Weiss." Sullivan's interruption was terse. "Do you want to call someone from your firm before you say anything further?"

"I admit my knowledge of criminal law has become a little rusty since I moved into the corporate field and away from the necessity of meeting with my clients in holding cells."

The attractively modulated tones held a hint of wryness, Bailey noted with a flash of faint surprise. Even at this moment, Tracy Weiss remained detached enough to see the irony in the situation.

"But no, I think I can dispense with the services of a fellow attorney for the moment, Mr. Sullivan." Tracy inclined that glossy head of hair graciously. "Or may I call you Terrence? Bailey, of course, I'm on a first-name basis with, but after hearing some of the lawyers at my firm lauding the results your agency produces, I feel that I know you, too."

"If you did, you'd be aware that I go by the last name only." He sounded impatient. "But go on. You were confessing to planning a murder." He shook his head as if in irritation at himself. "Or no—I was forgetting you're a lawyer and probably prefer the two-buck term over the nickel words the rest of us use. It's patricide, right?''

"Your tone's offensive, Sullivan," Plowright cut in. He moved to his daughter's side, almost but not quite close enough to touch her. "You have no official standing in this matter, so I'll thank you to remember you're here on my sufferance only."

"And what about me, Aaron?" Bailey looked curiously at the man. "Am I here at your pleasure, too? Are you about to have me thrown out because I don't have my party manners on?" She narrowed her eyes speculatively at him. "I happen to find *murder* offensive. We're not exchanging idle chitchat here over tea and cucumber sandwiches. Your darling daughter just confessed to wanting to *kill* you, for God's sake."

"Oh, dear." Beside her father, Tracy looked suddenly taken aback. Her eyebrows lifted like two perfect dark wings above the gray eyes, and although her glance encompassed both of them, Bailey had the distinct impression that her words were aimed at Sullivan. "Probably this is one of those times when the more exact two-dollar phrase should be used, in order to avoid any misunderstanding."

Her smile was politely apologetic, but as she moved to the chair in which her father had been seated earlier, she came close enough to Sullivan that he was forced to take a step back to allow her to pass. Bailey saw quick reassessment in his eyes, just as swiftly veiled.

"And creating misunderstandings is something you seem to do well," he said smoothly. "What say we try real hard to clear this one up? I'm with Bailey. If you weren't confessing just now, I'm damned if I know what the hell we've been talking about."

Tracy's legs were elegantly crossed, the dove-colored skirt sliding just barely above one knee, and her perfect posture didn't relax enough to allow her to sink back against the cushions of the chair. She reached for the half-full sherry glass that Aaron had set on the table and raised it to her lips, her lashes dark against the creaminess of her skin. In her own way she was as feline as Angelica, Bailey told herself with a trace of envy at the woman's unhurried grace and flawless beauty. But where Angelica was a Persian kitten, all fluff and innocence, Tracy was a Burmese—sleek, dark, and with her claws sheathed only because she had no need for them at the moment.

"I wasn't confessing, Mr. Sullivan. I'm not the type to bare my soul." Tracy's voice suddenly hardened. "But Angelica is. She came to me with what she thought was a foolproof plan to murder her husband for his money, and she assumed that I was as venal as she was. She asked me to help her, and I said I would."

"Again, you're not being real clear here, lady." Sullivan's eyes narrowed. "What are you saying—that you got cold feet and backed out of the deal after you played that little charade for Jackson's camera?"

"I'm saying that from the first I intended to betray her. I'm sure that's clear enough for you to relate to, Mr. Sullivan."

Whether it was a lucky shot, or whether somehow the woman had heard something about his past Bailey didn't know. But the claws were now out, she thought, taking in the politely questioning expression on the perfect features across from her. The claws were out, and Tracy had drawn first blood, judging from the tight set of Sullivan's jaw. Suddenly she was tired of playing nice.

It's time to show her what a tough street-tabby's claws can do, she thought coldly.

"Yeah, crystal clear, Trace," she drawled offensively. "Going back to those nickel words we laymen use, you're covering your sweet butt right now. Maybe Aaron can persuade himself that your involvement in this was totally innocent, but I can't. Angelica could never have come up with something like this without your help, and even if she had, at the first hint of a problem she would have panicked.''

"She did." Tracy lowered her gaze and looked down at her hands, now folded neatly on her lap.

For a moment Bailey didn't realize the implications of what had just been said. Then comprehension came, swift and shattering, and without consciously thinking about it she was suddenly on her feet and bending over the woman in the chair.

"You're lying!" she snapped, her face thrust close to Tracy's. "Hank Jackson was executed—*brutally*. My sister may have gone along with your scheme to eliminate Aaron if she thought he was about to discard her for another woman, but if she'd panicked, she would have run. She isn't capable of anything as cold-blooded as bringing a gun up to a man's face and deliberately pulling the trigger."

Bailey straightened and the hand that had been gripping the back of the chair fell to her side. Her eyes still held the expressionless gray gaze looking up at her. "But I think you might be."

"Try and prove it," Tracy said softly. "Somehow I don't think you'll be able to, Bailey, because deep down you don't really believe she's innocent, either. You can't forget she came to you first, and you're not so sure your little adopted sister would have had any qualms about eliminating *you* if you became a threat, are you?"

Bailey felt the blood drain from her face, but before she could muster a denial, Tracy stood. Ignoring Sullivan and her father, she walked slowly over to the display table and the Venetian globe that her father had replaced on its stand only moments before. She picked it up, handling it with care.

"I never thought she was serious. Knowing Angelica, I assumed this was simply another of her attention-getting ploys, but Aaron's right—she'd been acting odder than usual lately, and I decided to go along with her incredible plan just to see how far she'd take it."

With a delicate finger she followed the gold tracery on the surface of the glass ball. She looked up, meeting Bailey's eyes.

"By the time I got home from the Harris last weekend, I'd decided to tell my father. Before I could, I got a phone call from Angelica. She was worse than I'd ever heard her—raving on hysterically about how the investigator she'd hired suspected that she hadn't been totally honest with him, and that he'd somehow recognized me as Aaron's daughter." Tracy shrugged, the ball cupped in her palms. "I suppose it's possible this Jackson person might have known who I was. Anyway, I tried to calm her down, but it was impossible. She said that if you'd taken on the job as she'd hoped, she knew you wouldn't have betrayed her, but Jackson had said he was going to tell his boss the next morning and let him decide how to handle the matter. Angelica was terrified they would go to Aaron and inform him that his daughter and his wife seemed to plotting something against him. She begged me to come with her to Jackson's and get the photos from him, because she thought without them, he would have nothing to show Sullivan and the matter would go no further."

"That doesn't make sense," Sullivan said flatly. "If Jackson had come to me with doubts about a case, he wouldn't have had to back his story up with proof. His judgment would have been good enough for me, and I would have been on the phone to Aaron right away."

"It didn't have to make sense. Things seldom do, with Angelica." There was an edge to the softly modulated voice. "Ask Bailey what her sister's like."

She didn't want to be thrust into the position of having to confirm Tracy's assessment, Bailey thought. But she had no choice. Reluctantly she nodded.

"Angelica focuses on one thing at a time. It's possible she would have fixated on the photos and thought that all she needed to do to make things right again would be to destroy—" She stopped suddenly. Tracy was watching her with a small smile on her face.

"And I think that's what she tried to do, Bailey," she said softly. "But then something went wrong. Maybe the man didn't fall for her tearful charms, or maybe she let it slip that what she'd been planning was a crime so serious that he knew he couldn't keep quiet about it, no matter how much she pleaded with him. Except by then she wasn't going to leave without those photos. They're gone, aren't they?"

"Anything the police have told us is confidential," Sullivan said harshly. "Besides, like you said, Angelica wanted Bailey to tail Aaron last weekend. The woman's not dumb enough to think that her own sister wouldn't have recognized you at the Harris and immediately known that there was something suspicious about the whole setup."

"Whenever I was supposedly being seen or watched in the hotel suite I was to make sure I kept my face averted. I was the mystery woman, remember?" Tracy flicked a careless glance at Sullivan, ignoring the hostility in his tone. "Of course, we'll never know how it would have played out if Bailey had been the watcher and if Angelica realized that she'd recognized me and refused to keep quiet about it. You're lucky you turned down the job." This last was addressed to Bailey, but even as the brunette spoke she turned away to set the globe back onto its stand.

Bailey, still mentally reeling from the barbed implication in Tracy's comment, was watching her at the exact moment it happened. Just as she settled the globe gently into its concave holder, Tracy let her right palm tip deliberately sideways and the ball rolled out of her hands.

It fell to the granite floor, smashing into a thousand tiny slivers.

"Oh, *no!*" Tracy's eyes widened and she whirled around to face her father. "Aaron—I'm so *sorry!* How could I have been so stupidly *clumsy?*"

"No, that's not like you, is it?" Plowright said evenly.

Standing between the two of them, Bailey was aware of an undercurrent she didn't fully comprehend flowing between Aaron and his daughter. The woman had smashed the thing on purpose, she thought in stupefaction. Had her father seen how it had happened? Did he realize she'd deliberately destroyed one of his most valued possessions? His next words seemed to dispel that possibility.

"But accidents happen. Don't upset yourself about it, Tracy. I was probably too attached to the thing, anyway. That's never wise." Aaron's cool smile dismissed her protests. "I'll ring for Marta to sweep—"

"Oh, Mr. Plowright, your beautiful glass ball! How does this happen?" The appalled comment came from the stocky woman standing in the doorway of the library, and Bailey recognized Aaron's housekeeper, Marta. Plump hands were pressed to the woman's mouth in shock. "I will clean up, Mr. Plowright. But there is some man come to see you— he say he is from *police.*"

"Sorry to barge in on you like this, Mr. Plowright. Sullivan, Flowers." Striding past the flustered housekeeper, Donny Fitzgerald nodded briefly in the direction of his friend and Bailey, and his sharp gaze took in Tracy's motionless figure still standing over the shattered remains of the once-priceless bauble, but it was Aaron he approached, his expression grim.

"We're going to have to talk to your wife, Plowright," he said tightly. "If there's any way you can contact her, we'll do this quietly to save you the publicity, but if we have to we'll make it public. There's a warrant out for her arrest."

"Good God, man, have you lost your mind?" Aaron stared disbelievingly at the detective. "No one's dragging my name through the papers, least of all you. Does Bill know about this?"

"Commissioner Watkins?" Fitz's broad shoulders lifted. "I left a message with his secretary to tell him we were on our way to see you. I'm well aware you and he are golfing buddies, Plowright, but that doesn't affect my decision on this. I have to take your wife in for questioning, and the sooner I find her the better."

"What's my sister charged with?"

Fitz looked over at Bailey, and for the first time since he'd entered the room his rough-hewn features held a hint of uncertain sympathy. Then they hardened again, and when he spoke his voice was devoid of any warmth.

"We're charging her with murder." He looked suddenly tired. "There were fingerprints on the shower curtain Jackson's body was wrapped in. They've been identified as hers."

"Her prints were on file from when she was working. Apparently one of her employers insisted that anyone handling money had to be bonded, and they were taken then." Sullivan's gaze flicked briefly to the rearview mirror as he changed lanes.

It was early evening, and after hours of bad coffee and endless questions, they had finally been allowed to leave the police station and a frustrated Fitzgerald. After dropping his bombshell at Plowright's house, he'd reluctantly agreed to give Aaron a grace period of twenty-four hours to find his wife and deliver her to the authorities, but as he'd left he'd curtly asked Bailey and Sullivan to accompany him to the station. Once there, he'd spent most of the afternoon trying to get a handle on the personality of his prime suspect by quizzing Bailey about her.

The only thing those seven hours had revealed was that she really didn't know Angelica any better than anyone else did, Bailey thought heavily. Surely, as her sister, she should have been able to shed some light on why she'd committed such a terrible crime, but she hadn't.

"Even though Fitz thought Hank's death had nothing to do with what we told him about the fake tail job Angelica had him working on last weekend, he's a good enough cop so that he ran her prints anyway. He said he didn't believe it at first when the tech told him they were a match for the ones on the shower curtain."

Sullivan glanced over at her, sitting silently beside him in the darkened interior of the car. "Aw, hell, Bails," he said awkwardly. "I didn't think she was capable of it, either. Believe me, I never wanted it to turn out this way."

"I let her down." Her reply was quiet. "I wasn't there for her when she needed me, not just when she left that message on my machine, but for years. No sane woman would have done what she did, Sully, but I didn't see that she needed help. The signs must have been obvious, if even Tracy suspected something was wrong with her."

"If Weiss knew Angelica was losing it, then encouraging her in her crazy schemes was criminally irresponsible of the woman," Sullivan ground out. "I still don't totally buy her story that she always intended to tell Aaron.'' He frowned. ''They might have pulled it off, at that. It was just bad luck for them that Hank got a clear enough glimpse of Tracy to recognize her as Aaron's daughter.''

''A hundred-to-one shot,'' Bailey agreed dully. ''Despite what Tracy said today, most people don't know she's related to Plowright.'' She fell silent for a moment and then she looked up, her brow creased. ''But why come to me first? Even Angelica must have known how risky that was. All I would have needed was one quick glimpse of Tracy's face, and I'd have known immediately who she was.''

''And if you had, you would have gone to your sister, explained that her suspicions were groundless and kept your mouth shut about the unsavory relationship Weiss seemed to be projecting with her father,'' he said firmly. ''You certainly wouldn't have suspected that Angelica herself was involved in the charade.''

''She must have thought she could persuade Hank to keep quiet. It would have been her who brought that bottle to his house, I suppose.'' Bailey pinched the bridge of her nose tiredly, feeling the headache that had been threatening all afternoon start to throb in earnest. ''A couple of drinks to soften him up, then a breathless request to keep her little secret safe. She would have had no doubt that she'd have him wrapped around her little finger without even trying. Except Hank must have turned her down.''

''He was married once. His wife finally left him because of the drinking, and not long after that she was killed in a car accident.'' Sullivan turned into the narrow alleyway that led between the rug store and the Chinese restaurant to the minuscule sliver of parking lot behind the two buildings. ''He never got over losing Janine. In all the years I knew him, I don't think he ever showed an interest in any other woman.''

"Angelica would simply have seen it as a rejection of her. That might have been the real reason she snapped," Bailey said wearily, reaching for the door handle. "Or maybe I'm wrong about that, too."

"I'll come in with you." Opening the driver's door, he'd started to get out of the car before her voice stopped him.

"No, Sully. Let's say our goodbyes now, okay?"

Slowly he sat back in his seat again and swung the door closed. When he spoke, his tone was carefully neutral.

"This is it, Bails?"

"This is it," she said quietly. "We agreed to work together on this case, Sullivan, and then go our separate ways. The case is closed. I think it's better that we don't drag this out."

"You're always walking out of my life." Despite the dim light, she saw the brief flash of pain that crossed his features. "I wish this time I could have held on to you, honey."

"I wish that, too, Sully." Bailey hesitated. Then she reached over and lightly laid her fingers on the side of his face, feeling the tiny prickling stubble of his unshaven jawline against her palm. She held her hand there for a moment, and then she let it drop. "I'm glad I came back, even if it was only for these few days. I think some part of me always knew we'd never had a chance, but..." She didn't complete her sentence, knowing there was no need to explain.

"I never had a chance," he corrected her, his voice low. "I just let myself forget that for a while when I met you. You know I'm going back, don't you?"

"I knew." She shook her head suddenly, one quick angry movement, and felt the burn of tears behind her eyelids. "But I don't understand *why*. I don't think I'll ever understand, Sullivan."

"Try to, for my sake." Now he was the one who reached out. As Bailey attempted to avert her face from him, he gently held her chin and turned her to him. She blinked, hoping that that he couldn't see the brightness she knew was in her eyes. "Ainslie's just going to think I ran out on them like Thomas did. I'd like you to remember me differently."

"I don't think you're running away," she said, her throat tight. "I think you're going back to face the past. But the past *can't* be changed, Sully, no matter how hard you try. Why can't you see that?"

"Oh, I see that." She could feel his breath warm on her lips as he spoke. "I've always known I couldn't change what happened. That's what made it so hard to bear."

He sighed, and his hand slid along the line of her jaw into the hair at the nape of her neck. "I don't know how a man wins back his soul, Bails. I don't even know if he can. But I've got to try." She saw his eyes briefly squeeze shut, as if he was in pain. "I can't go on living with myself if I don't, and sooner or later you wouldn't want to be with me, either. I don't know if I could stand that."

"I thought I'd been beaten by a ghost—by Maria's ghost," she whispered, her eyes locked on his. "But you were never just haunted by one, were you? They're all around you, calling you back, and there's too many of them for me to fight. How am I supposed to take on a damned legend, Sullivan?"

"You can't. No one can." His fingers spread wide against the back of her head, as if he was cradling her. "I know the whole thing sounds crazy, Bailey—wild geese, lost souls, a flight into eternity. But behind the legend is a truth that can't be ignored. A soldier has to be able to depend on the man beside him, because sometimes that's all he has to depend on. And if men die because you didn't live up to that trust, then they've got every right to come back for you. I should have known she meant to betray us. I didn't. Five men died because of me.''

"And you're going back to even the number up, is that it?'' Bailey began angrily, but even as the words left her mouth Sullivan's finger was on her lips.

"You of all people know it's not that,'' he remonstrated quietly. "I'm not looking for death, but if the door opens and I have to walk through to make things right again, then I will.''

"You mean you'll trade your life for another's,'' Bailey said flatly. "That door only swings one way, Sullivan. I've never heard of anyone coming back.''

"I already did.'' There was an odd smile on his face, but his eyes were shadowed. "Who's to say I can't do it twice?''

"You were lucky once, but luck won't save you the next time,'' she said unsteadily. "It'll take something a whole lot more powerful than that to bring you back from where you're determined to go, Sullivan.''

She swallowed, suddenly wanting nothing more than to be alone with her thoughts. As if he sensed her withdrawal, he let his hand fall away from her and sat back in his seat.

"Take care of yourself, sweetheart,'' he said softly. "We'll probably run into each other again once or twice while Fitz wraps up this business with Angelica, but you're right—this is our goodbye.''

"You—you take care of yourself, too.'' She knew how foolish the words were even as she said them. Fumbling clumsily with the door handle, she remembered something and stopped, her hand going to the pocket of her jeans. "I meant to give this back to you,'' she muttered thickly, pulling out the small shell he'd insisted she take the night before. "Here—it's that good luck you were just talking about."

"So damned stubborn." He shook his head, and for a moment the wry grin that she knew she would always remember him with flashed out once more. "I told you, honey, it's yours now."

"What you said was if I had the shell, you'd stay close to me so I could be your charm, Sully." She pushed it at him. "That's not the case anymore, so you'd better take it back."

"Didn't you know? You'll never be farther away from me than my heart." This time he didn't smile, but only gazed at her as if he was imprinting every last detail of her face onto his memory, and Bailey knew she couldn't hold back the tears a minute longer.

"Goodbye, Sullivan," she said unevenly, stepping swiftly out into the cool night air, her movements jerkily awkward. She closed the car door behind her, and before it had even chunked shut she was walking as quickly as she could toward the side entrance of the building, her key already in her hand. She wasn't going to cry until she was completely alone, she promised herself fiercely. She wouldn't allow his last glimpse of her to be one of a shaking, sobbing wreck.

She inserted the key into the lock, and thankfully she heard the small click as the lock released. Without looking over her shoulder, she opened the door, stepped inside and shut it behind her in such shaky relief that for a moment she just stood there in the dark at the bottom of the stairs, her eyes closed and her back against the door.

She'd lost him. He was gone, this time forever. It was true—no woman could take on an army of ghosts and win.

All that was left now was to learn to live with that fact.

Slowly Bailey opened her eyes and pushed herself wearily away from the door, but even as her hand moved to the light switch beside her she froze.

"No lights, Bee. I've been sitting here waiting for you long enough so that I can see just fine. But if your eyes haven't adjusted yet, I should tell you that this is a gun in my hand." From out of the darkness came a nervous little laugh. "It's pointing at you, sis. And if I have to, I'll use it."

Chapter Twelve

"Guess what, Ang? I'm in no damn mood."

With a recklessness that surprised even her, Bailey grabbed at the glinting silhouette in her sister's hand, snatching the gun from her grasp before Angelica had a chance to tighten her grip on it. The safety was on, she saw with belated relief.

"I wasn't really going to shoot you, Bee. I just wanted to make you listen to me."

In front of her, Angelica's shadowy figure swayed. Bailey glared at her. "Is that how it was with Hank? Sorry, Ang, the innocent act stops working after you blow a man away in cold blood. Now get upstairs." She made an impatient gesture with the gun and with her other hand she reached for the light switch. "The police are looking for you, and if you think I won't turn you in, you're wrong."

As she spoke, she flicked the light on, but as the stairwell jumped into harsh brightness from the naked bulb hanging overhead, she bit back a gasp.

Angelica was dressed in a torn and filthy pair of sweatpants. Over top of them she wore a stained windbreaker that was several sizes too large for her. What was left of her makeup had obviously been applied several days ago, and around her eyes were rings of smudged mascara. But the most startling sight was her hair. Instead of the pale gold that she'd been blessed with since birth, it was now a flat, sheenless black.

"I know I look awful." Dull blue eyes met hers, and Bailey tried to keep the appalled shock from her expression. "I had to trade the clothes I was wearing for these three days ago. I needed some money to buy food. And I did my hair in a bus station washroom with a bottle of temporary rinse so no one would recognize me."

Bailey recovered. Her lips tightening, she shook her head. "It'll wash out. Believe me, a bad dye job isn't enough to make me feel sorry for you, Angelica, and if I were you, I'd start thinking up something a whole lot more pitiful to use on a jury." She clicked the safety off the gun in her hand and tossed the ring of keys she'd been holding to her sister. "I'll be a few steps behind you. When you get to the landing, unlock the apartment door, walk in and stand where I can see you."

It was slightly disconcerting when, without further protest, Angelica slowly turned and began mounting the stairs, one small hand gripping the banister as if she needed its support to pull her up. She stumbled, and Bailey tensed, suspecting some trick, but then she saw that the overly large tennis shoes her sister was wearing had no laces. The tongue was flapping from one of them, and it had tripped her up.

She frowned as Angelica continued a few steps ahead of her. The woman had killed a man. There was no way to overlook that fact. But still, the figure in front of her was so far from the pampered and groomed beauty she was familiar with, it was impossible not to feel a fugitive ache of pity for her. Where had she been? How had she been surviving?

Bailey halted as she saw her bend over the lock. "It's

the round brass one," she said evenly. "By the way, how did you get in downstairs?"

"I had my purse on me when I left Sunday night." Angelica's reply was muffled by the curtain of hair. "I still had the key you gave me last summer, but I couldn't find the one that unlocked the apartment. I guess I lost it."

"You lost it right after I gave it to you, remember? That's why I came home to an apartment full of dead plants," Bailey said dryly. "Get inside and then stop in the middle of the room."

Instead of complying, Angelica turned and looked at her. "I didn't do it, Bee. I know everyone thinks I killed that private eye, but I didn't. You don't have to treat me like some kind of criminal."

Bailey repressed a sigh. "Ang, we aren't kids anymore, and there isn't a Mr. Nobody around to blame things on like you did when you were five and you broke Mom's opalescent vase. They found your prints on the shower curtain. I don't think you're going to be able to talk your way out of this one."

She waited until she could just see Angelica halt a few feet inside the apartment entrance. Then she took the last stairs with as much energy as she could muster—which wasn't much, she thought tiredly—stepped inside herself and closed the door behind her, all without taking her eyes from the still, slumped figure in front of her.

"If you're hungry there's a box of cookies in the cupboard and milk in the refrigerator. Help yourself."

"That used to be our before-bedtime snack." Angelica gave her a small, crooked smile. "Remember our bunny pyjamas, Bee? Remember how Mom used to read us a different story each night from that book of fairy tales, and how she used to change all the scary parts so we wouldn't have nightmares?"

"I remember," Bailey said shortly. "Snow White didn't bite into a poisoned apple, she just got really sleepy because she'd been up all night, and there was no evil troll in Rapunzel, she just accidentally locked herself in the tower. But even when I was little I guessed she was leaving things out."

"So did I. I knew the world wasn't that safe, even in fairy tales." Angelica turned and brought down the box of cookies from the cupboard. After opening it, she crammed two into her mouth at once, at the same time taking the carton of milk from the refrigerator and pouring herself a glass. Bailey watched her silently.

She was starving, she thought unwillingly. There couldn't be much harm in letting her eat before making the call.

She blinked. There was a slightly schizophrenic quality to all this, she thought, feeling the dull throbbing of her headache notch up to a higher level. She was covering her sister's every move with a gun—possibly the same gun that had been used to snuff out a man's life, she realized sickly. On the other hand, she was still worrying about her as she'd done all their lives.

It's like Mom's version of a fairy tale, she told herself impatiently. *I'm trying to pretend that there's nothing terrible here at all, but I know there is. That body in the Dumpster was put there by her, and the fact that she's eating milk and cookies and talking about bunny pyjamas to me right now can't change that fact.*

And the fact that she was a killer didn't change the bond between them, she thought heavily. So it seemed as though the schizophrenia wasn't going to go away, for a while at least. A thought struck her.

"How did you manage to get him out of the house and into that Dumpster all by yourself?" she said, her voice hardening. "You used to have to get Marta to help you carry a couple of shopping bags, for heaven's sakes."

"Tracy helped me," Angelica mumbled, her mouth full. She brought the glass of milk to her lips and thirstily drank down at least half of it before she paused for breath. Wiping her mouth with the back of her hand, she went on, her tone hopeless. "Actually I helped her, but since my own sister doesn't believe me, probably no one else will, either, so what's the use in talking about it? I'm going to spend the rest of my life in prison, and Tracy's going to walk away scot-free."

The childish phrase was typically Angelica, Bailey thought slowly. So was the insistence on her own innocence. But usually her protestations were accompanied by tearful histrionics, not stated flatly, without any embellishment at all.

"What do you mean, you helped her? Are you saying she killed Hank?" Her eyes narrowed on Angelica's delicate features, searching for any telltale sign that her sister was lying.

"Of course she did." The lush lips, ringed at the moment like a little girl's with a mustache of milk, turned down miserably. "She set up everything from the start—that stupid plan to make it look like Aaron was having an affair, hiring an investigator so that we would have proof—*everything*. It was all her idea."

"And then you were going to kill Aaron, weren't you?" Bailey felt a familiar hopelessness steal over her as she watched the play of emotions on her sister's face. Angelica just didn't get it, she thought. At the very least, she'd been a party to planned murder, and she seemed unable to understand the enormity of the crime she'd been involved in.

But Aaron was still alive. If Angelica's story was true, and Tracy had killed Hank Jackson, then she was right. No matter how willing a participant she'd been, she didn't deserve prison while the main perpetrator went unpunished.

"She said he'd been seeing someone else already, that it was only a matter of weeks before he dumped me, and with those papers I signed before the marriage, I wouldn't get anything from him. All I had to do was to hire someone who could testify later on that Aaron had been with a woman at the Harris Hotel last weekend. She was going to take care of the rest—I didn't even have to know how or when she was going to do it. Honest, Bee, I was hardly even involved in anything!"

"You just told me you helped her dispose of a body, for God's sake." She tried to keep the anger from her voice without much success. "Listen to yourself. A man was killed, and instead of calling the police you helped his murderer, Ang. Maybe that's hardly anything to you, but to the rest of the world it's a serious crime. Were you there when she shot him?"

"No!" The mascara-smudged eyes widened in shock, whether real or feigned it was impossible to tell. "I don't even know why she went to see him Sunday night. She *knew* he was going to be turning over the report and the photos to me on Monday, like he was supposed to."

"Wait a minute. Do you mean Hank was still going through with this as if it was an ordinary job? He didn't suspect there was anything fishy about the setup, or tell you he'd recognized Tracy as Aaron's daughter?"

Angelica drained her milk before answering. "Why would he suspect anything?" she said peevishly. "You're as bad as Tracy, Bee. Both of you think you're so smart and I'm too dumb to do anything right. Although I guess it wasn't such a good idea going to you first when I needed to hire an investigator," she added, flushing slightly. "Tracy nearly went through the roof when she found out

I'd approached you, and she didn't calm down until I told her you'd passed on the job. But no, Hank didn't recognize her. He didn't recognize me, for that matter.''

''What do you mean, he didn't recognize you?'' Bailey didn't take her gaze off her sister as she sat down on the edge of the bed and toed off the sneakers she was wearing with a grimace of distaste.

''I look like a bag lady.'' Angelica shuddered daintily. Bailey took a deep breath, and her sister looked up at her. ''I don't know why we have to go over every little *detail,* for heaven's sake. He used to come into the Diamond when I worked there years ago. I didn't know his name, but I recognized him as soon as I met with him at the investigation agency. Vodka rocks, no twist, always a double.'' She bent over her foot again and massaged it gingerly. Slowly Bailey walked over to the counter and set the gun down.

She was telling the truth. Whoever had killed Hank had set the stage at his house to make it look like the man had gone off on a bender. But although Angelica might make any other mistake it was possible to make, up to and including trying to hire her sister to tail Aaron and his daughter, as an ex-cocktail waitress, she wouldn't have brought a bottle of rye to a vodka drinker.

That had been *Tracy's* mistake.

''Tell me what happened on Sunday night, and don't leave out anything.'' She pulled one of the hard-backed chairs from the table over nearer to the bed and sat down, leaning intently toward her sister. ''It's really, really important, Ang. Helping Tracy to move Hank's body was wrong, and going along with her plan to kill Aaron for money was even more wrong. But if you testify against Tracy, the prosecutor might cut you a deal, depending on how much you know.''

"She called me on my cell phone Sunday night—that's gone, too, now," Angelica said sulkily. She caught Bailey's eye and continued. "She gave me an address and told me not to tell anyone, but to come there right away. Oh, first she told me to call you and put on a big act about finding out for sure that Aaron was cheating on me. She said that would make things more convincing later on."

It had, Bailey thought with cold anger. It had bolstered Tracy's assertion that Angelica had gone hysterically over the edge.

"Go on," she said tightly. "You made the call to my machine and then what?"

"Then I went to the address she'd given me. I didn't even know it was Jackson's place until I walked in and—and—" For the first time Angelica's expression held real emotion. She tucked the black hair behind her ears with a nervous gesture. "Bee, she'd shot him in—in the—"

"I know." Bailey reached over and touched her sister on the arm. "What did she tell you when you walked in and found her with him like that?"

"Like I already said, Tracy thinks I'm stupid." Already the horror had faded from Angelica's features, to be replaced by indignation. "She said she'd gotten a call from Jackson himself about an hour before, telling her that he was going to inform the police that she was running some kind of scam on her father. She told him she could explain everything, and he agreed to talk to her, but when she got to his house she found the front door open. He was dead when she got there, she said." Angelica's raccoon-ringed eyes hardened. "I'm not *that* dumb, Bee. But what could I do? She had the gun she said she'd found by his body, and she told me that if we didn't get rid of him, the police might start digging into the case he'd been on that weekend and end up questioning me. I would have ended up telling them everything, and I knew it. So we wrapped him up in that shower curtain and dragged him out the side door to my car.''

"Tracy was wearing gloves and you weren't, right?" Bailey said heavily.

"She had those red driving gloves on that she always keeps in her Porsche," her sister agreed. "I wasn't even thinking about fingerprints. I just wanted to get that horrible job over with so I could go home and forget any of it had ever happened. Except I never did get to go home," she added unhappily. "After we did what we had to do in that awful alleyway, I drove her back to Jackson's house in my car. That's when she told me that she intended to put the whole thing on me—the plan to kill Aaron, Jackson's death, everything. She said my prints would be all over the plastic, and the police had lasers or something that would be able to find the smallest drop of blood in the trunk of my car. She said all she really wanted was for me to get out of her father's life, so if I disappeared for good, she wouldn't have me arrested. I didn't completely believe her—not the part about just wanting me out of Aaron's life. She wanted the money, Bee. She wanted it almost as badly as I did. But when it all went wrong, she figured that at least she'd get rid of the competition.''

"Well, you're not exactly her competition—" Bailey began, but Angelica interrupted her sharply.

"Believe me, I am. Any woman he looks at is the competition as far as Tracy's concerned. Sometimes she sounds as if she's his girlfriend, and sometimes she sounds like she hates him. That's why the money was important—because it was his, and she knew he'd never give it to her himself.''

"And why was it so important to you?" Bailey searched her sister's face curiously. "I know you're scared of being poor, Ang, but you would never have gone hungry or been without a roof over your head. I would have been there to help out, and eventually you would have married again. Why risk so much—your freedom, your future, your own self-respect—just for the money?''

''Because I wanted it bad enough,'' Angelica said flatly. ''I wanted it so badly that nothing else mattered, as long as I had a shot at it. You know what I came from, Bailey. When Mom and Dad adopted me I was just a little girl, but I was old enough to know I never wanted to go back to that kind of existence. I never will.''

Her voice, usually so breathy and childish, was grimly determined, and beneath the wispy black bangs her eyes were a cold blue. This was the real Angelica, Bailey thought slowly. This was the double-forged steel that had always been there, under the concealing frills and froth. Suddenly she had no doubt that her sister would have gone ahead with Aaron's murder, might even have done the deed herself if she'd had no other option.

''You don't understand, do you?'' Angelica was looking at her now, and with much the same curiosity. ''You haven't ever wanted anything badly enough to risk everything for it. You'd rather just open your hands—'' with a sudden movement she brought her own up, spreading her fingers wide ''—and watch what you want slip away.''

''That's not the way I play the game,'' Bailey protested heatedly, oddly shaken by the image. ''I play to win, dammit.''

''Maybe you do.'' Angelica shook her head, the dark hair making her look tougher than she'd ever seemed as a blonde. ''But it's still a game. And you're only playing. I wonder if you'll ever find someone or something that's worth a life-and-death struggle for? Probably not,'' she said dismissively. ''You let that Sullivan man get away from you last year, and if I ever loved any man as much as you obviously loved him, I would have gone to hell and back to keep him. But you were afraid to take the chance.''

''You know *nothing* about what happened between me and Sullivan,'' Bailey said tersely. ''What in the world would I have been afraid of?''

''Of giving it everything you had and losing anyway.'' Angelica stood up, shoving her bare feet back into the battered tennis shoes. ''You're not a fighter, Bee. I am. That's the difference between us.''

''That must be why you're on a Most Wanted list, and I'm not, then,'' Bailey snapped. She stood, too, and walked over to the phone. ''We'd better notify the police that you're here, but first I'll call your attorney. If you're going to testify against Tracy you'll need someone on your side who can cut you the best deal possible with the prosecutor. Do you have a lawyer?''

''Sure. I helped her dump a body a few nights ago.'' Angelica gave a bitter little laugh. ''Uh-uh, no deals. I'm tired of listening to everyone else's good advice, Bailey. I'm handling this my own way.''

''And what way's that?'' Slowly Bailey replaced the receiver on the phone. ''Ang, I don't think you realize the kind of trouble you're in. Aaron's got until tomorrow at noon to find you and hand you over to the police. After that, your picture will be on the six-o'clock news and on the front page of the evening paper, for heaven's sake. You can't hide forever.''

''I don't intend to.'' The toughness that Angelica had briefly shown seemed to have faded, and she darted an uncertain look at her sister. ''If things don't work out the way I hope, then I'll contact you myself by noon tomorrow, okay? I promise I will. But for now I need some money and the loan of your car.''

''Some money and my—'' Bailey stared incredulously

at her. "Do you think I'm crazy? That's aiding and abet-ting, for crying out loud. What's this big plan you've got, anyway?"

"I'm not telling."

Angelica's bottom lip stuck out stubbornly, and again Bailey was reminded of the little girl she'd once been—willful, spoiled, loved. She'd fallen a long way down, she thought, looking at the tired, smudged eyes, the cast-off clothing, the scratched wrists and swollen ankles. She might put her life back together after whatever prison term she was sentenced to serve, but it was unlikely that she would ever be a golden, adored princess again.

Silently she walked over to the table and got her wallet out of her purse.

"I've got about a hundred on me. Is that going to be enough?" She would probably look back on this as the stupidest thing she'd ever done, she thought wearily, hold-ing out the roll of bills to Angelica. She would never see the money again, it was quite possible that for the next three months she would be making the final payments on a car she didn't have anymore, and the next time she talked to Fitzgerald or Straub they'd be snapping cuffs on her and reading her her rights.

Except right now, Angelica's red-rimmed eyes were spilling over with tears, and for some dumb reason the risk was worth it.

"You always loved me, didn't you, Bee? Even when I was bad, you still never stopped loving me." Arms that felt too thin wrapped tightly around Bailey's neck. "I won't let you down. By noon tomorrow you'll hear from me one way or another."

"I'd better." Bailey cleared her throat, feeling a sudden rush of sadness, not just for the moment they were sharing, but for all the moments, now lost forever, when they hadn't been this close. "I'm still your big sister, you know. You don't want to get me mad, Angel."

"You used to call me that all the time. I missed it when you stopped, Bee." Angelica stepped back and knuckled her eyes, smearing the mascara even more. "Tomorrow at noon. I promise you'll hear by then, sis."

Maybe she would and maybe she wouldn't, Bailey thought a few minutes later, standing at the window and watching the taillights of her car disappear down the street to be lost in the rest of the traffic. But the bond between her and her sister had proved too hard to break, and she knew she couldn't have turned Angelica away.

"You haven't ever wanted anything badly enough to risk everything for it."

She frowned at the stray memory and let the blinds snap shut. Typical Angelica, she thought with a flicker of irritation. She had the habit of throwing up verbal smoke screens in an argument, whether there was any truth to them or not, but in this case she was definitely off base.

"You'd rather just open your hands...and watch what you want slip away..."

But she *hadn't,* Bailey told herself angrily. Even if she'd been unwilling to admit it at the time, she knew now that she'd come back into Sullivan's life for one reason, and one reason only—to see if there was any possible way the two of them could have a future together. In the end she'd known there wasn't, because Sullivan himself had no future, only a past and the ghosts of that past.

"What was I supposed to do?" Her whisper was edged with desperation. "Tell him that I'd take whatever he had to give, for however long I could? Tell him that even if I knew I would lose him tomorrow, I would still want every hour of tonight?"

The echo of her question seemed to hang in the air for

a long moment before it faded into silence. Suddenly and with total certainty, Bailey knew that if she didn't act she would hear it echoing in her mind for the rest of her years.

On legs that felt unsteadily weak she crossed the few feet from the window to the table where the phone sat. She picked up the receiver and punched in a number, noting with light-headed detachment that her hand was shaking. She listened for a few seconds to the buzzing rings on the other end of the line.

He wasn't at the office, she thought, cowardly relief flooding through her. He wasn't at the office, and it was too late now to call him at home. Maybe she'd try him again tomorrow, or maybe in the morning this insanity would have passed and—

"Sullivan."

The voice on the other end of the line sounded intimidatingly abrupt, and she was suddenly paralyzed with uncertainty. She cleared her throat, but no words came out.

"Bailey? Is that you, Bails?" The abruptness was replaced by sharp worry. "Is everything okay?"

"Everything's all right, Sully," she managed, her voice sounding more like a croak. "I just thought you should know that Angelica was here waiting for me when—"

"Hang tight, I'm on my way." There was a crackle of static on the line, and then she heard him curse. "I've got the office phone forwarded to my cell and I just went under a bridge. Are you still there?"

"I'm still here. But she's not." She closed her eyes, picturing him speeding through the night toward her. "I'll tell you all about it when you get here, Sully. I'll leave the side door unlocked, so just come on up."

She had no idea how far away he was or how long it would be before he arrived, she thought, replacing the receiver. For all she knew, she only had a minute or two. She went swiftly over to the small case, still unpacked, sitting where Sullivan had put it last night on the chair by the door. Flipping it open, she rummaged frantically around in it for the gold and pink shopping bag that held the most frivolous and ridiculous purchases she'd ever made in her life.

They looked like silk and satin and lace, she thought, apprehensively staring at the tiny thong panties and the garter belt dangling from her fingers. But they weren't. They were armor.

"No ghosts. No wild geese. Not tonight," she said softly. "Maybe he'll go back to you one day, but for tonight—"

She swallowed. Gingerly she drew the coffee-and-cream-colored bustier from the bag. The bag crackled. She jumped as if she'd been shot. Then she took a deep breath, squeezed her eyes tightly shut and sent up a wordless little prayer. After a moment she opened her eyes, her expression determined.

"But for tonight, the man belongs to *me*," she whispered fiercely.

Chapter Thirteen

Her call had been a lifeline.

Since he'd left her an hour and a half ago he'd been driving around aimlessly, trying to come up with some excuse that would justify him going back to her apartment tonight.

But when she'd disconnected, for a moment he'd felt a rush of blackness sweep over him, as if he'd been cut adrift in an empty, endless sea with no salvation in sight. As he'd tossed the cell phone onto the seat beside him he'd noted dispassionately that his hand wasn't entirely steady.

You fool, Sullivan, he told himself with sudden anger. *You were lost before she met you, so don't go expecting the woman to save you from yourself now. It's too late for that. It's been too late for a long time.*

He was through following in his father's footsteps. He'd never learned what it was that had stolen Thomas's soul from him, but even as a child he'd known that his father had left some part of himself on an old battlefield and had searched for it in vain ever since. He'd looked to one woman after another to complete him, but with nothing of value to give them in return, Thomas's only legacy had been one of pain.

Not Bailey, Sullivan thought bleakly. *I'm not Thomas,*

and I won't let myself do that to her. She deserves everything from a man, and one day she'll find the one who can give it to her.

That man wouldn't be him, Sullivan told himself tightly, mounting the stairs to her apartment two at a time. But that didn't change the fact that if he'd had a soul to sell, he would have traded it gladly for one last night of holding her in his arms.

Except that wasn't why she'd called him here. He had to remember that.

"The door's open." The muffled reply to his knock came from somewhere inside the apartment, but when he entered she was nowhere to be seen. He frowned slightly, his glance sweeping the place.

The blinds were closed, and the only illumination was the warm golden light coming from the large parchment shade that hung directly over her bed. The purple velvet spread—Bailey was the only person he knew who would choose purple, he thought wryly—took on a muted amethyst glow, while the rest of the room faded gradually away into shadow.

"Sorry, I was just getting changed." Her voice came from the minute hall that led off to the tiny bathroom, and looking up, he saw her coming toward him. She was bundled up in a fuzzy orange robe that looked comfortably old. It was belted thickly around her waist, and it trailed on the floor behind her as she padded into the room. Her hair was carelessly pinned up with a couple of amber claw clips, and the pieces that weren't secured spilled into her eyes.

He held back a smile. She looked like a small orange bear ready to hibernate. Even her expression was slightly bearish—her brows pulled together in a determined scowl, her chin lifted as if she was issuing a challenge to all comers.

But that was to be expected, he thought. She'd just had a run-in with her sister, and obviously it hadn't gone well, since Angelica had given her the slip.

"I gave her some money and loaned her my car," Bailey began pugnaciously. "Sit down, Sully, there's more."

"You *what?*" Sitting down suddenly seemed like a damn good idea, and he slowly lowered himself to the bed, his disbelieving gaze on the defiant figure in front of him. "For God's sake, Bails, you could be charged with—"

"I know, I know." She waved his protest away with a glare. "But she didn't do it, Sully. She was framed."

For the next ten minutes he listened intently to what she had to say, only interrupting her once.

"Double vodka on the rocks, no twist," he said tightly. "I'd forgotten, but she's right. That was Hank's drink before he swore off the stuff."

"That's what clinched it for me." Bailey was perched on the edge of a chair near the bed. She leaned forward. "I promised her I'd wait for her call before I got in touch with Fitzgerald, Sully. She said she had some kind of plan, but I think she just needed time to come to terms with the fact that she was going to have to turn herself in. When she contacts me tomorrow I think she'll be ready to tell her story to the police."

"And Tracy's not going anywhere." He shook his head, his eyes hard. "She thinks she's sitting in the catbird seat right now. I agree—let's not frighten her away until we've got the nets in place."

"There's not much we can do without Angelica anyway, and she seems to have acquired a talent for disappearing when she wants to." Bailey looked down at her lap, a silky strand of hair following the curve of her jawline. "Which leaves us with a good twelve to fourteen hours of just sitting around and waiting."

There was a husky note in her voice, and Sullivan suddenly was too aware of the fact that he was sitting on her bed, with her less than an arm's length away and probably wearing little, if anything, under that bulky robe. He felt an unreasonable spurt of irritation. Did the woman have any freakin' *idea?* he thought testily. Couldn't she tell what that voice did to a man? Sure, the fuzzy orange robe projected cute and cuddly rather than femme fatale, but that huskiness was lethally sexy, no matter what she was wearing.

He wasn't a saint, he thought glumly. This was going to be one hell of a long, hard night.

"I know what we decided earlier, but I'm staying." He tried to inject a certain detached briskness into his tone. "The foldout couch again, of course."

It was about five feet long and last night, after a few minutes of polite squabbling over who would take the bed, he'd finally overridden Bailey's objections and insisted that he would be perfectly comfortable on it. That had been a barefaced lie, Sullivan thought wearily, but then again, last night he hadn't felt much like sleeping anyway. Tonight was no different. He would lie there in the dark, listening to the sound of her breathing a few feet away, and wonder just how long it took for a man's heart to break completely in two.

Loosening his tie with one hand, he started to stand, but Bailey's palm shot out like a traffic cop's, halting him.

"You're sleeping in my bed tonight," she said, the husky note deeper. Actually, it sounded more like a croak, he thought quizzically. He shook his head firmly at her.

"Honey, we went through all this less than twenty-four hours ago. I'm not having you giving up your bed and taking the couch, and that's final. I told you, I've slept in worse—''

"I wasn't being altruistic, Sullivan." It *was* a croak, and now he saw that her face was pale, her expression set. "I don't intend to take the couch, either."

For a moment he said nothing. Her gaze was locked on his almost desperately, as if she had screwed all her courage up for this single confrontation, and more than she could afford to lose was riding on his answer.

And that answer would have to be no, Sullivan told himself harshly. It was one damn word and the sooner he said it the better.

The sooner he said it the *better,* he reminded himself a second later. He wrenched his gaze from where it had been lingering on the curve of her bottom lip, and blurted out the first thing that came into his head.

"Bailey, honey, what are you wearing under that god-awful robe?"

Her face flamed. "My stupid seduction outfit," she snapped. "I wanted to make it clear to you that this was *my* choice tonight, Sullivan, just in case you pulled that gallant and noble crap on me again." Awkwardly she fumbled with the thick belt of the robe, and then, with a movement almost too swift to catch, she flashed her robe open and closed at him. She blushed even deeper. "But when I got it on, I knew it wasn't me."

"From the little I just saw, it sure looked like you," he said, his throat dry. Now he was the one who sounded like a damn frog, he thought with a wince.

She shook her head, and the brilliant color receded slightly from her cheeks. "I'm no sex bomb, Sully. But I'm not some virginal girl who doesn't understand what it's all about between a man and a woman, either. I know this is all we get, and I want it anyway. I want you," she added simply.

Abruptly she stood, just slightly out of the diffused circle of light from the gently glowing globe. Pulling the robe open, she shrugged out of it, and it fell to the floor behind her.

"What the hell, I might as well pull out all the stops," she said with a crooked little smile that didn't reach those wide, shadowed eyes. "What do you say, Sullivan?"

He didn't say anything. He was incapable of saying anything. He wasn't even sure if he was still breathing.

She looked like a Christmas present, he thought incoherently—a Christmas present for a boy who'd been naughty all year, and wasn't intending to change that to nice in any foreseeable future. She was all satin and lace and ribbons that looked as if one little tug would be all that was needed to release the treasures they bound.

Creamy pale stockings were held halfway up her thighs by garter clips, each one with its own tiny coffee-colored rose. Above the paleness of the stockings, her skin was flushed and rosy. Sullivan felt his blood thicken as his gaze rose higher.

There was a coffee-colored triangle of lace between the tops of her thighs and the garter belt that encircled the lower part of her waist. It looked flimsy, and where it rose to ride over her hips it got even flimsier, ending up as little more than a gleaming satin band. Higher still was more lace, soft against the pink flush of her skin, and then her waist seemed to nip amazingly in.

Women didn't wear these under their street clothes anymore, he thought, and how could anyone blame them? A man had to have designed them. The bustier was boned and cinched, and the crisscrossed satin ribbons that laced up the front were pulled so tightly that, at the lace-strewn top where they ended, Bailey's breasts were impossibly uplifted into two creamy globes that seemed to be spilling out of the garment. She looked like a Victorian miss surprised in the intimacy of her boudoir by some unprincipled footman or groom, Sullivan thought, with him as the coarsely male brute who had violated her privacy.

He suddenly felt too big, too clumsy and too rough. He liked the feeling.

"I was right, wasn't I?" Her teeth sank into her bottom lip, and the clear hazel eyes clouded as she stared at him. "It's *not* me, is it? This was a terrible, terrible mistake, I just *knew* it would be."

At her stricken exclamation, the breath rushed back into his lungs so suddenly that it felt as if he'd been punched just under the heart. His gaze met hers, and slowly he rose to his feet until he was standing in front of her and looking down into those eyes that had always reminded him of clear water in a stream. Very deliberately, he brought his hands to her shoulders, gripping them tightly.

"You don't know one freakin' thing about men, Bailey," he said hoarsely. "Let me give you your first damn lesson."

He brought his mouth down on hers hard enough to tip her head back on her neck, but even as he did, his hands had slid up to cup her face, and he was supporting her. He needed to *taste* her, he thought with fierce urgency—he wanted his tongue in the dark velvet well of her mouth. He wanted her lips open and wet and swollen beneath his. Nothing had to make sense, and nothing had to be logical, because for this he didn't need to think or consider.

This was elementary. This was what he'd been made to do and she was the one he'd been made to do it with. A man could go crazy trying to deny it.

He was going crazy now anyway.

She tasted cool, as if he had stepped out into the middle of a sudden summer shower, thrown his head back to the heavens and was drinking in the rain. But the next moment he felt her stir beneath his kiss, heard a little sighing purr come from deep at the back of her throat, and all at once instead of rain he felt as if he was being filled with heat lightning. He was dangerously close to the edge, and it was way too soon, he thought dazedly. With an effort, he dragged his mouth from hers, lifted his head and looked down at her.

Her eyes were closed, but even as he watched, they opened. For the space of a heartbeat she just looked at him, her gaze brilliant and unfocused. Then the corners of her mouth, still soft from the pressure of his, lifted shakily.

"So you like the outfit? It's not too—too much?"

"Yeah, it's too much, honey. It's too much and you're too much," he said, finding it hard to keep his voice even. "I told myself I was going to do the right thing by you, but how the hell am I supposed to resist when you look like this?"

"You're not, Sullivan. You're supposed to give in." A tumble of hair was obscuring one hazel eye, and she gave a small, impatient shake of her head. Her expression grew serious. "I'm not asking for any promises. You've never said you loved me and I've never said I loved you." Her gaze darkened, but with what emotion it was impossible to tell. "But let's just give each other this one night, with no regrets," she said softly.

He'd never told her he loved her? Sullivan thought wryly. Maybe not in words, but how was it possible that she hadn't seen his fool heart pinned to his sleeve every time he looked at her? But she was right—maybe righter than she knew. He couldn't give her any promises beyond tonight. He hesitated, wondering just how much he should tell her.

The next moment she had grabbed him by the lapels of his suit jacket, and her face was only inches from his.

"Dammit, Sully—*no!*" Her eyes blazed furiously up at him. "Don't walk away from me this time, or I swear I'll never forgive you. You *want* me—I know it. And I want you. It took all I had to come to you like this, and the last thing I can take are any more of your misguided attempts to *shield* me!"

Her hair smelled of lily of the valley. When he'd ended things between them, for nights after, he'd slept on the pillow she'd used, pressing his face into that scent and pretending she was still there beside him, just inches away. Finally the scent had faded and even that little deception had been denied him.

He could deceive himself again. He could pretend this wasn't the last chance he'd have to make love to her. He could do all the things he'd once done with her, and she would do every sweet thing she'd once done with him, and the two of them together could turn the next few hours into forever.

He would just pretend that this night would never end, Sullivan thought, fighting off the sliver of pain that was trying to shaft under his defences.

"On one condition." He caught the errant honey strand of hair that had drifted once more across her forehead, and wrapped it lightly around his finger.

"What?" Through her lashes her gaze narrowed. He opened his own innocently wide.

"You keep all this on until I take it off, piece by piece, honey. Deal?"

This time when her teeth caught at her lip it was to hide a smile. She didn't succeed. "You know how to work all these little snaps and hooks and clasps, Sully?"

"One-handed, and with my eyes closed, darlin'," he promised her. He let the strand of hair spring free, and traced a light line down the side of her mouth, the line of her neck, past her collarbone and into the lacy hollow between her breasts, all without taking his eyes from hers. "I misspent my youth."

"Knowledge is never wasted, Sully," she said primly. The primness was ruined a moment later by a small gasp as he bent his head and flicked his tongue in the same intriguing hollow. He raised his head and looked at her.

"Yeah, that's what I thought, too. Kiss me, Bailey, and let's see how much we both remember."

She hadn't wanted promises or declarations from him, he thought, as her lips parted softly under his. He gathered her to him as gently as if she were made of spun glass, but then his embrace tightened almost fiercely. She hadn't wanted them, and he had no right to give them, so he wouldn't say it out loud.

But whether she knew it or not, he was telling her right now. Inhaling the scent of lily of the valley, Sullivan gave himself over to the night, the kiss and the woman in his arms.

As HE LOWERED HER onto the bed, Bailey felt herself sinking into velvet as if from a great height, felt it lap around her like a shallow sea. The next moment her eyes flew open in consternation as Sullivan released her and moved slightly away.

"I'm overdressed, honey." Shrugging out of his jacket, he carelessly tossed it onto the chair nearby. Not taking his eyes from hers, he undid the top button of his shirt and started to remove his tie, but she stopped him.

"Uh-uh, Sullivan." It had to be the garters and bustier, she thought. She'd never actually *purred* like this before. "You keep it all on, until I take it off piece by piece. That's the way it works with us modern women—equal opportu-

nity.'' Slowly she lifted one cream-colored leg into the air
and pretended to adjust the clip of a suspender.

His teeth gleamed white in the shadows. ''Bails, honey,
I'll go along with the equal opportunity thing, but definitely
not the modern woman part. Right now you look like some
Edwardian wanton posing for a postcard.'' As she started
to lower her foot demurely, he caught and held it lightly,
the blue of his eyes deepening. ''Except they didn't have
thongs back then. Is that what I see under all that lace,
darlin'?''

She felt herself blushing, and was grateful that the golden
glow from the lamp was too diffuse to do more than soften
the darkness around them. ''My first,'' she admitted unsteadily.

''I remember that sweet rump of yours.'' He ran his
thumb along the arch of her foot, and she caught her breath
as what seemed like a thousand tiny shocks tingled up her
leg to her inner thigh. ''I always thought it was a crying
shame to cover it up.''

Moving closer, he brought one knee onto the bed between her legs and let her foot slide up and over his shoulder. Through the thin silk of the stocking, she felt his mouth
moving along the length of her uplifted leg. His tongue
licked slow, steady circles up the curve of her calf, and as
she involuntarily bent her knee, she felt the heat of his
mouth as he kissed her there.

Somehow every sensation seemed heightened by the
cobwebby friction of the silk against her skin, moving
slightly with every stroke of his tongue, slipping delicately
under his hands as he slid them higher up her thigh. The
tingling shocks, so distinct and individual at first, had begun
to run together into a slow, melting heat, as if she was
gradually being immersed in warm, scented oil. Through

her lashes she saw Sullivan's thumb flick expertly at the rosetted clasp of one garter.

"You feel like satin," he said softly, looking up at her. "I want your skin against me, honey."

Slowly he stripped off first one stocking and then the other. Then his hands moved to the ribboned bow between her breasts and he gave it a little tug.

Bailey felt the lacing release. She brought her own hands up and fumbled with the tiny flat buttons of his shirt until all but the last few were undone. Then she stopped.

"You finish, Sully." She saw his quick grin and gave the noose of his tie a reproving jerk. "Some of us didn't misspend our youths," she said. "I was probably doing something worthwhile and uplifting while you were setting the land speed record for undoing bras."

"What a liar," he said mildly. He stood, his shirt open to his waist, and casually slid the knot of his tie down until it hung free. "The only reason you never learned how to undress a man is because you like to watch."

"There is that," she admitted, propping herself up on her elbows and tipping her head to one side. Their eyes met, and lazily he undid his cuffs. "It must be the voyeur in me," she said huskily. Without taking her gaze from him, she loosened the ribbons on the front of her bustier even farther.

Sullivan shrugged carelessly out of his shirt and let it drop behind him. His hands moved to his belt. "See, that's not fair, Bails." He frowned at her. "I get the reputation, but you're the one with the secret vices. Kinky lingerie. Voyeurism. Hell, the missionary position with the lights out should be enough for anyone. You missed a lace," he added, his voice slightly hoarse.

"Thanks." She hooked her baby finger under the errant ribbon and pulled it through the small gold eyelet that had

escaped her notice. "So you think I might need professional help? A sex therapist, maybe?" She unclipped the
center rosette on the garter belt around her waist, looking
up at him. "Plain white briefs," she noted. "Gee, you *are*
normal."

"Well, the red bikinis are for Valentine's Day only. Stop
twirling that thing around on your finger, I'm starting to
hope I'll get a free table dance, honey." He slid the zipper
of his fly down with excruciating slowness. "Yeah, a therapist might be your answer. But you want to get someone
with enough experience to handle your particular problem,
and that's not going to be easy." He planted one foot up
on the hard wooden chair beside the bed, his expression
troubled as he unlaced his shoe, removing both it and his
sock. He did the same with the other, before casually stripping his pants off.

Bailey stopped breathing. The briefs left absolutely nothing to the imagination. White against the dark tan of his
skin and the darker arrow of silky hair that vee'd from his
navel to disappear under the waistband, they seemed almost
criminally revealing. Maybe he bought them snug, she
thought weakly.

She swallowed. "So what should I be looking for?"

He raised an eyebrow. "It's like choosing any other professional, honey—a plumber, say, or an electrician. You've
got to ask questions. Does he take his work seriously?"

"You seem to have someone in mind. Does he?" She
sank slowly back onto the velvet spread, the front of the
bustier almost totally undone, and held her breath as Sullivan slid his thumbs under the waistband of his briefs.

"Very seriously," he said promptly. "Then you'll want
to know if he's got the time to do the job properly. The
guy I'm thinking about never rushes a project." He paused,
the waistband of his briefs still firmly in place.

"Well, sometimes that's a drawback," she complained with a small scowl. "Does he have anything else to recommend him?"

"Like I said, it's just like choosing an electrician, Bails." A strand of black hair had fallen across his brow, and he let it hang there. One corner of his mouth lifted, and he shoved the waistband of the briefs past his groin, down the leanly muscled thighs and to the floor. "You wanna make sure he's got the right equipment for what you need him to do. But you'll have to make your own mind up on that one, honey."

He was close enough so that when she reached out, the tip of her finger could just trace a light line down the dark vee of hair. She ran her fingertip lower into the denser thicket between his legs, and then carefully wrapped her palm around him.

She felt a tremor run through him. Looking up, she saw he was watching her through his lashes, his lips slightly parted. She stroked him again, and a muscle jumped at the side of his jaw.

"Bailey, honey, that's like smoking around a gas pump," he said tightly. "How about you let me hang on to my self-control just a little longer, okay?"

Slowly she lay back against the pillows, and the last ribbon on the bustier slid free, exposing her to his gaze. "But I don't want you to," she said breathily. "I want you to lose control, Sully. Isn't that what you want?"

He didn't immediately reply. Putting one knee on the bed beside her, before she knew what he was doing, he had effortlessly turned her over onto her front, the lacy bustier slipping from her to the floor. His hands nearly meeting around her waist, he pulled her derriere toward him, hooked one finger into the waist strap of the mocha-colored thong, and slipped it down her thighs, under her knees and off.

Efficiently he turned her onto her back again, and this time he was straddling her.

"Hell, yeah," he said with soft urgency. "I think I can just about manage that, honey."

He brought his mouth down on hers, and as his tongue penetrated her, Bailey arched her hips toward him. She heard his breath catch in his throat as he felt her move against him, and then his kiss deepened and he was entering her both ways at the same time. Her legs parted as he eased himself into her, and convulsively she clutched at his arms, her nails digging into his biceps. He paused and lifted his head, his eyes dark with concern as he gazed into hers.

"Should I stop?" he said, his voice unsteady. A strand of his hair brushed against her cheek, and she shook her head, wanting only to have him back inside her.

"No," she whispered. "Don't stop for anything, Sullivan. I want all of you."

His eyes met hers, and for a moment it seemed as if she could see past that blue, blue gaze to the innermost recesses of his very being. "You always did have me, Bailey. Whatever's mine to give you, it's yours," he muttered against her lips.

Before she could answer him, his mouth was covering hers again, and the other steady, piercingly sweet pressure was filling her. She *would* have to tell him to stop, Bailey thought with faint panic—she would have to tell him she wasn't able to take this, that he was too much for her—

He was completely inside her. The breath she had been holding escaped from her in a soft sigh. She felt him withdrawing and then moving into her, as perfectly fitted to her as if they were two parts of an interlocking whole, and suddenly the slight pain was gone and all that was left was the slow swirl of pleasure that was beginning to possess her.

She felt as if she had been turned to cream, she thought hazily—rich, sweet cream that was slowly being heated over a flame, becoming thicker and heavier and more intense as the temperature notched higher. She felt as if she was pouring herself around the man inside her, and as if he was melting into her.

She tried to open her eyes, but the most she could do was lift her lashes just enough to see his, fanned dense and inky against the hard edge of his cheekbones. It was important she tell him, she thought disjointedly. She knew the answer to everything now, and she knew how to make it all right. Above him like a small golden moon glowed the paper shade, and even as she looked at it, it seemed to expand and grow bigger, spinning dizzily around them both.

She was moving her head back and forth on the pillow, her teeth sunk into her bottom lip to hold back the cry of pleasure that was threatening to escape. She couldn't hold on much longer, Bailey thought disjointedly, feeling the rush of molten heat flowing through her start lapping at the last edges of consciousness. But before she let herself be swept completely over the edge with him she had to tell him—

"Oh, honey, I missed you." Sullivan's voice was a broken rasp above her, and as she dazedly looked at him, she saw the glazed desire in his eyes shimmer with an edge of terrible sadness. "In my dreams you always came back for me."

He dragged in a shallow breath and filled her again, his hair short damp spikes against her face and the muscles in his neck standing out like cords. Bailey felt herself receive him, felt the heat within her flare out of control, knew she had less than seconds left.

She brought her hands up to his face, her lips parted and

her head tipped back. "I always will," she gasped. "No matter how far away you go, Sully, I'll find you and bring you home. I *swear* I will, baby. I *swear* it."

She hardly knew what she was saying. All she knew was that she couldn't stand to see such pain in his eyes, and whatever it took to wipe it away she would do. But it seemed as if her words had meant something to him, because the edged shimmer in his gaze slowly sheened over with the dark blue glaze of pure desire that she knew so well. He caught his lower lip between his teeth, and that she knew well, too.

"Bailey, honey, we're going together now, right?" he whispered, his words barely audible.

"We're going together," she whispered back, her grasp on him tightening. "Take me there now, Sully."

He thrust again, and then again, and then she heard herself crying out incoherently, heard herself calling his name, heard him call her, and it was like falling, the two of them locked together like halves of a once-broken heart, magically made whole again. She felt the shuddering explosions deep inside her, saw fireworks cascading behind her closed eyes....

An eternity later, the last one lit up the velvet darkness of her consciousness.

She hadn't told him, she thought dazedly, but that was all right. She would tell him tomorrow, or the tomorrow after that, because this was the key that unlocked their future. It made perfect sense, and she didn't know why she hadn't realized it before.

He thought he'd lost his soul. But she was part of him, and he was part of her. She would share hers with him, she thought dreamily, feeling one last spasm run through him as his head bent to the hollow of her neck. He could have her soul, and then he would never, never have to go away and the legend would lose its hold over him.

She would tell him tomorrow, she told herself, his breath warm against the pulse of her throat.

BAILEY OPENED ONE EYE sleepily—only one, because the other was hidden behind a tangle of hair. The tangle stirred lightly, lifting from her brow and then settling down again across her lashes, and a second later she realized that it was Sullivan's warm breath she could feel on her cheek and in her hair. It was Sullivan's breath on her cheek, and it was Sullivan's strongly muscled arm wrapped possessively around her breasts, and it was his body, hard and smooth, that she was snugged tightly up against, from her back to her derriere and right down to her legs, trapped beneath one of his as if even in sleep he hadn't wanted to take the chance of her slipping away from him.

Through the matchstick blinds chinked full sunlight, and ruefully she blinked at the clock on the table by Sullivan's shoulder. Dear God—it was almost *noon.* She gave a guilty start, and beside her, Sully murmured something unintelligible in his sleep.

She shifted around in the circle of his arm until she was facing him, feeling a gurgle of pure happiness bubble up inside her and letting her fingertips trail down the line of his hip and then softly touch the thickness of hair at his groin. It was almost noon, but who could blame them for sleeping in? They'd made love all through the night and right into the dawn, time after time. It was entirely possible that they would make love again before they finally got up to face what was left of the day, she thought drowsily.

Something buzzed by her outstretched foot, and she jumped, her hand still on him. Inches from her startled gaze, Sullivan peered through a wayward strand of midnight-black hair.

"Woman, are you insatiable?" he growled sleepily. He blinked, and a slow smile spread across his features. "Gee, you're pretty in the morning, Bails."

The muted buzzing sounded again, and this time Bailey felt a vibration against her toes. She giggled, suddenly realizing what it was.

"Your cell phone must have fallen onto the bed last night," she said. "Hold on, I'll get it."

Pushing back the velvet spread, she heard the phone buzz again and she grabbed at a lump under a twisted sheet, just as a louder ringing sounded from beside Sullivan.

"You get mine, I'll get yours, honey." He grinned. "Take a message and I'll do the same." He rolled over lazily and picked up the receiver as she found his cell phone and flipped it open.

"Hello?" She hoped she sounded less husky than Sullivan did, she thought as she heard him answer her caller.

"Hi, darlin'. Terry Paddy there, by any chance?" The voice on the other end of the line seemed amused, and Bailey injected a note of brisk efficiency into her answer.

"He is, but he's on another line. Can he call you back?"

"Nah, the boy's obviously busy." The gravelly voice chuckled. "Listen, just give him a message, will you? Tell him the Dutchman wants him to fly out tomorrow, because he just lost one of his best commanders. There'll be someone at the Trinity Tavern with his ticket and his orders. Sully'll recognize him. Can you pass that on, sweetheart?"

"Ticket? Orders?" Bailey's lips felt frozen. "What's this all about?"

"Now that's between Sully and the Dutchman, darlin'." Again Sullivan's caller chuckled. "But you might want to give your soldier an extra special send-off, honey. The Dutchman's got a habit of losing men."

With a click he disconnected. Slowly Bailey flipped the cover of Sullivan's cell phone closed, staring at the thing as if it was a snake that had just reared back and struck her.

She could feel the poison spreading through her system already, she thought numbly. He'd told her he was going back, but he'd let her believe that his plans were still nebulous. He had to have put the word out weeks ago, she thought, an icy chill wrapping itself around her and dissipating the last of the warmth from his embrace. He'd been expecting this call, or one similar.

He'd known all this last night.

She turned to him, her eyes blinded by tears and her throat tight with pain, but before she could speak, his arms were around her and his hand was cradling the back of her head. Over his shoulder she saw that he'd hung up her phone.

"Bails, it's bad news," he said softly. "There's no easy way to break it, so I'll give it to you straight. That was Fitz." He stroked back the hair from her forehead with a gentle hand. "It's Angelica, honey. They found her in a motel room this morning. She's dead, Bailey."

Chapter Fourteen

"I blame myself. The signs were all there, dammit—the irrational behavior, the mood swings. I should have *known,* for God's sake!"

Aaron's features were pinched with grief. Bailey saw Fitz exchange an uncomfortable glance with Straub, and the younger detective cleared his throat awkwardly. Across the room Sullivan leaned against the door, his face unreadable and his arms crossed on his chest.

They were in an interview room at the police station that had been turned into a temporary office, presumably because of Aaron's status, she supposed. The rich weren't questioned, even delicately, in front of a roomful of detectives, ringing phones, and victims of other crimes shakily giving their statements.

Aaron's first stop had been the morgue, however, and even though Bailey had no fondness for the man, she knew that identifying his young wife's body had to have been an ordeal for him. Perhaps he'd really loved Angelica, she thought dully. But even if the rumors were true and he'd been contemplating divorce, this wouldn't have been the way he would have wanted his marriage to end.

She felt Sullivan looking at her. She didn't meet his gaze.

"Had you ever found drugs in her possession, Mr. Plowright?'' Straub asked diffidently. "Not necessarily heroin, but any kind of illegal drug?''

"Of course not. I would have packed her off to the best clinic available, if that had been the case, man.'' Aaron glared at Straub.

"We have to ask,'' Fitz said, his tone briefly apologetic. "I know it's an unpleasant subject, and this kind of investigation is never easy, especially on the family. But your wife didn't have track marks, so the needle wasn't her normal practice.''

"You think it was a one-time only use. Suicide, in other words.'' Sullivan's comment wasn't a question. He pushed himself from the door, his face grim.

"We think it's possible.'' Straub darted a compassionate glance at Bailey, but she didn't respond. He shrugged. "She hadn't been herself lately, whether because of a recently acquired drug habit or the onset of some psychological illness we can't say for certain yet. But she came up with this outlandish plan to hire Jackson to mount a surveillance operation on her husband and his daughter in order to create a mystery woman she could pin his murder on later. Not only that, but she actually shared this plan with Ms. Weiss, expecting her to go along with it.''

"She said Tracy came up with the plan,'' Bailey said woodenly. "Angelica agreed to it, but she told me only last night that it had been Tracy's idea from the start.''

"She also told you Ms. Weiss had killed Hank Jackson and forced her to help dispose of the body,'' Fitz said heavily. "But the only prints on that plastic curtain were your sister's, Bailey, and her car was found abandoned last night in an industrial area. We're still running tests, but there are definitely traces of human blood in the trunk. She must have ditched the vehicle right after she got rid of Jackson's body.''

"She should have come to me." Aaron's face was in chalky contrast to the unrelieved black of his suit. He shook his head. "She never would have been convicted of the man's murder. It's doubtful whether she would have been found fit to stand trial, for heaven's sake."

"Perhaps not." Fitz raked a hand through his thinning hair. "But the guilt might have led her to suicide anyway. She may not have been able to live with what she'd done."

"She told me she thought she knew a way she could work everything out. She said if things didn't go the way she hoped, she would contact me by noon today." Bailey heard the tremor in her voice. With an effort she steadied it. "Why haven't you questioned Tracy? Does anyone know where *she* was last night?"

"Not at the Brockton Motel, Bailey. Tracy was with me, going over one of my corporate files." Aaron's hand rested lightly on her arm, but his tone sharpened. "I don't blame you for not wanting to believe any of this about your sister, but Tracy's suffering enough already without you accusing her of God knows what far-fetched crime. She bitterly regrets not coming to me when she first learned of Angelica's plans."

"If she had, my sister might still be alive," Bailey said, her tone low and intense. "Tell your daughter for me that whatever else she escapes blame for, I hold her directly responsible for *that*."

"Your hands aren't entirely clean, either, Bailey," Aaron replied sharply. "The last one in this room to see Angelica alive was you. You could have turned her in last night yourself, so keep that in mind when you're assigning respons—"

"Watch yourself, Plowright," Sullivan cut in, his jaw tight. "Pointing the finger at anyone might not be the wisest move for you to make."

"And what's that supposed to mean?" Aaron's gaze jerked up at the man standing over him.

"It's no secret that your marriage had run its course." Sullivan gave him a flat stare. "If nothing else, Angelica's death is damn convenient for you, isn't it?"

"All right, Sully, that's enough." Glowering, Fitz shoved back his chair, but Aaron forestalled him.

"No, Detective. Maybe it's best we get this out in the open right here and now." He turned back to Sullivan. "I'd hoped my marital problems weren't common knowledge, but since they appear to be, then yes, it's unlikely that Angelica would have remained my wife for much longer. But even if there was the slightest hint of foul play, why would anyone suspect me of wanting her dead? Good God, man— I divorce my wives. I don't do them in."

"This isn't a question I was intending to ask at this time," Fitz said diffidently. "But since you yourself want to clear the air, Plowright, isn't divorce an expensive proposition for a man in your position? With a smart attorney, your wife might have been looking at a settlement worth millions."

"I loved Angelica when I married her, Detective, but I didn't go into the union blinded by passion," Aaron said frostily. "If it's necessary, my lawyers can provide you with a copy of the prenuptial agreement she signed. It was ironclad. My wife would have left our marriage with exactly what she brought into it."

He shoved back his chair and glanced discreetly at the Rolex on his wrist in much the same way, Bailey thought, as he would in dismissing a tedious business meeting. "Unless there's anything else you need from me, Detectives, I'd like to get home. Despite what's been said here, this is a mournful occurrence for both myself and my household. My staff's been given the day off to grieve for a mistress they were very fond of, but unfortunately that leaves me with the unhappy burden of handling those matters that can't be delayed. You'll let me know when the body can be released to the funeral director, Detective Fitzgerald?''

Exactly as if he was adjourning a meeting, she thought bitterly as she got to her feet and turned to the door. But as if he could read her mind, Aaron stopped her with a conciliatory hand on her arm before she had taken more than a couple of steps.

''We've never been close, Bailey,'' he said somberly. ''That's probably more my fault than yours, and maybe you're right to lay the blame for the breakdown of my marriage at my feet, too. But I *did* adore Angelica once. She was the most exquisite thing I'd ever seen, and during the first few weeks of our whirlwind courtship I was totally enchanted with her. I was thinking of those days only last night, in fact. The restaurant where Tracy and I dined used to be Angelica's favorite when we were dating.''

He gave a small, helpless shrug. ''I was feeling a little melancholy anyway, knowing that it was probably over between us, and the place brought back memories of happier times. I even got the piano player to sing 'Moon River.''' His gaze, usually so wintry, softened. ''That used to be our song,'' he added quietly.

Watching him, Bailey found herself wondering if she'd misjudged the man. Was it possible there was a streak of sentimentality in him after all?

''That's touching, Plowright.'' Sullivan's voice was harsh. ''Too bad your maudlin impulses didn't extend to offering the woman a fair divorce settlement. She might not have been driven to do what she did. But I guess there's a world of difference between that and slipping a piano player five bucks so you can indulge in a few moments of auld lang syne, right?''

The pensiveness that had shadowed Aaron's expression was gone so completely that Bailey wondered if she'd only imagined it, and in its place was an oddly assessing look, as if he was taking a moment to size up Sullivan's strengths and weaknesses. Grieving widower or not, the man was still a ruthless tycoon who had made his fortune knowing just how to disable his opponents, she thought uneasily. It was reckless of Sullivan to antagonize him this way.

But she kept forgetting that reckless was Sullivan's trademark, she reminded herself starkly.

"Your insults seem to have an unusually personal edge to them today," he said, meeting Sullivan's hard gaze thoughtfully. "Does your jaundiced view of my character have anything to do with your realization of your own shortcomings? After all, we must have something in common—if things had turned out differently for both of us, we might even have been brothers-in-law." He glanced at his watch again and smiled thinly. "But even if my wife hadn't just tragically died, that possibility would likely never have become reality, I suppose. Some men just aren't the type to settle down, are they?"

Bailey was close enough to Sullivan to hear his harshly indrawn breath as Aaron's shot found its mark, but a sideways glance at him showed nothing more revealing than the tense set of his jaw. When he spoke his tone was even.

"Some men aren't, Plowright. But facing that fact to avoid destroying anyone else might be a better way of handling it than to keep losing wives, don't you think?" He turned to her, his voice softening. "Fitz says he'll get a written statement from you later, honey. Let's get out of this place before I do something I might regret."

His choice of words couldn't have been less fortunate, she thought, sharp pain lancing through her. "I don't see that happening, Sully," she said dully. She turned back to the man watching them. "You'll inform me about the funeral arrangements, won't you, Aaron?"

"Of course," he agreed. He pressed one of her hands between both of his. "I'll be holding an informal wake at the house this evening. Drop by and we'll talk of happier times, Bailey."

"Happier times?" Sullivan ground out as they drove from the parking lot a few minutes later. "He couldn't be any happier. A divorce might have dragged on for months, but this way he's become a free man overnight."

"That's still not a motive for murder, even if he didn't have an alibi," Bailey said listlessly. "I'm sure he wouldn't have risked mentioning that prenup to Fitz if it didn't exist. Aaron said it himself, Sullivan—a divorce would have cost him nothing. I don't much like the man, but I don't think he's a murderer."

"You think she killed herself, don't you?" He looked over at her searchingly, and slowly she nodded.

"I think she must have. I'll admit I suspected Tracy, but Aaron wouldn't give her an alibi just because she's his daughter. That's not the way the man operates." She shrugged. "And if Angel killed herself, then it must have been for the reason Fitz suggested."

"Guilt over murdering Hank?" Sullivan looked unconvinced. "But what about the bottle of rye? What about everything she told you last night, for God's sake?"

"I think my sister spun me a fairy tale last night, Sully." Bailey gave him an uncompromisingly direct look. "As you know yourself, I'm gullible enough to swallow that kind of story." She turned away from him and fixed a stony gaze on the passing traffic, willing herself not to cry.

"I didn't spin you a story, Bails." His voice was quiet. "You knew I was going back."

"I knew," she agreed leadenly, still not looking at him.

"What I didn't know was that your arrangements were already in place."

"I wasn't expecting that call so soon, either." The light at the intersection they were approaching turned amber, and he swore under his breath as he braked for it. "But you said you understood why I was doing this, Bailey. You said you accepted—"

"Then I lied, too!" Whirling around to face him, she heard the thickness in her own voice and felt the tears that she'd vowed not to shed spill over, but suddenly she couldn't hold them back any longer. "Everyone else lies, Sully, so why not me? I thought I had more *time,* dammit! I thought I could persuade you not to go. I thought I could convince you to *stay,* to build a future instead of throwing your life away on the past!"

"You might have done, at that." There was raw pain in his voice. "But you wouldn't have liked the man I eventually became, Bailey, and in the end I wouldn't have been able to stand him, either."

Behind them a car honked impatiently. Sullivan's mouth tightened, and he put the Jaguar in gear. Bailey looked down at her hands and saw the salty sheen of teardrops on her clasped fingers.

"What will it take for the debt to be paid?" she said in a low tone. "Last night you said you wouldn't go looking for death, but that's the price, isn't it? Nothing less will do."

He didn't answer her, and after a moment she wiped her eyes with the heel of her hand and looked up. "I'm going to have to learn to live without you, and I might as well start now," she said distantly. "Drop me anywhere downtown, Sully."

"I'll take you to your apartment." They were only a few

blocks away, and already he'd started to edge over into the turn lane. Bailey shook her head.

"I'm not going home. I'm going to work." She saw the brief confusion that crossed his features and shrugged impatiently. "I don't know about your agency, but at Triple-A Acme a case isn't closed until every last loose end's tied up. I'm going to Le Lapin D'Or."

"The restaurant where Aaron says he had dinner with Tracy last night?" He frowned. "But I thought you accepted his story."

"I do."

Her voice was completely steady again, Bailey noted, and her tears had dried. This wasn't so hard. If she took it one day at a time, and there were three hundred and sixty-five days in a year, sooner or later hiding the pain would become second nature. She could do this.

She looked at him and felt her heart turn over in anguish. She laced her fingers together even tighter.

"I do believe him. But Angelica was my sister, and I owe it to her to check this one last detail."

"Then I'm going with you, Flowers." Sullivan's tone brooked no argument. "We're partners on this case, and I don't like loose ends, either."

Trying to dissuade him when he'd set his mind to something was impossible, she thought in frustration half an hour later. Despite her protests, he'd simply walked into the restaurant with her and within minutes had struck up a conversation with their waitress as if he'd known the woman for years.

"Oh, I know Mr. Plowright well." Setting their drinks down on the table, the petite redhead smiled. "A very distinguished-looking man. He used to come here quite often with his wife, but we haven't seen him much lately."

"Was he here last night?" Bailey knew her question

sounded too abrupt as soon as she'd said it, and she wasn't surprised when the woman hesitated.

"I told you, honey, it's next week." Sullivan grinned ruefully at the redhead. "My wife here is certain I fouled up a telephone message. I'm sure we weren't supposed to have dinner with him last night, but it might be a little embarrassing to tell the great man we can't remember exactly what the arrangement was."

The woman smiled, her manner once again relaxed. "I got off early yesterday, but I could ask Pamela. She's the hostess. Let me check with her."

"Thanks, I fumbled that one," Bailey muttered ungraciously. She took a sip of the white wine she'd ordered and set the glass down again, knowing it would only bring on the headache she could feel threatening.

"You've got a personal interest in this," Sullivan said mildly. "It's understandable that you're eager to get some answers."

At the far end of the room a tuxedo-clad man strolled over to the white baby grand piano and lifted the instrument's lid. He pulled out a bench and sat down and after a moment began warming up with a few snatches of show tunes.

"Who's the Dutchman?" That made two questions in a row that she'd blurted out, Bailey thought, annoyed at herself. But Sullivan, although he hesitated, finally answered her.

"He's a broker," he said briefly. "Of men," he added, seeing her blank look. "Over the years he's built up a list of contacts, and when someone needs mercenaries, they get in touch with him and he calls men like me. I was off his list for a few years, but a few weeks ago I told him I was available again."

"And he has a habit of losing men," she said flatly,

recalling the mysterious caller's words. Sullivan's expression didn't change.

"He brokers high-risk assignments," he said neutrally.

Before she could question him further, their waitress returned, smiling apologetically. "Pamela *thinks* she remembers seeing Mr. Plowright last night," she said dubiously. "But she says she can't be certain. We had several large parties in here, and things were pretty hectic for a while. I'm sorry we couldn't help you more."

"Not to worry." Sullivan's tone was easy and untroubled. "I'll see if I can finesse the information out of his dragon of a social secretary without giving myself away."

As the woman was called over to another table, Bailey reached for her shoulder bag and pushed back her chair. "That's that, then," she said. "It's not as conclusive as I'd have liked, but I guess there's not much more we can do. No, don't get up, Sully."

She stood. Their eyes met, and for a long moment they simply looked at each other, saying nothing.

He was *such* a handsome man and his eyes were so very, very blue, she thought, a rush of love filling her and the tears rising painfully in her throat. She'd thought a few days ago that he hadn't looked any different from the day she'd first met him, and now he never would. In her heart he would never grow old, never lose that charmed luster, and would always be looking at her with that wry, sexy grin that never failed to disarm her completely.

She never wanted to know, she thought anguishedly. If she ever saw Ainslie walking down the street, she would turn and go the other way as fast as she could. She didn't want to hear the news when it came. She wanted to remember him this way and never, never know.

She put her hand out and touched his cheek lightly.

Swiftly he caught it and held it there, his gaze locked on hers.

"We already said goodbye, Sully," she whispered. "We just never said we loved each other." She bent over quickly and pressed her lips to the corner of his mouth, and then, just as quickly, she straightened and turned on her heel.

She had taken only half a dozen steps when she heard him call her name, and she paused, looking back over her shoulder at him. He hadn't moved. His eyes were still fixed on her.

"We never said it, Bails," he said softly. A corner of his mouth rose unevenly. "But we always knew, didn't we?"

Her throat had completely closed up and her vision was obscured by a sheen of tears. Bailey nodded blindly. "Yes," she managed. "Yes, baby. We knew."

And then she was walking away, and she didn't look back again.

Chapter Fifteen

Aaron Plowright closed the door on the last of the somber crowd of friends and associates who had come to support him in his fresh bereavement. They hadn't been there because of Angelica, Bailey thought, glancing up at the full-length portrait of her sister that had been hung over the enormous spray of roses and white lilac on the heavy carved mantel. They would have known from the first that she wasn't a permanent fixture in their world.

"She was lovely, wasn't she?" Tracy drifted to her side, a small glass of Armagnac held delicately in her hand. She was wearing black, as behooved her status as unofficial hostess at her father's late wife's wake, and the color made her skin seem almost milky-white. "I know Aaron's told you how devastated I was to hear of her suicide. I hold myself responsible, in part."

"I do, too," Bailey said coolly. "But you acted as you thought best at the time."

When Aaron had phoned her a few hours ago and repeated his invitation, she'd declined with the excuse that the police were still holding her car, since it had been the last vehicle Angelica had used and had been found at the motel where she'd died. That had been a mistake. He'd immediately brushed her protest aside and had insisted on sending a driver for her. But she was glad now that she'd come. Her sister deserved to have one sincere mourner here for her, and the elegant woman standing beside her, despite the black dress she was wearing, certainly felt no real grief at Angelica's death.

"Brandy?" Crossing the room to them, Aaron was holding a cut-crystal decanter. He poured a snifter for himself and looked up inquiringly.

"No, thank you," she demurred. "I really should be on my way soon, Aaron. There's no need to get Manuel out again tonight, though. I can call a cab."

Most of the servants lived out, but she'd learned that Aaron's driver had a spacious apartment over the massive garage not far from the main house. Still, Bailey thought, the man had probably settled down for the evening.

"He's paid to drive for me," Aaron said with a slight frown. "Why would I let you call a taxi?"

"When you have the kind of money my father has, the world is suddenly much simpler, Bailey," Tracy said with a light laugh, holding out her glass.

He looked at her and then turned away, replacing the heavy stopper in the decanter and setting it on a side table. "It's been an emotional day, my dear," he said smoothly. "There's coffee in the next room."

There were undercurrents here that she didn't understand, Bailey thought with mild distaste. She had no desire to understand them, either.

"If you don't mind, I think I'll just freshen up before I leave, Aaron." Her smile not directed at either of them, she set the glass she'd been holding all evening down beside the decanter, and hesitated. Tracy interpreted her confusion.

"There's a powder room upstairs, the fifth door on your left," she said, her voice once again coolly controlled.

"When you come back down I'll ring Manuel to bring the car around."

Another tiny flexing of her newly acquired power, Bailey thought tiredly, crossing the imposing hall and mounting the gleaming steps of the grand staircase that had formerly graced an English baronial manor, as Angelica had once excitedly told her. At the thought of her sister, she felt an aching sadness. It wasn't as piercingly sharp as the anguish she'd been holding back all evening after leaving Sullivan. Nothing could equal that, she thought, her hand gripping the banister for support. These hours of interacting with strangers without betraying herself had been an ordeal that she was only too ready to end. But although what she felt for Angelica was worlds away from that wrenching pain, it was still something that would haunt her whenever she remembered the perfect child her adopted sister had once been.

This would have been the dream for Angelica. This luxurious existence would have been the summit she had striven for so single-mindedly, even as a little girl. Bailey paused by a half-open door, frowning slightly. She'd only seen Angelica's bedroom once, but she was almost positive this was it. Aaron's was farther down the hall, she remembered. Giving the door a light push, she looked in.

The room was decorated in pink and cream. Satin and lace festooned every upholstered surface, and on the bed was an enormous china doll, its skirts spread out over the masses of tucked and pleated pillows.

The little girl who'd been abandoned in a motel room had eventually returned to her roots, Bailey thought in sharp pity. But for a while she'd created for herself the childhood she'd never had. This room was a child's room. Feeling as if she was intruding, she started to back out of the doorway.

Then she stopped, her gaze frozen on the corner of the photograph protruding from the stiffly ruffled skirts of the china doll on the bed.

The next moment she had tossed the doll aside. Hidden underneath it was a handful of photos, and before she'd even riffled swiftly through them she knew what they depicted.

"Mystery woman with her arms around Plowright's neck, kissing him. Mystery woman lying on the bed while he's sitting on a nearby chair. Mystery woman wearing a robe and nothing else..."

One by one the photos matched up with the descriptions of Tracy and her father on Hank Jackson's list. They had been stolen from him after he'd been murdered, Bailey thought sickly. And then they'd been hastily hidden here in a dead woman's bedroom, where no one would intrude.

Angelica had never returned to this house after Jackson's murder. She'd left when Tracy had called her and told her to meet her at the man's house, and from then on she'd been on the run, which meant that she hadn't hidden these photos here.

"I wondered why you were taking so long."

Bailey whirled around at the calm voice. There in the doorway of Angelica's bedroom was Tracy, her expression composed. In her hand she was holding a gun, and even as Bailey's gaze darted to the windows, she leveled it on her.

"For heaven's sakes, you'd be dead before you got halfway across the room," she said impatiently. "Don't convince me that Angelica was the smart one, please."

"You'll never get away with this killing, Tracy." With an effort Bailey kept the tremor out of her voice. "Your father's downstairs."

"Actually I was curious at your delay, too." Aaron stepped into the room with an expression of distaste on his patrician features. "God, this room is claustrophobic," he muttered. He looked at Bailey and gave a theatrical shrug. "Well, our secret is out. That's what comes of having a gumshoe in the family, I suppose. I'm sorry you felt the need to snoop, Bailey—by the way, what exactly did you find?"

"She found the photos." For the first time Tracy sounded slightly nervous. "I had to hide them somewhere," she snapped. "How was I to know the woman would wander all over our house?"

"*My* house, my dear," Aaron corrected her tartly.

"You were in this together," Bailey said incredulously. "But *why,* Aaron? You could have divorced Angelica, you said it yourself! You had no reason to kill her."

"I had two, and they were both good ones. Heavens, Tracy, stop waving that damned cannon around," Aaron interrupted himself. Taking the gun from his daughter, he turned back to Bailey.

"The first reason was that she had wanted to kill me. The second reason was that your darling sister was a whole year younger than everybody thought she was.

"A year younger?" Bailey frowned, confused. "She was *four* years younger than that fake ID she bought said she was. You knew that."

"For God's sake, we're not talking about her little scam to get work as an underage cocktail waitress." Aaron sounded impatient. "We're talking about the fact that the birth certificate that was obtained for her when she was found abandoned never matched the hospital records of her birth. Some social worker made a mistake."

"And therefore the prenup wasn't valid," Tracy elaborated curtly. "She was a week away from her eighteenth birthday when she signed it, which made it worthless. Unfortunately by the time of the wedding, she'd had that all-important birthday, and the marriage itself was legal. I uncovered all this when I was drawing up the divorce papers for my father. Admittedly, I was checking every detail, but we couldn't take the chance of Angelica's lawyers finding the same loophole. We're wasting time here. I'd like the photos now, please." She held out her hand for them, but Bailey didn't move.

"So she was only four when she was left in that motel room by her mother," she said, her gaze shadowed. Then her voice hardened. "But I still don't understand. The setup at the Harris, hiring Hank Jackson, creating the existence of a mystery woman—you're saying that was all Angelica's idea?"

"My God, you *are* the dumb sister." Tracy glanced at her father, but he didn't return her smile.

"There's no need for boorishness," he said with a frown. "And I really don't think it serves any purpose to fill you in on all the details, Bailey. You understand that you won't be leaving this house, don't you?"

"Like you said, Aaron—I'm a gumshoe. The gun in your hand was a clue," she said woodenly. "But since that's the case, what would it hurt to satisfy my curiosity?"

Aaron sighed. Then he inclined his head graciously. "Very well. But for God's sake, let's get out of this chocolate box of a room and go downstairs. I for one could use another drink."

He didn't mean to kill her here, Bailey thought dully as, followed by Tracy and Aaron, she dutifully descended the staircase and at Aaron's nod, led the way into his study.

"I discovered the problem with the prenup when my father asked me to start drawing up divorce papers for him," Tracy said, brushing a speck of lint from her skirt and perching on the arm of the wing chair. "There was no question of letting Angelica rob him of millions, of course, so we knew we would have to get rid of her."

"I was a trifle disconcerted when I learned how eagerly she'd jumped at the possibility of getting rid of *me*," Aaron added dryly, downing a mouthful of brandy, the gun in his hand trained on Bailey. "I was even more disconcerted when I realized that if my daughter had truly been in cahoots with my wife, the plan Tracy had concocted might actually have worked." He raised an amused eyebrow, and to Bailey's surprise, the brunette flushed.

"It had to have seemed as if it might have worked, Aaron," she said sharply. "I know we were painting a picture of Angelica as unbalanced, but it was necessary to convince the police that she would have gone through with it if I'd agreed."

"Point taken, my dear, point taken," he said placatingly. "Which was why that Jackson fellow had to die. We needed her completely discredited."

Bailey's temper flared. "Hank Jackson was an innocent bystander in all this. How could you talk your way into the man's house and kill him, Tracy? What the hell runs in your veins—ice water?"

There was an awkward silence. Aaron broke it with a small cough, as if she'd committed a social gaffe and he was attempting to cover it up for her. "That was me, I'm afraid," he said. "I showed up on his doorstep and told him he'd been made a party to blackmail, and rather than call the police I was willing to discuss the matter with him. I even showed up with a bottle of hootch, as I believe it's commonly called. I'd heard he was a drinker." He shrugged.

"He'd won that battle," Bailey said coldly. "He was a decent man who didn't deserve to be killed just to set the stage for the murder you really wanted to commit."

"I'm not a monster." Aaron's tone sharpened. "It was necessary. Just as it was necessary that you be the one to dispose of the body with Angelica," he added edgily to Tracy.

"I know, Aaron." She raised her eyebrows. "I was on cleanup detail, since you couldn't ask Marta or Manuel to do that particular job for you. And I was the one who had to contact one of my less desirable clients to make a drug buy from him, as well as being the one who had to watch your wife inject herself with an overdose. As I said earlier, Bailey, when you have the kind of money that my father has, someone else takes care of all your little problems for you."

Bailey ignored the other woman's last remark. "How did you get her to do it?" she asked shakily. "I found it hard to believe Angelica would have chosen that way to die even if she was racked by guilt. She had a horror of drugs that stemmed from her childhood. But if she wasn't suicidal, how did you convince her to inject herself, damn you?"

"Because I told her the alternative was to end up the way Jackson had," Tracy said coldly. "She had an even greater horror of having her beauty destroyed."

"She'd been contemplating *my* murder, after all," Aaron protested. "Of course, being Angelica, she thought she could wrap me around her little finger again with a few tears—I was actually surprised she took so long to contact me. We had quite a long chat when she called last night, you know," he added offhandedly to his daughter.

Bailey saw the elegant figure stiffen. Then Tracy smiled. "No, I didn't know. Whatever did you find to talk about?"

Aaron set his snifter down on the table beside him casually. "Oh, this and that. She was trying to win my sympathy, naturally, so she was attempting to convince me that you'd been seriously considering going through with my murder.''

The gray eyes, so like his, widened in amused surprise. ''Oh, dear.'' There was a hint of humor in the low voice. ''I hope you weren't *too* convinced, Aaron.''

''You know, I rather think I was,'' her father said pensively. He raised his gaze, his eyes suddenly glacial. ''What she said bore out suspicions I already had.''

''You can't be serious.'' Slowly the elegant legs uncrossed, and Tracy started to stand. ''Aaron, I'm your *daughter*. How can you—''

The shot caught her high in the chest, spinning her around, and even as Bailey leaped to her feet the slim figure slammed into her from the force of the bullet. Instinctively Bailey's arms went around her, but Tracy's momentum carried them both to the floor.

''Exactly. You're my daughter,'' Aaron said softly, his gun still raised and his posture ramrod straight. ''You and I think the same way, my dear, except that if I'd been in your position, I would never have lost my nerve. I would have had more respect for you if you'd followed through with your plan.''

''For God's *sake*, Aaron.'' Bailey looked up at him in horror. ''You can't mean to stand there and watch your own flesh and blood die. Give me something to stanch the flow, dammit!''

But even as she spoke, she heard the woman in her arms take a harsh, gasping breath. Looking down swiftly, she saw the ominously dark stain running from the corner of the pale rose mouth, saw the pinpoints of light start to fade from those pain-filled gray eyes. Tracy's gaze met that of the man standing over them.

''But I never wanted your respect, Father,'' she whispered fiercely, as another, darker gush of blood welled up. "I wanted your *love*."

On this last, gasped word, a spasm shook the slim frame so convulsively that Bailey's grip around Tracy tightened in an attempt to keep her from striking her head on the granite slabs of the floor. A final gout of blood rushed forth, and then Tracy's anguished gray gaze, still fixed desperately on her father, glazed over.

Bailey's shaking fingers sought to find a pulse at the side of the white neck. There was none. Hardly knowing what she was doing, she carefully released her hold on the body, letting it sink back down onto the granite. Then she passed her hand over the perfect oval of a face, gently closing Tracy's eyes.

She had blood on her own skirt, she realized numbly. With an awkwardly automatic movement, she fumbled in the pocket of her tailored skirt for a tissue, but instead her questing fingers closed around a small object that at first she couldn't identify.

Then she knew what it was. She had transferred Sullivan's shell from her pants pocket to her jacket when she'd changed her clothes a few hours ago, she remembered. Somehow the talisman had seemed a link to him, even though in her heart she'd known that he was gone from her forever.

She'd told herself that when he finally found the absolution he sought, she wouldn't want to know, but now ironic fate had decreed that she be the first to walk through that open door into eternity. Plowright was going to kill her. He probably had some story already in mind that would convince the authorities that she'd fired the shot that had killed Tracy, and that he had then wrestled with her for the gun in a desperate struggle to save his own life, a struggle that had ended in her violent but accidental death.

She'd inadvertently laid the framework for any lie he might concoct with her own outbursts earlier today, blaming Tracy for Angelica's death. An unhinged sister, an emotionally volatile confrontation—she could almost hear Aaron's broken recounting of his version now. The man was a superb actor, as witnessed by his performance at the police station only hours ago.

So he would kill her. If she lifted her gaze she might well see him leveling the gun on her at this very moment, see his finger tightening on the trigger. But she wouldn't die—not completely. Some part of her would live on, as long as Sullivan kept her safe in his heart, Bailey thought, a deep calm settling over her. Her fingers stroked the faint ridges of the shell in her pocket, and she raised her head, looking up into the face of her murderer.

"Despite my daughter's gibes, you're smart enough to know what happens next," he said with a slight frown. "I hold no grudge against you, Bailey. I'll make it quick."

She should have said the words, Bailey thought with sudden sadness. He'd said he'd always known anyway, but she should have told him.

"I love you, Sully," she whispered inaudibly. Aaron raised the gun in his hand. His finger tightened on the trigger. Bailey closed her eyes and saw those blue, blue eyes, that smile that could always make her heart turn over. "I always did," she said softly.

"Goodbye, Bai—"

Aaron's farewell was drowned out by his shot—a shattering, violent explosion of sound that filled the air around her, just as she'd imagined it would...

...except that she *couldn't* have heard the shot that had just killed her, she thought, her eyes flying open and her head jerking up in confusion.

The scene that met her shocked gaze seemed for a second

to be a tableau, a crystallized moment of time amazingly frozen and stilled against all laws of gravity and physics. Glittering shards of glass hung in the air, glowing so richly that they seemed like jewels strung on invisible thread. Aaron too was frozen, his hand gripping the gun that was still pointed at her, but his face was turned toward the inwardly shattering Tiffany window, his features blank with incomprehension.

"No! Damn you, Plowright—no!"

Time resumed, sped up, raced forward as if to make up for its split-second immobility, and all of a sudden spears of glass were flying into the room, creating a deadly frame around the figure moving through them toward Aaron.

"Bailey, get *down!*" Sullivan's anguished gaze locked on hers for a heartbeat, his eyes burning and his face already streaked with blood. Bailey's breath caught in her throat, and her ribs felt as if they were being squeezed by a giant hand.

"Sully, watch *out!*" she screamed, as out of the corner of her eye she saw Aaron swing the gun around and fire blindly through the veil of glass at the man now only feet from him.

This time there was no mistaking the deafening explosion for anything other than what it was. Even as she saw Sullivan bringing his own weapon up, Bailey felt the thunderclap of sound split the air and saw the impact of the bullet drive him backward. His neck arched agonizingly up, the tendons in it standing out like rigid cords, and then he was falling.

"No!"

Bailey heard the scream slice through the reverberations of the gunshot and realized dimly that it was coming from her own throat. Scrambling to her feet, she slipped on the slick pool surrounding Tracy's lifeless body, but she got up again, her eyes wide and horrified.

"Sullivan!" Falling to her knees beside him, heedless of the glass beneath them both, she bent over him, her heart lurching with fear. His eyes were closed, and under his tan his face was bloodless, but as she pressed her thumb to the side of his neck she could feel a thready beat.

He was alive, but just barely. Already the front of his shirt was a brilliant crimson, and as her terrified gaze sought and found the center of the stain, she realized that the wound would soon be a fatal one. Only immediate medical attention could save him.

"I'm not looking for death, but if the door opens and I have to walk through to make things right again, then I will…"

He'd taken the bullet meant for her, Bailey thought frozenly. Terrence Patrick Sullivan had traded his life without hesitation.

"Not if I can help it," she said hoarsely.

She rose and turned in one fluid motion, her hands outstretched, her fingers curved like talons, and she saw the shock that passed over Aaron's good-looking features. Then his face contorted in rage and for the third time his gun hand came up, just as she felt her foot slip wetly on the polished granite and knew helplessly that she had failed.

"I don't think so, Bailey," he snarled. Swiftly he aimed and pulled the trigger.

His arm flew up, his aim going wild and his gun's explosion drowned out by the shot that had come just a split-second before it. He fell to the floor, his shirt red with his own blood, and even as his head smashed backward onto the stone, Bailey knew he was dead.

She spun around in time to see Sullivan's blue gaze fade and his own just-fired gun slowly fall from his grasp.

"Madre de Dios!"

The shocked exclamation came from the doorway, but before she could react, the slim dark man had hastened to Sullivan's side, his face grave.

"We have to call an ambulance, Manuel." Bailey was already heading for the telephone on Aaron's desk, her legs barely supporting her and her hand at her mouth. "I can explain what happened here, but we have to get him to the hospital right now."

"I already called." The liquid consonants hinted at a slight accent. "They should be here any minute."

Aaron's erstwhile chauffeur gave her a brief glance and then turned his attention to the man lying in front of him. Bailey stumbled back to them, falling on her knees beside Sullivan's prone body and seeing with dread that the crimson stain had now seeped through the thicker material of his suit jacket. She ripped off her own and wadded it up into a hasty pad, handing it to Manuel, who held it firmly against the wound. Immediately the edges of her jacket turned red.

"I am outside the garage having a small cigar, and I see a man coming over the fence. I tell him he is trespassing on my employer's estate." Manuel kept his troubled gaze on the barely perceptible rise and fall of Sullivan's chest. "He says his name is Terrence Sullivan, and the woman he loves is in danger. I do not understand all of what he is telling me—some kind of crazy talk about a moon river, and the piano player told him he is just getting over a bad cold and cannot sing the high notes this week, so Plowright lied." He frowned. "It makes no sense, but that does not matter, because as soon as I see him I realize that I know this Sullivan. He is a man to be trusted," Manuel said simply. "I phone 911 like he tells me and then I run here."

"You know Sullivan?" Bailey had been carefully blotting the worst of the blood from the jagged cuts near the closed eyelids, but now she looked up swiftly. "How do you know him?"

Manuel's somber expression softened. "My brother told me about him in his letters. I had gotten out of my country, but Enrique had stayed behind to fight. He told me there was a man teaching them in the camp—a soldier. Enrique said this Sullivan was a man of honor and bravery. The only photograph I have of my brother is of him and Sullivan laughing together at the camp."

Manuel shrugged, as if there was no more to be said. "Enrique did not survive the war in my country," he said quietly. "But my brother was a good judge of men, it seems."

Chapter Sixteen

Bailey never later recalled the trip to the hospital, only that it seemed to take forever, and that once or twice during the ride the paramedics darted quick looks at her before bending urgently over Sullivan again. They were in constant contact with the emergency room at Mass General, and she caught just enough of their curt transmissions to fill her with numb fear.

Please, God, let him live, she prayed soundlessly, her eyes never leaving his bloodied body. *Don't let them take him—please don't let them take him.*

She knew she was a little out of her mind. She had to be, because all at once it seemed perfectly possible that somewhere high in the night sky a skein of wild geese was circling lower and lower, their mighty wings cutting the air with a rush of sound, coming for the soul of an ex-comrade.

"You're his wife?" Without waiting for an answer, the attendant who'd spoken went on as the ambulance careened into the hospital's emergency driveway. "You can follow us in, but don't get in the way. Every second counts."

Bailey nodded numbly. Moments later the back doors of the ambulance flew open, and as the stretcher that Sullivan was on was hastily unloaded, another team from the hospital took over with grim haste. The young man who had spoken to her nodded.

"Get in there. It's not really allowed, but…" He didn't finish his sentence, but as his glance slid away from hers Bailey knew what he hadn't wanted to say. Stumbling through the sliding glass doors, she saw the stretcher being wheeled into an anteroom off the corridor just ahead, and she ran after it.

"The man's lost a hell of a lot of blood. Anybody know what his type is?" The speaker was a wire-thin black woman in the white coat of a doctor. Curtains had been drawn around the table where Sullivan had been laid, but not fully. As Bailey looked in she saw another, younger woman cutting the leg of his pants to well beyond his knee. There were three other people in the small room, each one busy with some preassigned task.

"I think he's O-negative," she said, her voice unsteady. "Look just under his hairline on the nape of his neck—it's tattooed there."

The thin woman looked up sharply, and then nodded. "Lyle, find the damned tattoo, pronto. And you—" She flicked Bailey a quick glance. "You can stay there as long as you don't go hysterical on us. We're doing everything we can to save your husband's life, honey," she said less brusquely.

The next moment her attention was once again focused on her patient, her manner efficiently capable but her eyes grimly shadowed.

At some point Bailey's lips began moving almost soundlessly, and her hand crept to the pocket of her skirt, her fingers wrapping tightly around the small shell.

"'You will not fear the terror of the night, nor the arrow that flieth by day, nor the pestilence that walketh in darkness,'" she murmured, her eyes fixed on the cluster of white coats that blocked Sullivan from her view. A heart monitor had been hooked up to him, and the screen on the wall was visible. To her it seemed as if the green spikes that signaled his heartbeat were spaced ominously far apart. She saw the doctor's lips purse, heard her snap out an order. Bailey's own heart skipped a beat and her lips stopped moving.

"'...nor the destruction that wasteth at noonday. A thousand may fall at your side, ten thousand at your right hand—'"

She looked up through blurred eyes and saw Manuel standing beside her. He touched her lightly on the shoulder.

"—but it will not come near you," he finished quietly, meeting her gaze. "Words of strength, I think," he said. "You must stay strong, Bailey."

She nodded, not trusting herself to reply, and he went on in an undertone. "The police came just after the ambulance. A Detective Fitzgerald brought me here and persuaded the hospital staff to let me wait with you."

"*Defibrillators*—stat!"

Bailey's attention jerked to the stainless steel table where Sullivan lay, and the sudden tense activity that surrounded it. Then her frightened gaze flew to the monitor on the wall. The green line blipped once. It went flat, and from it came a high, monotonous tone. The sound filled the room like a scream.

"He's gone into cardiac shock, dammit! Stand back!"

The wiry doctor had two implements in her hands that looked incongruously like irons. She rubbed their surfaces together, deep grooves suddenly carved at the sides of her mouth, and then bent forward and laid them on his chest. Through a chink in the wall of nurses and technicians Bailey saw Sullivan's body buck convulsively. The doctor stood back. The green line didn't move.

"Again—*clear!*" she snapped, and for a second time Sullivan's torso jerked upward, but the high-pitched tone still filled the air, and the line stayed flat.

"Manuel, they're *losing* him!" Bailey cried helplessly, her horrified eyes fixed on the grim tableau being acted out in front of them. He pulled her to him, trying to turn her away from the sight, but she twisted in his arms, unable to look away.

"They are doing all they can," he said tightly.

"*Clear!*"

It was a nightmare, Bailey thought frantically. It was a terrible nightmare, and although it seemed to be unending, sooner or later she would wake from it.

"*Clear!*"

She *had* to wake up from it. She couldn't stand this any longer—that horrific noise, the unmoving line on the monitor, the mechanical bucking of Sullivan's body every time the voltage ran through—

"He's gone. I never get used to this, dammit." Slowly the doctor handed the paddles to one of the nurses and wiped a trembling hand across her eyes. For a moment she stood motionless. Then her lips tightened, and she looked at the watch on her wrist.

"Time of death, 8:47. Mark it down and I'll initial—"

"*No!*" The scream ripped so violently from Bailey's throat that she could taste blood, and she tore herself from Manuel's protective grasp. She pushed past a nurse and slammed up against the hard steel edge of the table. "*No,* damn you! He's not dead! He *can't* be dead—try again, dammit! *Try again!*"

"Sugar, he's gone." The woman put her hand out, but Bailey shrugged it off and bent over Sullivan.

"He's *not*—" Her words choked off. His eyes were closed and his skin was pale, but that was how he had looked just after he'd been shot. Except now there was some undefinable difference, and with a dull sense of horror, Bailey realized that the body she was looking at was empty. There was nothing there anymore. It was no longer Sullivan, because Sullivan had been taken away from her.

"Somebody shut that thing off," the doctor said, and almost immediately the monitor fell silent.

But she could still hear a high-pitched tone, Bailey thought crazily. She could hear it, and it was getting fainter and fainter, as the wild, lonely cries got farther away. They would be heading into eternity. They had got what they'd come for.

"*No!*" she whispered hoarsely as the room around her started to spin and her world turned to black. "No, I won't let—"

"Somebody catch her, she's fainted," the doctor snapped out, but as her whole world went dark Bailey was beyond hearing anything.

THE DARKNESS WAS COLD—so *cold.*

That was the first thing Bailey noticed. The second thing she noticed was that she wasn't alone.

"You can't take him back. This was the way it was written for him long before you came into his life. Long before I did, for that matter."

She was as beautiful as everyone had always said she was, Bailey thought. But why had no one ever thought to mention the fear in her? It hung around her like an almost tangible thing, and the heavy perfume she wore was completely overwhelmed by the sharp scent of despair.

I once was afraid of her. I once thought she was stronger than I was, that she'd won. But she was always afraid of someone like me, she thought wonderingly.

"I sent him here. With my last breath I sealed his fate, and you can't do anything to undo that."

The charmingly inflected voice held a note of desperation, and suddenly Bailey knew that the speaker had no power at all. "You didn't send him here," she said pityingly. "You only sent yourself, Maria."

She moved on, and whether it was her imagination or not, it seemed as if the temperature had lost some of its bone-chilling quality. Gradually the darkness became a swirl of mist.

It was hard to judge just how far she had gone, she thought, because of the fog that surrounded her. Time wasn't moving, because time didn't move here. Time and space were concepts that she could barely recall. Far above her she thought she could hear a thin, wild cry, but before she could look up a second voice was speaking to her.

"Bee, is that you?"

She looked as she did in her portrait, Bailey saw, not as she had the last and final time they'd met. She sounded confused.

"Mama left me, Bee. She went away and forgot about me, and I've been looking for her ever since." The child-like voice trailed off, but then she spoke again, her tone lower and more intense. "Do you know the way out of here, Bee? Can you take me with you?"

"You know the way out, Angel," Bailey said as gently as she could. "You have to find your way back yourself. Besides, there's someone else I promised to find, and I have to keep looking."

"I know." The voice was fading behind her. "He's up ahead, Bee. But you'll have to hurry."

She knew she had to hurry, Bailey thought, travelling forward through the mists. She didn't belong here, and she only had a certain allotted period to pass freely through this place. She didn't know how she knew this, but she did.

"Do you have the shell, darlin'?" He sounded so much like his son that at first Bailey thought her search had come to an end, but then she saw the differences, and as she did he read her thoughts. His laughter was low and touched with regret. "Yes, he's a better man than I ever was. But he made some of the same mistakes, didn't he, darlin'?"

"He made his own mistakes, and he tried to put them right," she told him. "And yes, I have the shell. Are you asking for it back?"

"No, I don't want it back. I learned it could only protect me if I gave it away to him."

She knew she had to get going again, but once more he sounded so like the man she was looking for she couldn't turn away. "Why are you still here?" she asked softly. "What keeps you?"

"I wanted to help him if he needed me," Thomas said, and his voice seemed to grow fainter, even though she hadn't moved. "I think I can go now that you've come for him. Give him the shell, Bailey. But you're running out of time…the legend can still take him."

Even as his words faded away completely she heard it, too—the high, wild cry above her, growing louder and traveling faster than she could through the tattered remnants of the fog. She heard the beat of strong wings, and thought she could feel the rush of their presence passing over her. She was nearly there, she thought fearfully. But even so, was she too late?

She *couldn't* fail him, she thought desperately. She'd made a vow, and although at the time she'd had no idea how much would be required of her to keep that vow, or how far she would have to travel to insure she kept faith with him, she couldn't falter now. She had this one chance only to defeat them, and if she failed they would have won forever.

She could see them circling just ahead in the grayness, a ghostly vee-shaped flight, their mighty wings outstretched and their eerie, lonely call chillingly seductive.

Bailey closed her eyes in sudden defeat. She wasn't strong enough, she wasn't fast enough, she couldn't *do* this, she thought hopelessly. She was going to lose him.

"You've got the shell... As long as we don't let each other out of our sight, honey, we're both protected."

He'd put his faith in her. He had loved her so much that even now he couldn't leave her, and she loved him so much that she didn't intend to let anything take him away from her. Her eyes flew open.

The shell was in her hand, and she raised her clenched fist above her head, the pain in her bursting forth in a flood. "The arrow that flieth by day," she said, her cracked voice rising and strengthening, her gaze burning through the fog like fire. "I won't *let* you come near him! This is stronger than whatever power you have over him, and you know it!"

She was so close to them now that the world was full of the sound of their cry, as if they were trying to drive her back with their screams, and the wind from their wings slammed into her with the force of a hurricane. Bailey felt herself falter, and using all her strength, she brought her clenched fist down, fighting against the wind that threatened to pry her fingers open. Only a corner of the shell protruded from her grasp. She brought it to her lips.

"Sully, I love you," she whispered, the words ripped away immediately by the fury around her. "I love you, Sully, and I know you love me, too," she said softly. "With all your heart...and with all your soul."

The screaming rose to a crescendo; the wind blew her to

her knees. Bailey felt the tears pouring from her like a river, washing away the pain in a cleansing flood.

And then everything suddenly disappeared—the noise, the wind, the clinging tendrils of fog, and she knew they had gone. Slowly she got to her feet.

"You said you'd come for me, Bails." She looked up, and there he was—blue, blue eyes and that heart-stopping smile, just as she always saw him in her heart. "You're a very stubborn woman, honey. I knew you would."

"It's not your time yet, Sully," she said, her gaze fixed on his. "We have a whole life to get through together first."

"I know." He reached over and touched her cheek as if to make sure she was really there. "And we have another life to watch unfold, honey. She's going to be a girl, and she's going to be a handful."

Bailey's breath caught and her eyes widened. "She's part of us already?" she said wonderingly.

"We'd better never tell her what part a satin rosette and silk stockings had in her creation, Bails." The corner of his mouth lifted in the wry smile she knew so well. "But we have to get back now. You go first, and I'll be right behind you."

"You promise?" There was a flicker of worry in her question. Sullivan gave her a gentle push.

"I promise."

His voice was getting fainter and she suddenly couldn't keep her eyes open any longer. She felt her lashes drift down onto her cheeks, felt everything start to recede, began to smell again the sharp scent of antiseptic and the coppery tang of blood.

"I love you, Bailey," she heard him say from a long way away, as the darkness surrounded her again and she let herself be drawn into its embrace.

"I SAID SOMEBODY CATCH the woman—she's fainting, for God's sake!"

Bailey swayed and then stood, gripping Manuel's supporting arm for balance. She looked at the woman in front of her.

"One more time," she said quietly. "Give it one more try, Doctor."

The lines of exhaustion on the tired face deepened. "We've got another one coming in any second," the woman said shortly. "I'm sorry for your loss, but my job is to try to save the living." She drew a fine-boned hand across her eyes wearily, her voice softening. "I don't like to lose them, either, but I don't have time to grieve."

"One more time," Bailey insisted with flat stubbornness. "Humor me, Doctor."

"Someone get her out of here, for God's sake." Sighing, the wiry figure turned away. "And get an orderly in here to mop up this blood before I break my—"

"One more *time,* Doctor!" Her face white, Bailey grabbed the woman by the shoulder and spun her around. Angry dark eyes met hers, but she didn't flinch. "He's the man that I love and I'm carrying his child—so give it one last *try,* for God's sake!"

The dark eyes held hers. Then the woman wrenched herself from Bailey's grasp. "Give me the damn paddles again and switch the monitor on," she snapped, pulling the sheet off the body on the steel table. "Everyone get the hell out of my way."

The screen above her flickered and then glowed green in an unwavering line. Bailey bit her lip and tasted blood as the now-familiar noise came thinly from it, monotonous and unchanging.

"Clear!"

Stepping forward, the thin woman pressed her lips together grimly and the next moment Sullivan's body bucked violently upward. She stepped back.

The monitor line didn't move. The flat high tone continued. With a sudden sigh the doctor handed the paddles to one of the male nurses.

"I know it's hard, but there's nothing more I can do," she said, her tone final. "Your man's gone, and you're going to have to let me get on with my job. Get your friend here to take you—"

A steady beeping sound came from above her, and the doctor whirled around to look at the monitor. Bailey's gaze was already on it, and as she saw the regular spikes appear on the green line, she clutched at the edge of the table for support. Then she looked down at him.

His eyes opened. His gaze met hers. One corner of his mouth lifted in the ghost of a grin.

"You brought me home, Bails, honey."

His voice was so weak she had to strain to hear it, but she knew what he was saying from the look in his eyes. She felt her own fill with tears.

"Oh, Sully!" she said in a shaky rush. "I knew you were coming back, but—" The tears spilled over uncontrollably, and her eyes suddenly darkened. "They're gone, aren't they? It's all over now for good, isn't it?"

"It's all over, honey." The blue eyes were unshadowed and clear. "I love you, Bailey. I love you with all my soul."

"I love you, too, Sully."

Suddenly remembering, she pressed her hand to her stomach. It was flat, as it would be for some time to come, but she was in there, already starting to grow, Bailey thought. She felt a fierce rush of pure happiness, so overwhelming that she gave a tearful little laugh. She bent over him and put her lips near his mouth.

"And you're right," she whispered. "We'd better not tell her about the rosette and the stockings."

She saw him grin and felt his hand go around the back of her head, pulling her closer, and then the world around them faded as their lips met.

Behind them, the doctor took her incredulous eyes from the monitor. She looked down at them, and some of the weariness seemed to lift from her. She glanced at her watch.

"Lyle, scratch that last entry—or no, leave it." She shook her head in resignation. "Underneath it write 8:49. Put that down as the time he came back and I'll initial it." She glared around her, blinking rapidly. "What the hell is everyone standing around crying for? Get these two out of here—we've got work to do, people!"

Epilogue

"…take Terrence Patrick Sullivan as your lawfully wedded husband?"

"I do," Bailey said in a soft, clear voice.

"Oh, great, now I'm going to blub," Ainslie muttered to Tara as she saw her far-too-handsome brother kiss a far-too-radiant Bailey a few feet away. She fumbled in her purse on the pew beside her, and then gave up in frustration. What did it matter? she thought, the happy tears streaming down her face. People cried at weddings. Even the wiry black woman a few rows over, who looked like she didn't have a sentimental bone in her body, was damply smiling at the newly married couple. Even Quinn McGuire, an old friend of Sully's whom Ainslie had never seen do much more than crack a small smile, was wearing a broad grin, his massive arm wrapped tightly around the shoulders of his very pregnant wife Jan.

"What are they doing now, Auntie Lee?" Tara leaned forward, trying to see past the flowers and the candles. Ainslie looked up and felt the tears slip down her cheeks in a fresh flood.

Bailey had chosen her veil with this moment in mind, but still she felt the fine silver chain catch on the tulle.

Sullivan grinned at her and maneuvered the chain safely until it encircled her neck.

"Now you," she murmured, hardly aware of the church-ful of people watching. He inclined his head slightly, his gaze never leaving hers, and she slipped an identical silver chain, so fine it was hardly visible against the tan of his skin, over that glossy midnight-black hair and around his neck.

She'd found it a few hours after they'd transferred him from emergency and into a regular ward. She'd been sitting beside him, watching him sleep, and she'd drawn it out of her pocket and stared at it wonderingly on her palm. It had been the way it was now—two perfect mirror-image halves of a shell. The break had been clean, cutting straight through the original hole in it.

Thanks to a friend of Manuel's who was a jeweler, now each half had been mounted securely and strung on its own silver chain. But if you placed them side by side, Bailey thought lovingly, they still fit together to make one perfect whole. She smiled up at Sullivan and closed her eyes as he brought his mouth to hers again.

"Isn't it romantic?" Tara sighed gustily beside Ainslie. Sullivan's sister watched her big brother kiss the woman he'd looked for all of his life, and smiled through her tears.

"Nah, pumpkin, it's not romance," she said gruffly, wip-ing her eyes with the back of her hand inelegantly. "This is the real thing. What they've got is true love, and that's a lot harder to find."

Sully looked like a man who'd found his heart's desire, she thought. Bailey looked—Ainslie squinted suspiciously, and then her eyes widened and she smiled. Bailey looked just the tiniest bit pregnant, she decided, which explained why the wedding had been arranged in record time. She turned to her niece again, no longer caring about the tears.

''A whole lot harder to find, pumpkin,'' she said softly, her gaze going to Bailey and Sullivan. ''But if you do, never *ever* let it go.''

Harlequin truly does make any time special. . . . This year we are celebrating weddings in style!

To help us celebrate, we want you to tell us how wearing the Harlequin wedding gown will make your wedding day special. As the grand prize, Harlequin will offer one lucky bride the chance to **"Walk Down the Aisle" in the Harlequin wedding gown!**

There's more...

For her honeymoon, she and her groom will spend five nights at the **Hyatt Regency Maui.** As part of this five-night honeymoon at the hotel renowned for its romantic attractions, the couple will enjoy a candlelit dinner for two in Swan Court, a sunset sail on the hotel's catamaran, and duet spa treatments.

A HYATT RESORT AND SPA   Maui • Molokai • Lanai

To enter, please write, in, 250 words or less, how wearing the Harlequin wedding gown will make your wedding day special. The entry will be judged based on its emotionally compelling nature, its originality and creativity, and its sincerity. This contest is open to Canadian and U.S. residents only and to those who are 18 years of age and older. There is no purchase necessary to enter. Void where prohibited. See further contest rules attached. Please send your entry to:

Walk Down the Aisle Contest

In Canada
P.O. Box 637
Fort Erie, Ontario
L2A 5X3

In U.S.A.
P.O. Box 9076
3010 Walden Ave.
Buffalo, NY 14269-9076

You can also enter by visiting www.eHarlequin.com
Win the Harlequin wedding gown and the vacation of a lifetime!
The deadline for entries is October 1, 2001.

HARLEQUIN®
Makes any time special®

PHWDACONT1

HARLEQUIN WALK DOWN THE AISLE TO MAUI CONTEST 1197
OFFICIAL RULES
NO PURCHASE NECESSARY TO ENTER

1. To enter, follow directions published in the offer to which you are responding. Contest begins April 2, 2001, and ends on October 1, 2001. Method of entry may vary. Mailed entries must be postmarked by October 1, 2001, and received by October 8, 2001.

2. Contest entry may be, at times, presented via the Internet, but will be restricted solely to residents of certain geographic areas that are disclosed on the Web site. To enter via the Internet, if permissible, access the Harlequin Web site (www.eHarlequin.com) and follow the directions displayed online. Online entries must be received by 11:59 p.m. E.S.T. on October 1, 2001.

   In lieu of submitting an entry online, enter by mail by hand-printing (or typing) on an 8½" x 11" plain piece of paper, your name, address (including zip code), Contest number/name and in 250 words or fewer, why winning a Harlequin wedding dress would make your wedding day special. Mail via first-class mail to: Harlequin Walk Down the Aisle Contest 1197, (in the U.S.) P.O. Box 9076, 3010 Walden Avenue, Buffalo, NY 14269-9076, (in Canada) P.O. Box 637, Fort Erie, Ontario L2A 5X3, Canada.

   Limit one entry per person, household address and e-mail address. Online and/or mailed entries received from persons residing in geographic areas in which Internet entry is not permissible will be disqualified.

3. Contests will be judged by a panel of members of the Harlequin editorial, marketing and public relations staff based on the following criteria:

   - Originality and Creativity—50%
   - Emotionally Compelling—25%
   - Sincerity—25%

   In the event of a tie, duplicate prizes will be awarded. Decisions of the judges are final.

4. All entries become the property of Torstar Corp. and will not be returned. No responsibility is assumed for lost, late, illegible, incomplete, inaccurate, nondelivered or misdirected mail or misdirected e-mail, for technical, hardware or software failures of any kind, lost or unavailable network connections, or failed, incomplete, garbled or delayed computer transmission or any human error which may occur in the receipt or processing of the entries in this Contest.

5. Contest open only to residents of the U.S. (except Puerto Rico) and Canada, who are 18 years of age or older, and is void wherever prohibited by law; all applicable laws and regulations apply. Any litigation within the Province of Quebec respecting the conduct or organization of a publicity contest may be submitted to the Régie des alcools, des courses et des jeux for a ruling. Any litigation respecting the awarding of a prize may be submitted to the Régie des alcools, des courses et des jeux only for the purpose of helping the parties reach a settlement. Employees and immediate family members of Torstar Corp. and D. L. Blair, Inc., their affiliates, subsidiaries and all other agencies, entities and persons connected with the use, marketing or conduct of this Contest are not eligible to enter. Taxes on prizes are the sole responsibility of winners. Acceptance of any prize offered constitutes permission to use winner's name, photograph or other likeness for the purposes of advertising, trade and promotion on behalf of Torstar Corp., its affiliates and subsidiaries without further compensation to the winner, unless prohibited by law.

6. Winners will be determined no later than November 15, 2001, and will be notified by mail. Winners will be required to sign and return an Affidavit of Eligibility form within 15 days after winner notification. Noncompliance within that time period may result in disqualification and an alternative winner may be selected. Winners of trip must execute a Release of Liability prior to ticketing and must possess required travel documents (e.g. passport, photo ID) where applicable. Trip must be completed by November 2002. No substitution of prize permitted by winner. Torstar Corp. and D. L. Blair, Inc., their parents, affiliates, and subsidiaries are not responsible for errors in printing or electronic presentation of Contest, entries and/or game pieces. In the event of printing or other errors which may result in unintended prize values or duplication of prizes, all affected game pieces or entries shall be null and void. If for any reason the Internet portion of the Contest is not capable of running as planned, including infection by computer virus, bugs, tampering, unauthorized intervention, fraud, technical failures, or any other causes beyond the control of Torstar Corp. which corrupt or affect the administration, secrecy, fairness, integrity or proper conduct of the Contest, Torstar Corp. reserves the right, at its sole discretion, to disqualify any individual who tampers with the entry process and to cancel, terminate, modify or suspend the Contest or the Internet portion thereof. In the event of a dispute regarding an online entry, the entry will be deemed submitted by the authorized holder of the e-mail account submitted at the time of entry. Authorized account holder is defined as the natural person who is assigned to an e-mail address by an Internet access provider, online service provider or other organization that is responsible for arranging e-mail address for the domain associated with the submitted e-mail address. **Purchase or acceptance of a product offer does not improve your chances of winning.**

7. Prizes: (1) Grand Prize—A Harlequin wedding dress (approximate retail value: $3,500) and a 5-night/6-day honeymoon trip to Maui, HI, including round-trip air transportation provided by Maui Visitors Bureau from Los Angeles International Airport (winner is responsible for transportation to and from Los Angeles International Airport) and a Harlequin Romance Package, including hotel accomodations (double occupancy) at the Hyatt Regency Maui Resort and Spa, dinner for (2) two at Swan Court, a sunset sail on Kiele V and a spa treatment for the winner (approximate retail value: $4,000); (5) Five runner-up prizes of a $1000 gift certificate to selected retail outlets to be determined by Sponsor (retail value $1000 ea.). Prizes consist of only those items listed as part of the prize. Limit one prize per person. All prizes are valued in U.S. currency.

8. For a list of winners (available after December 17, 2001) send a self-addressed, stamped envelope to: Harlequin Walk Down the Aisle Contest 1197 Winners, P.O. Box 4200 Blair, NE 68009-4200 or you may access the www.eHarlequin.com Web site through January 15, 2002.

Contest sponsored by Torstar Corp., P.O. Box 9042, Buffalo, NY 14269-9042, U.S.A.

PHWDACONT2

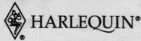